MEGAN R. REES

ISBN: 979-8-9933021-0-2

First edition 2025

Book Cover: Lyndsey D. Graphics
Interior Artwork: MgsDesiigns
Editor: Wren L. Helgren of Helgren Editing
Formatter: All The Proof Editing

Contents

In the Land
of
MYGIN FORMHAIN
Arielelan Forest
Eirarin
Caryen
Strunheld River
Strunheld
Lake Relcrios
Falenole
Delvaria
Relcrios River
Formhair Ocean
N
W E
S

CHAPTER

One

Princess Filibria took a deep breath as her palms cupped the ornate chalice. She lifted it, the weight balancing her focus. Centuries of women in these halls had held this chalice before her, wearing away the carven designs on the silver surface. Centuries of women had intoned the same words Filibria did now — but she would only say these words once in this hall.

"Drink of the cup and may peace bind you together as smoothly as the wine flows."

Without looking, she knew her mother, sitting to her right, had mouthed the words with her. The thought gave Filibria strength while she passed the cup first to her father, the King of Delvaria.

His eyes burned with pride when he took the cup from her, drank and handed it back. Her mother was next for the cup. Her fingers wrapped around the stem, giving Filibria's hand a quick squeeze.

"My peace weaver," Queen Bryn whispered. Warmth flowed through Filibria, reinforcing her smile.

Filibria took the cup from the dais after her siblings had drunk from it and passed it through the crowd, weaving the invisible bond of peace between them all. Focusing on her task kept the doubts, the fears, at bay. This hall was filled with echoes of peace. A strong bond, well tended by her mother, existed. Filibria was only weaving her own strands into the tapestry — before she left.

When Filibria returned to the dais to place the empty cup before her father, the hall erupted into a cheer. Filibria bowed before her parents when they rose.

"We have seen Princess Filibria weave peace with the grace and wisdom of the women before her," the King said. "The Kingdom of Delvaria sees her and acknowledges her as the next peace weaver. These halls accept her to be an ambassador of peace to the lands around us. May she weave as deep a peace as the women who walked before her."

"May it be," the hall responded with enthusiasm.

Filibria's poise began to melt when she sat down. Her years of training had gotten her around the hall, carrying the cup and not spilling a drop. Now it abandoned her as the feast continued in her honor.

It was only ceremony, she knew. Her father spoke as if she had just been approved for the role. As if he had not already arranged a peace marriage for her. As if that marriage was not in a week. The thought sent chills through her. Many women had been sent from these halls to marry into neighboring kingdoms to keep peace, but no peace weaver had ever been sent from these halls into the Kingdom of Eirarin...the sworn enemy of Delvaria.

Filibria begged leave from the feast to escape to her room. She locked the door behind her and sat down on the bed, not trusting her feet to hold her up anymore. She buried her trembling hands in her lap. A sob of panic escaped from her throat. Peace weavers had always been a pawn for their kingdom, but never to this level. Her father was sending her into danger; the fate of Delvaria would rest solely on her shoulders — and she was marrying a stranger.

Filibria knew how to keep her calm, to control her emotions and put on whatever face she needed in public. But when she was alone, without expectations from others, she always crumbled. Marriage meant either she would always have to keep a brave face, or she would crumble in front of him. Her husband would be able to see how unsure, and how scared she really was. And to love him meant she would not be able to control her emotions. Love was wild, unpredictable. It would endanger her front. If she had to keep herself together and put on a good face for the sake of peace, that meant she could let no one, not even her husband, see the real, scared her. Only a few had seen that side of her.

A knock sounded on her door.

"I am indisposed," Filibria called out.

"Filibria?" It was her mother. The concern in the voice on the other side of the door almost broke Filibria. "May I come in dear?"

With a sigh, Filibria stood and unlocked the door before returning to the edge of her bed. Her mother slipped in and looked her over.

"Talk to me," the Queen said as she sank onto the bed next to Filibria.

So many thoughts swirled through Filibria's head. Why now? Why Eirarin? Who was the prince she was marrying? What if she could not bring peace to the centuries of hate and strife?

"What if I fail?"

Queen Bryn took her hand and was silent for a while. Filibria knew her mother was struggling for a reassuring answer...because there wasn't one.

Both kingdoms sat on a vital trade route. Delvaria blocked Eirarin from exporting their wood and woven products across the sea to the south, and Eirarin blocked Delvaria from exporting metals and precious gems further into the continent of Mygin Formhain. Furthermore, without Eirarin's wood, Delvaria could not build ships to sail to other countries. What ships they already had were old and battered, in need of much repair. They had planted forests to remedy the lack, but the forests were still too young. Pride, greed, and misunderstanding had roiled up generations of war and strife between the kingdoms. The hate and prejudice was so old, no one could even remember what had started it. It had sucked both kingdoms dry.

But all that had changed in the past month. The King of Eirarin had sent a proposal of a peace-weaving marriage. Delvaria's princess to the Prince of Eirarin.

The two kingdoms were so closed off to each other, the royal Delvarian family were not even aware that Eirarin had an eligible prince. No one knew anything of him—not even his name.

To Filibria's surprise, her proud father had accepted the proposal and to keep chances of betrayal or attacks at bay, there would be two weddings. The prince would ride to Delvaria and wed Filibria in her halls, then bring her to his kingdom and wed there too, but their families would not meet. Filibria would be an ambassador for Delvaria, weaving peace through passing the cup in the Eirarin halls. She would be a face of the enemy to make them human again. Then, eventually, when the countries opened more, she would weave peace by passing the cup when they visited each other. Beyond that, she would do her best to serve her new husband and tie the bloodlines with a child. Her steady wisdom would keep the King of Eirarin and her father from ever going to war. Or so everyone hoped.

"You remember how I was married in the middle of a battlefield?" the Queen asked finally.

Filibria nodded. Her mother, from another kingdom, was a blade bride, trained to be a peace weaver, but married in the middle of war without pomp and circumstance.

"I was scared and...unprepared. I felt betrayed because my father had not told me of his intentions to marry me off so soon. I did everything I could to sabotage my relationship with Delvaria, with your father. But then I became pregnant with your brother and suddenly I saw how important peace was if I wanted to raise a family well. My situation was not ideal, just like yours, but I fought it and it still worked out. I think if you go in willingly, it will work out." She squeezed her daughter's hand. Filibria knew her mother enough to see the sadness hooded in her eyes, the fear for her daughter in her grip, and she knew it would not simply just work out. Her mother had fought for the position, for the honor surrounding it; Filibria would have to too.

"I just wish I had more time with you, to learn from you."

"I know."

"What if I don't love him? You've taught me how to control my emotions, how to appear happy, but what if I never have feelings for him?"

"If feelings never come...the marriage will still work. It is for duty, not love." The Queen's voice was heavy with sadness. "But I hope that is not the case for you. I hope you find love like I did."

Filibria shifted on the bed, still clinging to her mother's hand, still full of fear and questions. "How am I supposed to have time for a husband if I have to work to keep peace between the kingdoms? Or time for children? How did you do it?"

Her mother laughed. "When you love him, you will find time. But until then, showing love to your husband shows your peaceful side. It will make the kingdom respect you. By showing you can accept one of their own, you prove you can accept them all. And children—you will want to spend as much time as you can with them. Before...before they grow up and leave you." The Queen embraced Filibria. "I love you, Filibria. You did well tonight, as I am sure you will do in the future. Rest now. Malda will be up soon to help you to bed."

As her mother left, Filibria fought the urge to pull her back, to ask her questions late into the night until she had all the answers. But she knew deep down there were no answers, so she watched her mother walk away and did nothing.

Malda, Filibria's handmaiden, arrived soon after. Dear Malda had been raised alongside Filibria, becoming her constant help when she was old enough. It was more of a friendship than a maid and princess relationship, and Filibria was grateful for it.

"You were wonderful tonight," Malda said as she turned down the bedcovers.

Filibria only sighed. "A week, Malda. A week."

"I know."

"I wish you were coming with me."

"I know." Malda pursed her lips, a sign she was holding back a rant. She disapproved of the entire arrangement and had made it obvious over the past couple days. But as the wedding drew closer, she knew ranting would help nothing. Filibria needed encouragement.

"The seamstress finished your dress. Would you like to see it?"

"Not tonight." Filibria had already seen the dress. There was no time for her to have a wedding dress of her own made, so they had altered her grandmother's wedding dress to fit her in time.

"Would you like to play your harp for me tonight?"

Filibria looked at the instrument in the corner and was suddenly reminded it was too big to take with her. She would be riding a horse to Eirarin and nothing but a few essentials could come with her. Her harp had been with her ever since she was a small child. She knew every curve of the wood, every dent and blemish in its well worn surface.

Swallowing a lump in her throat, Filibria shook her head. "I'm ready to sleep now."

Malda paused, as if she wanted to dig deeper, but sensing Filibria's pain, she acquiesced.

"Goodnight then." She dowsed the brazier and left.

Filibria lay in the dark. Seven days until she was married, until she shared her bed with a strange man. Not just a stranger, a former enemy. Maybe she would have to sleep with a dagger under her pillow.

CHAPTER

Two

"Do you see the prince?" Malda asked. A forgotten hairbrush dangled from her hand as she pressed up behind Filibria on the staircase. Malda could always be relied upon to neglect duties in the face of nosiness.

Filibria closed an eye to squint through the arrowslit in the stone. Ten men, dressed in bright reds and golds, paced the courtyard far below. Their hands rested on their hilts, their heads swiveling at the slightest noise.

"No," Filibria sighed. "He must have already gone in." She tried to mask her disappointment. She was doing this for duty, not love, she reminded herself. Still, it would have been nice to see whether the foreign prince was handsome or not before she descended the staircase to marry him.

"Or he never existed in the first place!" Malda smacked the brush against the wall for emphasis. "What if I was right and it is only a ruse to attack the castle?"

"With ten men?"

Malda shrugged. "There could be more concealed in the wagon they brought. Eirarin is a crafty enemy."

Was it the bodice crushing her lungs, or the fear? Filibria let the deep window ledge hold her up, ignoring the dirty rocks against her white dress. She watched the men clad in red, such a foreign color; the color of blood, the color of war, the color of strife. Would the prince be wearing red? It would clash against her white dress like blood on snow...like war staining peace.

The week had gone by too fast for Filibria. She could only now cling desperately to each minute before it slipped by. Within the hour, she would be married.

"I think—" Malda gasped as Filibria clapped a hand over her mouth; the maid's eyes widened at the sound of footsteps far below them.

"Quickly," Filibria hissed. Malda gathered up Filibria's skirts and practically pushed her up the winding stairs and into her room. Inside, Malda arranged the dress and began tugging at the loose laces.

"Careful," Filibria gasped, laughing a little when the laces yanked at her breath. "Not too tight. I may faint already today."

"You will be fine," Malda assured her.

"But what if I do faint? Or trip? Or say the wrong words?"

"Shh. One step at a time."

Filibria fiddled with the sleeves draping too far over her wrists. There had not been enough time for the castle seamstress to finish. There had barely even been enough time to pack. Filibria's eyes wandered over her bare room. Only tapestries, too faded to be of worth, and her worn harp, too cumbersome to transport, remained. She could not look at her harp without wanting to cry. Everything else waited in trunks down in the courtyard. She had spent every night of her life in this room. She did not know a life beyond these castle walls.

"There," Malda said with one last tug of Filibria's laces. "Now for your hair."

Filibria picked up a mirror, gifted to her by her mother. It had been used in the training of always keeping a smile on her face, even when she did not feel like it. She did not feel like it now. Her lips were curved, her dimples showing, but her green eyes remained dull. No amount of practice could remove the fear of her uncertain future from them. She tipped it back to watch Malda deftly braiding her hair. The maid's lips were pressing into a thin line, her brows scrunched in worry.

When Malda caught sight of her reflection, she replaced her expression with a smile.

"You look beautiful, Filibria."

"Thank you..."

The door opened just then and Queen Bryn, followed by a flock of attendants, entered. The small room filled with skirts and overpowering perfume, further shattering Filibria's reverie.

Filibria turned to face her mother.

The Queen attempted a smile. "Look at you, Filibria. A proper bride. A peace weaver. Turn for me, daughter."

Filibria's skirts rustled over the stone. Too much swirling white. The skirt was too long, the corset too tight. Malda had laced in every last inch.

"Stand tall," Queen Bryn said. "You are a bride going to her wedding, not a prisoner to the block. Be graceful, yet confident—and smile. It will hide your fear." Her mother's teaching washed over her. It had all led to this moment. Filibria must not show emotion. Emotion held no place in her duties. She would marry. She would keep peace. And one day, like her mother, she would be queen and raise her own daughters to be peace weavers.

Far below, from the bowels of the castle, a horn sounded. Malda stirred into action, breaking the solemn air.

"We must hurry. Are you ready Princess Filibria?"

Filibria nodded.

Everyone knew she was lying.

"Filibria, a peace weaver." The Queen held out a hand. Filibria accepted it and they walked together, for the last time, out of her room.

She tried to relax on the descent to the main hall, running her fingers over the worn tapestries, each picture burned into her memory. She counted each step down the stairs and through the corridor, worn by generations of her family's feet. This was her home, but only until the day was over. Filibria forced the lump down her throat and held her head high.

No emotions, only duty—for her kingdom.

Even before they reached the Great Hall, they ran into people overflowing from the crowded room. Never in her life had Filibria seen so many people: servants, knights, chiefs, lords, merchants, farmers, all mixed and packed together, in her home—not even on Vow Days or Feast Days. The curiosity of such a monumental event, and the chance to catch a glimpse of the dreaded enemy, drew people like flies to a manure pile.

From outside the hall, the tension between the two kingdoms hung heavy like the smell of unwashed bodies surrounding her. The Eirarin guards stood stiff, their unease pressing against her heart...a reminder of what she was going into.

The benches and tables had been removed, leaving only standing room, and not much remained of even that. The walls had been scrubbed clean and washed white with lime. Heavy green garlands, decorated with summer flowers looped over the beams and curled down the columns on either side of the hall.

Filibria froze in the doorway.

A trumpet sounded and everyone turned to catch their first glimpse of the peace-weaving bride.

Every face, even the familiar ones of dear servants and castle friends, blurred when Filibria took her first step into the room. The splashes of gold and red registered in her vision, their tunics and shields bearing Eirarin's symbol, the talon of a bird of prey. Her kingdom's enemy, right here in her halls. No, not enemies. Allies. Today, the Eirarins would become their allies. The word echoed in Filibria's head, foreign.

A path cleared across the room to the dais where her father waited. His gaze landed heavily upon her. Though the other eyes did not penetrate, his did, but he gave her a small nod.

As Filibria focused on the rest of the dais, she caught her first full glimpse of her betrothed, the elusive Prince of Eirarin. He had never stepped foot outside of his own country, never ridden into battle beside his father. No one even knew his name, but none of that mattered.

He wore white, like her.

When she saw him, Filibria wished the circumstances had been different. If only she could have met him before this, to get to know him. Surely, he felt the same. She could see her own silent panic and reluctance mirrored in his face when their eyes met for a moment, and in the uncertainty of his stance. But neither he, nor his name, mattered. He was royal and of marriageable age. Nothing but a pawn for his kingdom, like Filibria. She was marrying into Eirarin for peace, not love; marrying the kingdom, not its prince. The thought hardened her resolve, reinforcing each step down the aisle.

"Princess Filibria," her father boomed to the audience. He lifted his hands high. "Daughter of Delvaria, bride of Eirarin. Filibria, peace weaver."

The words sent a shiver through Filibria's entire being as she walked forward. Cold sweat broke out on her skin. The deafening cheers from the crowd drowned out her thoughts.

"May she bind our kingdoms in peace and prosperity like her mother did before her!" the King shouted.

"May it be!" The crowd responded enthusiastically.

As Filibria reached the foot of the dais, her father held out his hand and led her up the steps. He took one of her hands and one of her betrothed's, placing her hand in his. Was it her imagination, or did her father's hands shake a little, clinging to hers longer than need be? Surely not.

Filibria turned her concentration to the new set of hands holding hers. The prince's hands were long, firm, and cold. They trembled, just as hers did. Filibria met the man's eyes again. They were green, like her own. He was scared, but he managed a slight smile. Now Filibria was the one to drop her gaze.

The King draped a white silken wedding cord braided with gold over their joined hands, wrapping it around several times.

"I swear—" the prince began—voice was soft and low, "to take this Delvarian princess to be my bride. My heart and hearth shall be hers until the day we die."

"I swear," Filibria said, "to take the Eirarin prince…" Her tongue floundered over the words. "To take…to take the Eirarin prince to be my husband. To the end of my days, I will bring peace to his heart, his hearth, and his kingdom."

Then together, they intoned, "We swear by peace and love to stand, heart to heart, and hand to hand, as one until the end. May it be."

"May it be," the crowd echoed.

Gently, the bride and groom slipped their hands free, pulling at the ends of the cord. It came away, dangling between them in a perfect knot. The crowd cheered again.

Trumpets sounded. Queen Bryn mounted the dais, bearing a mead-filled goblet. "Drink of the marriage cup," she said, passing it to the prince. He took it, drank, and then held it out for Filibria. She also drank from it, aware that he was watching her.

The King took the knotted wedding cord and held it up. His voice rang through the hall. "May our countries unite this day, just as these two unite before us and may they secure peace between Eirarin and Delvaria for the rest of their lives, just as this knot is secured between them."

"May it be," the crowd replied.

A servant reverently took the cord and placed it in a gilded chest. It would travel with the new couple to be displayed in the halls of Eirarin to be proof of their binding.

The King turned to his daughter, his eyes misty. He opened his mouth, as if to say something, but then closed it and turned back to the cheering crowd.

As custom demanded, Filibria's new husband gave her three gifts. In standing with tradition, the first was from him, the second from his mother, and the third from his father to signify their acceptance of her. The prince's gift was a silver necklace, set with shimmering blue stones, and the second, a rich samite cloak. His fingers shook, buttoning it at her neck.

"My mother wove it for you," he whispered.

Filibria admired the intricate embroidery across the shimmering fabric. She had never seen anything like it.

"It is beautiful," she whispered back, making him smile a little.

The third gift, he promised, waited for her in the courtyard. It was from his father. Each gift her husband presented stiffly and dutifully; Filibria accepted them in the same manner.

In exchange, Filibria's father called up her dowry. Three men, carrying small chests, stepped onto the dais. They threw open the lid of one chest and Eirarin guards swarmed around it.

"The royal dowry of Filibria," the King said. "Three chests of gold, as King Dalen requested."

The captain of the Eirarin guards stepped forward and bowed. "Captain Wrestan, highest rank of the Eirarin guard. I will ensure the safe delivery of this treasure to King Dalen." His men lifted the chests and carried them away. "Be certain King Dalen will be pleased," Captain Wrestan said with a last bow.

The prince barely glanced at the chests.

"More precious than this dowry is the hand of your daughter," the prince replied. Was his tone genuine, Filibria wondered.

The hall erupted into a long cheer. The Delvarians pounded fists and pommels into the tables, tossing their hats into the air. The two kingdoms had been bound. For the first time in generations, the weary kingdoms would have peace with each other. Young men would grow old instead of die on the battlefield. Trade would once again flourish and fill the coffers. Hopefully.

Filibria was now a married woman, but her head refused to process it. Later would be feasting in her honor, but she and the prince would not be there. They would already be riding for Eirarin. She glanced at her new husband. His eyes were widened by the celebration around him. As if he felt her gaze, he turned to look at her. Immediately, warmth crept up Filibria's face and she turned away.

"Trinlys." The softness of the voice was almost lost in the din.

"Sorry?" Filibria turned.

"Trinlys. My name is Trinlys. Your father did not say it in the ceremony."

"He…We did not know it," she admitted.

The prince's eyes clouded with concern. "I am sorry. It might have been a little more comforting to have at least known my name. I knew yours." His voice was so gentle, like warm honey; his tone so sincere.

Filibria only nodded. Her brain fumbled through anything to say to keep the conversation flowing. But as she opened her mouth to speak, Malda appeared to retrieve her so she could prepare for the journey.

In her mother's chambers, Filibria's handmaidens removed her wedding dress, packing it away. It would be used for the next peace weaver in the kingdom, whoever she may be.

One of the handmaidens draped the samite cloak over her arms, marveling at it.

"It has been many, many years since a piece of Eirarin weaving has been in these halls," Malda said, taking the cloak from the maid and carefully packing it away.

"Yes, and the kingdom of wood and weaving gifted the princess of metal and gems a necklace." One of the maidens snorted in laughter. Titters ran through the handmaidens at the irony of it.

"I wonder what the last gift is. It must be large if he could not bring it into the hall." The maids set about speculating suitable large gifts while they laced Filibria into her traveling dress. They became distant chatter as Filibria retreated into her head to process what had just happened. She was married. To a stranger.

"The rogues let no one go with you." Malda huffed, breaking through Filibria's thoughts. She yanked at the laces, as if they were around the neck of the offending kingdom.

"You know I cannot take anyone with me. It is the law," Filibria said, "and you know how badly I wish you could come with me."

Malda then snorted. "Do they care not for their women? You are a princess. If anything befell you on the dangerous road, there would be war. Who will look after you?"

"Malda, fretting will do no good. We cannot know their ways." Filibria gladly focused on pacifying her childhood friend. Anything to distract her from the looming departure.

"It is not befitting to ride with only men. And on horseback too! Barbarians, the lot of them."

"Well, the prince is her husband now," another maiden, Uni, spoke up.

Malda glowered.

"And they are horse riders," Filibria added quietly. "It will do me good to learn to ride as they do. Besides, the roads are too rough between the kingdoms, unpassable for wagons. But soon that will change with the coming peace." She squeezed Malda's hand, but Malda only huffed.

"What did you think of him, the prince?" one handmaiden asked Filibria.

"He's handsome enough," Uni spoke up first, "but he's so thin. I wonder if he is sick? I had imagined a tall, strong warrior. Instead, he's pale and thin, like a scholar or a merchant. Not fitting for a prince."

"She was not asking for your opinion, Uni," Malda gently rebuked, turning to Filibria.

"Trinlys. His name is Trinlys," Filibria said.

The name rippled over the girl's lips as they tried it out. "He was...quiet, shy."

Filibria paused, remembering his smile. "I think he will be nice." Or perhaps she had misjudged warmth where there was only quiet disinterest. "At least his voice makes me think he will be nice. It is so gentle."

"His mannerisms and his voice don't matter," Uni protested. "What did you think of his looks?"

"He...He does look a little like a scholar." With reading and writing low on the list of priorities in Delvaria, scholars were rare and often frowned upon, but they had always fascinated Filibria. "He looks kind. But I don't remember much," Filibria said.

Uni groaned. "Did you even look at him?"

"I did." But when Filibria tried to recall his face, only his scared green eyes surfaced in her memory. She shook her head. "I don't really want to talk about him right now."

Malda draped a traveling cloak around Filibria's shoulders and fastened it at her throat; her fingers slow, trembling.

"What if he doesn't like me?" Filibria murmured.

"Filibria, I have known you since we were children. No one can help but like you." Malda tipped Filibria's chin, so their eyes met. "And besides, he is not entitled to love you. Just serve him well. Keep him and the kingdom happy."

"But what if *I* do not like *him*? What if I cannot bear living with him?"

"Hush now," Malda said, "and have courage." She snapped her fingers to ward away fate. "May your fears be unfounded."

"She's here," Uni murmured. The crowd of handmaidens melted into the corners when Queen Bryn stepped into the room. This would be the last time she saw her mother for a very long time, Filibria realized. She suddenly had so many questions for her mother, but time had run out. Instead, Filibria memorized her mother's face, freezing it into her memory; each line of life etched on her face, each hair greyed with wisdom, but most of all, her grey eyes deep with compassion and love. No one else looked at Filibria like that.

"Are you ready, my daughter?"

Filibria nodded.

Her mother took her hand and squeezed it. "You are a peace weaver now. Bind our kingdoms together as I have taught you. We need your peace—more than ever in these days. Remember, it is not a role. It is your identity."

"I will do my best, Mother."

"And..." The Queen paused as if hesitant to make any promises. "And if you bind the kingdoms close enough, perhaps the borders will open. Perhaps...perhaps we might see you again."

Filibria fell into her mother's arms. All the tears she had suppressed the entire day released in a flood.

Queen Bryn gently released her daughter. Tears flowed down her own cheeks. She took Filibria's face in her hands. "Be brave, child."

"I will."

CHAPTER

Three

DEAR CARNA, THE OLD castle steward, waited outside the Queen's chambers to take Filibria to her husband. For longer than she could remember, Carna and his wife had always been there for her. They had parented her almost more than her own parents had. Carna held out his arm and Filibria slipped her hand into the crook of his elbow.

"Your father is still in the hall," Carna said. "Would you like to say goodbye?"

Filibria shook her head. All the goodbyes that mattered had been said. Her father and siblings would not even notice she was gone. For all they cared, she had left already. As for the castle staff, they had already said all the goodbyes that were proper.

"Alright then." Patting her hand, Carna led her through the castle. "Oh, wait a minute." He stopped and fumbled in the bag at his waist. "My wife and I have something for you." Carna pressed a green stone into Filibria's hand. "As a wedding gift. Should you ever need to, you can always sell it for some money of your own."

"Thank you." The stone dug into Filibria's hand as she squeezed it. She wanted to throw her arms around Carna's neck and give him a hug like she had when she was little. But she was grown now—and married—so she had to restrain herself.

Out in the courtyard, the soldiers from Eirarin waited for her. Some stood on edge near their horses and some were already mounted. A small crowd of castle staff formed a wary half circle, their backs to the castle. Prince Trinlys stood between the two, now bound to both. A look of relief crossed his face when Filibria appeared.

Carna must have felt the increase of pressure from Filibria clutching his arm, for he gave her another discreet pat on the hand.

"May you find the same peace you have set out to give," he said before transferring her hand to the waiting prince. "Treat her well, Prince, and you will be blessed. Safe travels to you both."

The prince bowed. Then Carna and the castle staff retreated, leaving Filibria alone with the Eirarins. Would she ever see the old man again?

Prince Trinlys took the reins of a horse and led it towards Filibria.

"This is your third wedding gift, my lady. She was bred in the royal stables and her sire is the greatest horse in Eirarin." He passed the reins to Filibria. "You will ride her today. She is yours to name."

"Thank you." The horse's coat shimmered like gold silk in the sun. Its beauty far surpassed anything in her father's stables, or any other horse she had ever seen before. Filibria rubbed the mare's nose as it sniffed at her. She knew how precious horses were to the Eirarin's. This gift was worth more than any of the others the prince had given her. The honor overwhelmed her.

"Let's ride out," Captain Wrestan barked. "We must ride hard if we are to make it home tonight." His horse danced beneath him, mirroring his master's impatience.

The prince cupped his hands to give Filibria a leg up onto her horse. She paused. She could have mounted the horse without his help, but to say something would only make it more awkward. Putting a hesitant hand on his shoulder, she stepped into his hands. Trying her best not to kick him, she swung her leg over the horse and settled into the saddle. Trinlys straightened and smiled at her, wiping his hands off on his pants.

When Captain Wrestan sounded a horn, Trinlys quickly mounted, and the cavalcade rode out.

The pastures and fields around Falendle gave way to the young forests further north. The trees quickly swallowed up all sight of the city and its small castle. Soon only a brown ribbon of road unraveled behind them; this road tied Eirarin and Delvaria together. Just like how Filibria now tied them together. Filibria craned for a last look until finally a bend swallowed up the last glimpse of the city.

"You will see it again someday," the prince spoke softly. "When the ties between our kingdoms are strengthened, we can ride the road in safety as often as we wish." He had ridden quietly up beside her and now watched her intently.

"I hope." But it was not her home anymore. Filibria set her face to the road ahead. Only the future mattered now.

Filibria gave her attention to her surroundings, marveling at the vast amount of trees. They cut off the harsh daylight so that the light was soft and green, the air cool. Even though the trees were still too young to use in ship or house building—the reason they were being grown—they still almost met above the wide road. Filibria had never been in a true forest before. She decided she liked it, but was also glad they would not be spending the night in one.

They rode hard, as if pursued, away from the castle. Only when they were well out of sight of the capital did they slow to preserve the horses.

When the excitement of riding wore off, boredom set in. Filibria had always considered herself a good rider. But next to these men, she soon began to ache at their pace. None of the men talked to her, or even looked at her, including her new husband. She snuck a glance at him, riding with his face set to the road, grim and silent. Was he not curious about her? At least, unlike her, he had surely heard of her existence. Or was he simply not good at starting conversations? Maybe his words dried on his tongue like hers did. What a pair they would be. Doomed to silence forever. He did not even talk to his own men. Instead, he rode a little behind them, outside the circle of their words.

Filibria eavesdropped on the conversations, but it was like most conversations between men, concerning either women or war. Once, the words "trade routes" caught her ear, Filibria spurred her horse ahead to catch the end of the conversation.

"Soon this road will be bustling with trade," one soldier said.

"Aye, it will be good to see gold flowing into the kingdom again."

"Taxed gold," the one soldier spat, "but only for a while." He glanced quickly over his shoulder. Seeing Filibria, he dropped his voice and she heard no more.

The words twisted in her stomach. What did they mean by that? She watched the prince. If he had heard any of the conversation, he did not show it on his face. He was lost in his own world.

Was her only worth in this marriage for trade routes? Granted, they were important, being the main source of conflict between the two kingdoms.

The condition of the road drew Filibria out of her head. Once, generations ago, it had been a wide paved road, but the stones had been dug up to build walls and houses, leaving exposed dirt. Undergrowth had overtaken it until only two narrow tracks, old wagon wheel ruts, remained. It became apparent why they could not bring a carriage. Even the wagon carrying her dowry and belongings struggled to make it over the road. Several times, the captain swore he would abandon it, but every time, the prince dismounted and coaxed the horses to pull harder.

The prince apologized each time they had to stop and free the wagon or move a fallen tree from the road.

"I did not realize my country was like this," Filibria replied, in shock. The further they rode from the capital, the more the land deteriorated. Hamlets shrunk, fields became overgrown, distinguished only by crumbled stone walls, before giving way to more young forests. It was no secret Delvaria was not rich, but so much disrepair and dilapidation appalled Filibria. What did the Eirarins think of such squalor? None of the men betrayed any emotion as they picked their way over the broken land.

As the afternoon waned, they passed by several burned remnants of houses, already reclaimed by tangling vines. Further on, a whole hamlet was razed to the ground, barely one stone still atop another and all darkened by the biting tongue of fire.

"What...happened here?" Filibria asked, her mouth agape. If reports of the burned villages had reached the capital, she had not heard them.

Trinlys shifted on his horse before answering.

"We are nearing the border," he said softly, "but this happened a long time ago and there has been little trouble since."

"Eirarin...did this?"

"Yes," he mumbled, "but it will be safe to rebuild. No doubt these roads will be soon cleared. Thanks to you."

"I never knew." Filibria shook her head in wonder. "I knew there was war. But..."

"But it seemed so far off?" Trinlys finished.

"Yes—but real people lost their homes. People died."

"On both sides," Trinlys said. Was there tension in his voice? If so, he removed it when he added, "But no more." He smiled. "On the Eirarin side, people are already living again in houses close to the border. You will see."

Filibria was not sure what she expected the border to look like. On the Delvarian side, it consisted of nothing more than a low stone wall. A wooden barrier blocked the road where Delvarian soldiers waited for the cavalcade. Filibria recognized them, but she could not remember their names. They would be the last Delvarian faces she would see for a long time. The soldiers moved the barrier aside, letting them ride past.

They rode through a small section of land Wrestan referred to as "no man;s land" before coming to another barrier. Red pennons flew from flagpoles and men dressed in Eirarin livery lounged against the barrier. They stood to attention when the cavalcade approached and Wrestan rode ahead to exchange words.

Soldiers stepped forward to search the wagon. They started pulling the chests of Filibria things out onto the road. When they threw back the lids, their intentions to search all of her personal belongings became apparent.

"Surely that isn't necessary," Trinlys protested.

"It is the King's orders," Captain Wrestan snapped. His tone challenged the prince argue it further.

"I'm sorry," Trinlys whispered to Filibria as her garments and undergarments were tossed into the bed of the wagon. Filibria only held her tongue and stared at the road straight ahead. Her face burned.

When they were satisfied she was smuggling nothing, they tumbled Filibria's things back in and closed the lid.

Two soldiers moved the barrier and motioned them through.

Filibria was now in Eirarin. She looked around at the new land; though the mountains of Delvaria faded into the horizon behind her, nothing much had changed.

"Welcome home," the prince said, turning in his saddle to smile at her. "We will be in Caryen by sundown."

Sundown, not too far off. Filibria had not realized how close the two kingdoms were. Eirarin had always been a distant, ominous threat, but now that she was riding through it, it was only a day's journey from one capital to the other. How easy it would be to move an army over the border before alarms could be raised.

Comfortable within their own border, the cavalcade slowed a little. When they reached the first stream, the captain halted, allowing everyone to dismount and water their horses. It felt good to slip from the saddle and feel solid ground again, though her legs refused to support her at first. Filibria clung to her horse for a minute, refusing to admit her weakness. Thankfully, the men paid her no mind. She led her horse to the stream and settled on the banks while it drank, pulling off her boots and sinking her feet into the cool water. When she glanced up, she caught the captain staring at her. He did not look away when she met his dark eyes.

"Perhaps we should blindfold her," Captain Wrestan suggested. "It would not do for her to memorize the way back."

"She is a bride, not a prisoner," the prince replied, his tone level, but his face had flushed at the suggestion. The hand on his rein tightened.

"But she is still of the other kingdom. Not bound by true blood yet."

Trinlys's face colored as he blustered through his words. "Vows are strong enough. She will ride free. Besides, if she wanted to find her way back, there is a wide road leading all the way from one kingdom to another."

The soldiers laughed in agreement, making the captain's face darken.

Wrestan glared at Trinlys, but the prince won, because when they mounted again, too soon in Filibria's opinion, she rode without a blindfold. Nevertheless, the company fell around her, hemming her in.

When they passed through the first village, Filibria knew she was not home anymore. Her definition of poverty had been redefined. Squalid wooden houses pressed against the dirt streets. Ragged children scattered before the horses and carriage to regroup and gawk behind them. Gaunt housewives turned out of the doors to watch the prince, and their new princess ride through. Every face was blank.

The two kingdoms, in their greed and hatred, had bled each other dry, cutting each other off from trade to the north and south. In the process, they had hurt their people. Her role was important, Filibria realized. Not simply for there to be no more war, but so that both kingdoms could flourish in peace.

Between the villages and forests lay barren fields. Boney livestock reached over roadside fences to graze on what little grass the ditches had to offer. A blanket of grey dust lay over everything and soon coated the travelers too.

Unlike Delvaria, the condition of Eirarin did not change the further they rode into the kingdom. In some places, entire forests had been chopped down, leaving rotting stumps protruding from the land.

The soft golden rays of sunset did nothing to improve the landscape. The forest stretched dark shadows over the road, but soon the forest fell away, leaving eerie stretches of quiet bogland. A thick fog rose from the damp, shrouding the road and the sleeping hamlets they passed through. A chill came with it, forcing the company to stop and retrieve their cloaks from their packs.

They were almost home, Trinlys promised, and a warm fire would be waiting.

As a full moon poked over the horizon, they finally saw the capital, a blaze of lights through the mist. Only one league more—then Filibria would be home.

CHAPTER

Four

THE KINGDOM OF EIRARIN may have been poor, but the capital, Caryen, was not. Even in the foggy darkness of twilight, Filibria could make out the vast stone castle, perched like a bird of prey atop the hill, surrounded by high walls. The city rambled below it in crooked lanes and the bottom of the hill was encircled by another strong wall. But the city had outgrown its borders, spilling out and over into the countryside. Delvaria was rich in quarries and mines, so Filibria was used to stone houses, but in contrast, Eirarin exported wood, so the houses were tall, narrow wooden structures, leaning against one another like drunken men supporting each other down the street. The further up the hill, the bigger and wider the houses; some even had gardens out front. Even the shabbiest of the houses boasted glass windows, rippling with dampened firelight.

The horses' hooves on the wide cobbled roads echoed against the houses and in the alleys as they climbed the slope. A dead hush lay over the town. Once or twice, Filibria thought she saw a shadow in a window, only for it to disappear when they passed. She shivered and pulled her cloak around her. Though she dreaded reaching the castle, she would be glad to be out of the dark. Even in familiar places, like her home, she had never welcomed it.

The gate to the castle was shut when they arrived. Torches burned in the gatehouse above, but it took several shouts to rouse the guards. Unseen hands turned gears and the portcullis rattled open into dark shadows above. The spikes protruded like teeth as they rode into the mouth of the courtyard.

An old ostler, holding a torch, waited for them. The men dismounted and led their horses to the stables, leaving Trinlys and Filibria alone. When Filibria slid from her saddle, her legs did not catch her. Before she could fall, Trinlys appeared at her side and caught her elbow.

"Thank you," she said shakily.

"Not used to the saddle for so long?" He laughed, then sobered. "I'm sorry we rode so hard. I would have broken up the journey if I could have had a say, but the men were scared to stay too long in your kingdom." Realizing he was still supporting her elbow, he let go quickly, hiding his hands behind his back.

"That is the furthest I have ever ridden," Filibria replied.

"Thankfully, you will not have to again for a long while. Never, when the roads are mended, for then you shall have your own carriage."

So many promises. Was he trying to pacify her? Or trick her into a sense of security?

The ostler took their horses away to the stable while Trinlys led Filibria towards the castle. Even though her legs held her, every step hurt.

"Mother Brylla should still be up. She will take you to your chamber and help you in any way you need."

As Filibria followed her husband through the dim halls, she caught glimpses of the many rooms. Firelight glinted off gilded beams and polished weapons on the walls, and between the weapon displays hung rich tapestries. Fires smoldered in the large fireplaces where dogs dozed in the warmth before them. Several of the beasts lifted their sleepy heads in mild interest when Trinlys and Filibria passed. One dog jumped up and padded towards them—a huge, wolf-like dog. Trinlys fell to his knees in front of it, wrestling the dog's head in a fond embrace.

"This is Keayn," he said lovingly, as the dog licked his face. "and she missed me. Yes, she did, didn't you girl?"

Filibria stood aside, unsure of how to react.

As if remembering himself and his duties, Trinlys sprang back to his feet, wiping the dog hair and slobber off his face and the front of his tunic. With an apologetic smile, he gestured forward and took the lead.

They climbed four flights of winding stairs to the top floor of the castle—the private floor, Trinlys informed her. Up here were the chambers and solar belonging to the royal family, whom she would meet tomorrow. The floors on this level were carpeted in thick woven material. Filibria had never seen anything like it. It muffled her footsteps and also helped to keep the constant chill of so much stone at bay. Eirarin truly was a kingdom of weaving and textiles.

Trinlys led Filibria to a big oak door and knocked. Immediately it swung open, light seeping into the hall from around a plump figure.

"You have arrived!" the woman said as she took Filibria's arm, drawing her into the room.

"Mother Brylla will tend to your needs," Trinlys managed to say before he was shooed off and the door closed in his face.

"Let me take a look at you, you poor cold thing. A soft bed, warm clothes, and a bite to eat is what you need."

The woman standing before Filibria was the most motherly-looking person she had ever seen: comfortably round, with a head of greying hair pulled back into a large bun. Scents of cinnamon and fresh bread emanated from her simple study clothes. In front of the woman's eyes were two bubbles of glass, suspended across her nose and over her ears by a piece of wire. Filibria tried not to stare too hard at the contraption, but Mother Brylla caught her at it.

"Glasses," she said, shoving them up her nose. "A new invention to help you see better. The scholars in the high city of Dlegcalgon came up with them. I have a cousin there who got me a pair." She touched the wire proudly.

"Now"—Mother Brylla stopped, her hands on her hips as she gathered her thoughts—"a proper introduction: I'm the chief cook, chief chambermaid, and in charge of most things around here. Everyone except the King, of course, calls me Mother Brylla, even though I am mother to no one." Mother Brylla led Filibria towards the roaring fireplace. "This is to be your room. The prince is just down the hall. Tomorrow you will be expected to act in your role as a married woman, but for tonight, you get to be by yourself."

Filibria's face flushed with heat. "He has a separate room then?" The question, loaded with relief, slipped from Filibria before she could catch it.

Mother Brylla chuckled. "Wouldn't want too many heirs."

Filibria's blush deepened.

"There is no hurry. He is as scared as you are. The bedding ceremony is tomorrow, though after it you may still keep to your own room."

Filibria's heart sank. The bedding ceremony: where their marriage would be made complete. It was necessary to fully tie the bond of peace, she reminded herself...but the dread would not leave her.

As Mother Brylla bobbed around the room, talking, preparing the bed, and helping Filibria undress, Filibria took the chance to look around her new room. She missed the curving walls of her old one, tucked away in a tower. This room was also much bigger.

Instead of Devarian colors, the room was decorated in the reds and golds she was slowly becoming accustomed to. Red was in the canopy over her bed, and in the curtains over the window nook. Filibria touched the coverlets. Woven of fine gold thread, they matched the cushions in the window and on the chair. Along one wall was a carven cupboard and a mirror framed in worked flowers and vines of gold. The most significant difference from her old room was a desk, complete with fresh ink, pens, and parchment.

When Filibria walked to the desk, Brylla said, "You would be allowed to write to your family, I'm sure."

Filibria ran her finger through the pen's feather.

"I can't write," she admitted. Reading and writing were not considered essential skills in Delvaria. Even her own father could not and left it to his trusted scribe. Delvaria believed everything was best communicated through oral word. Written ones were not to be trusted; for the intent behind them could easily be mistranslated.

"Well, the prince can both read and write—and I'm sure he would be happy to teach you if you'd like. Come now, your bed is ready. Can I get you a bite to eat? Oatcakes and honey? Some warm milk?"

Filibria shook her head at the suggestions. "Sleep will suffice."

Mother Brylla's face softened. "Of course, dear." She removed Filibria's shift, replacing it with a soft nightgown. "Tomorrow will be a long day. The King is hosting a feast in your honor, and then a tournament, also in your honor. Unless it rains, of course. Let's hope for that. You will have a bath in the morning, and we will bring you a new dress. No doubt you'll also be a fair bit sore tomorrow, but we'll take care of you. We aren't a kingdom of riders for nothing." Mother Brylla pulled back the coverlets, allowing Filibria to crawl into the inviting bed.

Mother Brylla doused the torches. "Good night." She closed the door behind her, wrapping the room in quiet warmth.

Despite the weariness lapping over Filibria's body, she could not sleep. Everything ached, her heart most of all. She watched the firelight flickering over the walls and gilded ceiling. This was her new home. For better or for worse, fate willing, she would live out the rest of her life within these stone walls. The reality refused to sink in.

Somewhere within these walls, her new family rested. King Dalen, sworn enemy of her kingdom, slumbered next to his wife, surely only a couple chambers from her's. And Trinlys, did he sleep? Or did he lie awake like she did, trying to envision their future?

As the firelight dimmed, the tears came. Always her life had been predictable and certain, but now she could see no further than the next day. Years of peace weaving lay ahead of her. Beyond that, she would be a wife and a princess. Later, she might be a mother and a queen. It was the life her mother had followed and her mother's mother before her. But right now, all her duties felt so far off, so large and uncertain—so...overwhelming. Filibria buried her face into the pillows and wept.

CHAPTER

Five

Despite the banquet being an evening event, Mother Brylla and a host of women woke Filibria early.

When Filibria stretched to roll out of bed, she had to clamp her mouth shut to keep from crying out. Every muscle in her body screamed from the previous day's ride. Mother Brylla tried her best to look sympathetic, giving the princess a small smile.

"We've set a hot bath for you, dear. Just the thing you need." She slipped a firm arm under Filibria's shoulder, helping her towards a large wooden tub by the fire. Brylla and a maid eased the nightdress off of her. A floral fragrance wafted up from the steaming water as Filibria sank in.

Nothing in a long time had felt so good as the warmth enveloping Filibria. A sigh slipped out as she leaned against the edge; her stiffness leached away.

Mother Brylla smiled.

"The water was boiled with special herbs from the garden. A secret recipe only a few know. It will have you feeling fresh and limber in no time."

Filibria lost track of time while she soaked. Mother Brylla and her minions moved quietly around the room, disappearing out the door every so often to reappear with a brush, jewelry, or pots of colored powder for her eyes and cheeks. They tidied up her already spotless room, smoothed the bed down, and spread their preparations out over the coverlet. They did not talk to her while they worked and only glanced curiously in her direction; Filibria ignored them. When she closed her eyes, she could imagine herself back in her old room, with Malda puttering around. But Malda always talked, or complained, or ranted. These women were too quiet, and the silence summoned too many thoughts to Filibria's head.

She didn't want to leave the bath, but time was slipping away. Mother Brylla left the handmaidens to dry Filibria off while she went to attend to a few feast details down in the kitchen. She returned just as the maidens finished drying Filibria's hair, and she did not return empty-handed.

"A bite to eat to keep you on your feet until supper." Mother Brylla set a large platter of food on the desk. "When we start dressing you, there will be no time. You will get away with eating in your room today, but all other meals you are expected to share with the royal family in the Great Hall. The King will not be pleased if you miss one." Mother Brylla's serious tone frightened her.

"I will try my best to always be on time," Filibria promised meekly.

"A horn will sound before each meal to summon people. As long as you hear it, you will be good."

As Filibria ate the provided oatcakes and cheese; the maids stood around the room, trying their best not to watch her. No one talked. Did no one in the kingdom like conversation?

The chambermaids swooped in when she finished her last bite. They spent the rest of the morning fixing Filibria's golden hair into intricate braids, manicuring her nails, and painting her face—then they brought in her dress. It was white, trimmed with golden threads, with sleeves that ended past her wrists and draped to her feet. The neckline was lower than anything Filibria was used to, and the waistline, loose. While some of the women fussed with the laces, others placed a coronet on her head and wove her braids through it. They secured a thin veil to the back of the band.

As a last touch, Mother Brylla handed Filibria a small bouquet.

"Flowers have meaning here in Eirarin. Every flower we give one another sends a message. The Queen had this made for you from her own garden. The little blue flowers are dandlehocks, symbolizing hopeful love. Ferns are for peace, not just within your marriage, but the kingdom too. Same with the dark blue flower, the malina, which symbolizes loyalty. The white buds are girshel, symbolizing children and fertility."

Filibria counted ten of the white buds and hoped it was not prophetic.

"And finally, the little pink flower all on its own is hope. Every bride in the kingdom gets a bouquet like this. You got more for loyalty and peace than most."

Blues, whites, and pink—such delicate little flowers. Filibria touched them. But what about duty? What flower symbolizes duty?

"You'll learn the flowers soon enough," Mother Brylla prattled on, almost as if she had heard Filibria's thoughts. "We don't take it too seriously, but it is fun for sending little messages. Especially to your lover." She winked. "And speaking of him, he's been waiting outside a while for you." Mother Brylla took a step back to survey her work. As a last decoration, Filibria fixed a smile on her face.

"You're a brave girl," Mother Brylla said quietly. She opened the door, gesturing Filibria out. "I will see you in the Hall," she promised.

Trinlys stood in the hallway, once again also dressed in white. Keayn, his dog, stood proudly at his side. Trinlys smiled when Filibria hesitantly took her place beside him.

"You look lovely. I hope you were able to rest well."

Warmth crept over Filibria's face, and she was glad for the dim light in the passageway; nevertheless, she ducked her head.

"Thank you. I did."

He offered her his arm, and she took it, noting for the first time the strength and sturdiness it had to offer. If he was scared, he did not show it like he had on the dais in Delvaria. Together, they made their way down the stairs into the crowded Great Hall. When they stepped through the threshold, a hush fell and all eyes turned to them. Filibria reinforced her smile.

A horn blew, calling everyone to rise. On the balcony, the minstrels struck up a tune as the couple started walking. Though the Great Hall was smaller than the one Filibria was used to, the walk to the dais stretched on forever. At the high table, atop the dais, sat the King Dalen, imposing in his crimson cloak and heavy gold crown. Filibria had grown up hearing her father's rants against this man and even now, distrust stirred in her. To his left sat the Queen, a plain but friendly-looking woman.

The King and Queen rose to their feet when the new couple mounted the dais.

"Welcome, my new daughter, to the halls of Eirarin." King Dalen spread his arms wide. Though the gesture was meant to be friendly, his face remained impassive and cold. "May you bring unity between our two kingdoms for generations to come. May this union tie Eirarin and Delvaria together for the rest of time. May our kingdoms finally have peace. And may the trade routes open wide to fill our coffers." The hall cheered coarsely, banging on tables and shouting praise.

Filibria curtsied. "I thank you, King Dalen of Eirarin, for your generous hospitality and your reaching arm of peace. I promise to serve the Kingdom of Eirarin for as long as I live. And I promise to bind our kingdoms together in peace." The words, well-practiced, flowed easily from her mouth, portraying more confidence than she felt. Her training was truly coming into play now.

A servant stepped forward bearing the gilded chest from Delvaria. The Queen opened it and held the knotted marriage cord high.

"It is tied! They are united."

The hall cheered. The Queen set the cord back into the box and took up a chalice in front of her. "Let them drink of the marriage cup of our halls to complete their bond."

Filibria took comfort in the familiarity of passing and drinking from the same cup. Eirarin customs did not differ much from her own country; at least, she was not floundering about what to do.

"May this family be bound together by the strong ties of marriage and may these kingdoms be bound likewise," the Queen said.

"May it be!" the people in the hall shouted.

That ended the formalities, freeing the newlyweds to take their place at the high table.

Trinlys led Filibria to the empty chairs. He pulled a chair out for her, seating her between his chair and a young girl. Yet another mysterious royal heir. His sister, Filibria guessed.

A pale, gangly boy brought water for Filibria to wash her hands, and when each course came around, he set some of it before her.

"My name is Jarin," he whispered to her over the din of the hall as he served her the first course of soup. "I'm a page from the outer province, where my father is a lord. The Queen is letting me serve you. I am to help you at mealtimes, fetch you for meetings, and assist you when you go out."

"Thank you, Jarin."

He smiled, but when the Queen looked over and frowned, he shrank back into the shadows behind Filibria's chair.

The feasting lasted throughout the whole evening. Ale flowed freely until the smoky room stank of it. People drifted in and out of the hall—talking, laughing, quarreling, drinking and eating. Others settled at the empty tables to play chess or dice. In the center of the room, jugglers and acrobats entered to the rhythm of music from the balcony above. Filibria, the prince, and the rest of the royal family stayed on the dais. It was almost like an invisible barrier lay between them and the room below. Only the King did not notice it. He grew merrier as the feast and toasts progressed. Chiefs, knights, soldiers, and commoners came to the foot of the dais to toast the King and congratulate him on the marriage. They hardly glanced at the new couple or the rest of the royal family.

Halfway through the meal, Filibria noticed Captain Wrestan sitting on the other side of the young girl. He would get up occasionally to wander the room, joining in games, or toasting. He too ignored the family, though he glanced once or twice at Filibria. His look was cold and it stabbed fear into Filibria's heart. No ordinary captain ever held a place at the King's table.

The girl, who bore a strong resemblance to the prince, fidgeted and twisted around in her chair to take everything in. She met Filibria's eyes more than once and they both half-smiled in sympathy. The girl did not eat much, and neither did Filibria. She pushed her food around the platter but only ate a bite or two. Beside her, Trinlys had finished eating long ago and kept his eyes trained on the table right in front of him. Filibria dare not look at him. Was he as bored as she was?

When dinner finally finished, servants swarmed in, clearing tables and moving them to the edge of the room. In the center, they spread fresh rushes over the floor. The acrobats disappeared, musicians struck up a dancing tune, and a young couple stepped out onto the floor. While everyone laughed and clapped, the couple danced. The floor soon filled with dancing people until the circles of dresses and bright colors spun around and around, dipping and weaving through each other and the columns of the hall.

"Do you dance?" Trinlys whispered. Instead of waiting for an answer, he held out his hand.

Filibria just stared at him. Her only lessons in dancing had been informal. And the thought of dancing in this room full of judging eyes? With a man she barely knew? She'd rather spend another day in the saddle, but...it *would* look good to the people. Like she had no fear. Resolutely, she placed her hand in his. If he felt her shaking, he said nothing. Instead, he led her around the table and down off the dais. A lull fell in the festivities. The crowd pulled aside, letting the prince lead his bride into the center of the room. The musicians struck up another tune, and everyone began to dance.

At one point, swirling through the crowds of people, Filibria glanced towards the dais. The King was glaring at her and the captain was missing.

But Trinlys's arm was firm around her waist, the other on her shoulder. Filibria allowed herself to sink into the rhythm as he led her through each move with sureness and dexterity. Slowly, everything else around her faded until it did not matter. Before she could help herself, a smile formed—a real smile. The music shifted, indicating it was time to change partners. Reluctantly, Trinlys's hand slipped from her waist and he twirled her gently. Right into the captain's waiting arms.

Trinly's hand on her shoulder clamped down suddenly, as if to pull her back, but it was too late. The captain grabbed her waist, forcing her close to him. She lost the rhythm and her feet faltered, almost tripping.

"Careful there." The captain breathed into her ear. Trinlys, his arms around another girl, was disappearing across the room. The crowd swallowed him up.

Wrestan's fingers dug into her waist, trapping her in his arms. Her body went taut in response to his movements, fearful.

"You've got quite a position to fill here, Princess." His dark eyes never left her face, though she refused to look up at them.

Filibria did not answer.

He moved stiffly, as if performing a drill, not a dance. Filibria wished for Trinlys back, wishing for his sure, safe arms to be around her while she stumbled over the captain's feet. Only his firm grip kept her from falling.

"Watch where you step," he whispered as the song ended. "We wouldn't want anything happening to you." For a second longer, the captain held her...then he let go with an exaggerated bow.

"Until we meet again, my lady."

Filibria could not get away from him fast enough. She forced her way through the crowd until several clusters of people lay between her and the captain. Only then did she slow to scan the unfamiliar faces for Trinlys. As she searched, he met her in the middle of the room. Instinctively, he reached towards her, to claim her, but remembering himself, he pulled back. His eyes were strangely dark and cold. Could he be jealous of Wrestan? The captain had done nothing wrong, yet his actions clearly shook Trinlys as much as they shook her.

"I have never seen him dance before," Trinlys said weakly. Filibria searched his flushed face. Was it anger? Or perhaps an apology?

"You are a much better dancer than he is," she replied. She could still feel the unpleasant touch of his hands on her waist.

When Filibria and her husband returned to the dais, the Queen was waiting for them. The hour Filibria had been dreaded was here.

"It is time for you and the prince to retire. Mother Brylla is waiting in your room to prepare you."

Cold fear stabbed through Filibria. When she glanced over, Trinlys's face was pink, like her own must be. He looked at the floor, avoiding her gaze.

A serving man escorted Trinlys away while the Queen took Filibria up to her room. Mother Brylla and several other handmaidens were waiting within. The Queen left her in Brylla's capable hands, promising to return when she was ready.

Mother Brylla said nothing while she helped Filibria out of her dress into a simple silk nightgown, pulling a cloak around Filibria's shoulders as a finishing touch. When she fastened the cloak at Filibria's throat, she met her eyes.

"You're shaking, lass."

Filibria nodded.

"He is a gentle lad; he will not hurt you."

Filibria could only nod again.

"Now come." Mother Brylla, along with the Queen, led Filibria down a hall to the prince's room. He stood outside his door, draped in an identical cloak to hers.

Filibria could not make herself meet his eyes. He held out his hand and she took it, allowing him to lead her inside his room. She did not take in any of the room's contents, only the bed, as a small crowd followed them into the room.

Filibria and Trinlys stood at the foot of his bed, still holding hands. The Queen stepped forward with a simple silk cord.

"As this cord binds you," she said, wrapping the cord slowly around Filibria and Trinlys's joined hands, "may you be bound tonight."

"May it be," the small crowd echoed solemnly. Firelight flickered over their faces, Trinlys's face, and over the bed. It should have been warm, but Filibria only felt the chill of dread clinging to her body.

Filibria's hand shook against Trinlys's, cold and clammy.

Still bound, Trinlys and Filibria climbed into the bed. The curtains were drawn around them and the people filed from the room. Trinlys let out a long breath.

Filibria still did not look. She felt Trinlys fumble at the cords, releasing their hands. He moved away from her and a moment or more passed before he spoke.

"You can leave when the halls are clear and go back to your own bed. That is, if you want to."

"They won't...?" Filibria glanced towards the door.

"No one needs to know. They will all be in bed soon."

"Thank you." Filibria drew her arms up around her knees. She did not dare lean back against his pillows. Trinlys sat fidgeting with the corner of the blankets.

"I think it is a stupid tradition," Trinlys said. Silence. "Love should not be forced."

"It's not love," Filibria said simply. "It's politics."

"Well, it shouldn't be. Marriage should only be for love. Do you think some ever find love? In politics, I mean."

"Some." Filibria thought of her own parents. Forced to get married on a battlefield for the sake of their kingdoms, they had hated each other, but they fell in love and have been ever since.

Trinlys was quiet, as if lost in thought. He played with a thread on the edge of his blanket.

Filibria did not dare move. She hoped he would not bring up love again; it made her uncomfortable, more so than sharing the bed with him in silence. She could hear his steady breathing. Her chill gave way to uncomfortable heat, but she dared not move.

"You should be safe now," Trinlys said after what felt like an eternity.

Filibria slipped out of bed and fled from the room. She did not even look back at her husband. Did not wish him goodnight. Why was he doing this? Filibria wondered. Why was he being kind to her? Breaking rules for her?

CHAPTER

Six

Filibria woke the next morning to the chatter of women. At first, she thought she was back in Delvaria, but then the unfamiliar voices reminded her of where she was. The heaviness settled back in her heart. She did not want to open her eyes.

"Get out of here! Shoo," Mother Brylla said to the other women. "I am more than capable of getting her ready myself. Go on now." Silence settled in the room once the door closed.

"I know you're awake," Mother Brylla said, "and I know what happened—or rather what did not happen—last night."

Filibria groaned into her pillow.

"Don't fret about it," Mother Brylla said briskly, "I don't hold to the tradition. People need time, but don't let anyone else know or there will be trouble. A marriage is not true until it is finalized. And I have news that will no doubt make you happy. The tournament has been postponed because of the rain, but the Queen has requested that you breakfast with her in her chambers."

Mother Brylla pulled back the covers. The fire had died in the night and the chill hit Filibria's body. She wanted to pull the covers back up and sleep her heartache away. Instead, she forced herself out of bed, shivering.

Filibria stared out the window while Mother Brylla laced her into a simple lavender dress. A heavy fog, like the one outside, lay over her mind. Rain streamed down the glass and thunder rumbled over the land. She loved rain, today more than ever; it protected her, like a blanket, from the outside world.

"You can trust me, Filibria," Mother Brylla said, "but not the other women; too many eyes, ears, and wagging tongues. I sent them out and I'll take care of you myself from now on. I'm here for you for whatever you need; a shoulder to cry on, a heart to hold secrets, a store of wisdom for your dilemmas. Bring them to Mother Brylla and I will help you as I am able."

"Thank you."

"You must promise me to at least try to get to know Trinlys. He'll be with me in the kitchen today—alone with his books."

The subtle invitation hung in the air; Filibria did not respond.

Mother Brylla finished tying the last ribbon in her hair. "There! You look beautiful, dear."

She had to be lying. Filibria knew her face was pale and drawn from the past few days; no amount of makeup could hide that.

"Jarin is waiting outside the door to take you to the Queen's chamber."

The page eagerly led Filibria down the hall to the section of the castle belonging to the Queen. He opened the door for her and bowed.

The Queen's private chambers were the brightest in the castle. Light streamed through a large window, illuminating the colorful dresses of the ladies of the court and their serving women. Like all the other rooms in the castle, there was so much red. Against the wall were two looms. The thumping rhythm of the flying shuttles set the beat of the room. Women talked and laughed as their fingers flew over embroidery hoops. The Queen reclined on a couch, playing chess with one of her maids. She sat up when Filibria entered.

"Please sit." The Queen gestured to a cushioned stool in front of a low table covered in food.

Filibria obeyed. The women were silent now, watching her. No doubt judging her botchy, tear-stained face.

"Please, eat. Usually, everyone breakfasts in the hall, but I thought you might appreciate a little privacy, even if it means I steal you away from your husband."

A few of the women snickered, causing Filibria to blush.

"Thank you. I am honored. Your chambers are beautiful."

Filibria picked up a plate, gathering an oatcake or two, and several slices of fresh fruit. Anything to keep her busy and hide her embarrassment. Once she settled back into her chair, the other women swooped in on the food. They all settled down to eat quietly, once again watching Filibria.

When they finished, the Queen opened the conversation with trivial questions concerning the Delvarian wedding, such as the length, amount of guests, and other things Filibria could not remember.

"I suppose it has been many years since a wedding has been held in your halls?" she asked Filibria. "Your mother being a blade bride, that is."

"Yes," Filibria said with some astonishment. Her mother's fame had traveled far, if even Eirarin knew of her parents' wedding on the battlefield. "I was fortunate to be married in a dress in a hall, and not in armor on the battlefield."

"Indeed, but it still took much courage, I am sure."

Filibria ducked her head. "Thank you. It is my duty and I am honored to fulfill it." The words sounded so ceremonial—so hollowed. But if the Queen noticed or thought such, she said nothing, only skipping on to the next subject.

"Ah yes, about your duties. I have no doubt your mother trained you well in the role of a peace weaver?"

Filibria thought back to the grueling years of reciting feast oaths until she had memorized them all, learning to hide her emotions, learning the hierarchy of the hall: who held the highest positions and who not to anger. Hours and hours of lessons. "She did."

"Good." The Queen smiled. "You will not be expected to perform them all yet. We will give you time to adjust to your new life—and give us time to adjust to you. We have never had a peace weaver grace these halls. We commissioned the best craftsmen in the land to make the various goblets for passing peace. Of course, we have the common stirrup cup for parting and hunts, but nothing beyond that. We have all had to brush up on the culture." The Queen laughed at Filibria's surprised look.

"I am not a weaver, dear, though I have dispensed the gold to the warriors and passed the cup. I belong to Eirarin. I am my husband's cousin. He married me because Eirarin needed a Queen. I am not like your mother, nor am I like you. Brave is never a word I'd use to describe myself. It would be like pulling teeth to leave my home to come to a neighboring kingdom, wed or not. It must be so strange for you."

"If you have never had a peace weaver, then why now?" Filibria asked. In Delvaria, it was such a sacred and solemn tradition, with every eldest daughter married out of the kingdom and the younger daughters married to lords in the provinces. Even the sons married princesses of other kingdoms and the younger sons were sent to train far away. Peace was revered above all; she could not imagine a life where peace weaving did not exist.

"I do not know, to tell the truth," the Queen responded quietly, "I run the castle and keep myself to the doings within the walls, not outside. Those are for my husband."

"You never go out?"

"For the occasional hawking party and such, but my husband prefers I stay in the castle. And there is nothing beyond these walls for me anyway," she said, as if trying to justify the unfairness of her previous statement.

She reminded Filibria of a caged bird, locked away for the rest of her life and resigned to the fact. Would Filibria end up like her?

"I oversee the women of the castle and most importantly, the weaving. Do you know how to weave?"

"No." Filibria watched the women at the loom. They were so swift with their fingers, yet they talked and laughed with each other like it was easy work.

"Then we will have to teach you. Eirarin is famed for its weaving and every woman at least knows the basics. I will teach you myself sometime."

"I am honored. Thank you."

"You may return to your room now if you wish. But please, explore the castle; it is your home now too. And if you ever need anything, my room is always open to the women of the court. Tonight, I would be honored if you joined us in the royal solar. You are part of the royal family now, so it is your place as much as ours. We merely relax and talk before bed."

"Thank you." Filibria rose stiffly, curtseyed, and fled the room. The Queen made her feel welcome, but she was nothing like Filibria's strong mother. More like one of the chattering chambermaids. Still, Filibria needed friends and allies and the Queen was eager to love her.

Back in her room, Filibria curled up on the window seat against the cold glass. Her father's castle did not have glass. It was too expensive. Glass was for boasters who had money and a large army to protect the castle, but glass was beautiful. Filibria traced the rain droplets down the panes. They flowed like her own tears. Without meaning to, she fell asleep.

"Filibria?"

Filibria's face was pressed up against the cold glass. Mother Brylla touched her shoulder.

"You'll catch a cold. If you're sleepy, come to bed."

Filibria shook the sleep from her head. "What time is it?"

"Well, you missed most of the evening dinner. The King was none too pleased. Neither was Trinlys, though he was mostly worried. He's asked about you a couple times today. I assured them you were still tired from your journey. But if you want, you can still join them."

Filibria did not want to. After avoiding the bedding ceremony, being with Trinlys—acting like a dutiful wife—felt like a lie, but she knew she needed to spend time with them. They were her new family after all. And she had to do her best to not anger her new father-in-law. Peace between their kingdoms relied on it. It would not do to have a war started over a missed meal.

"I will join them."

Mother Brylla smiled and helped her change into a fresh dress.

Dinner was much more subdued than the feast the day before. Since the King still had his guests with him who were waiting out the storm, the food was plentiful and the hall was packed with visitors.

Filibria kept her head down all the way across the room. She was aware of the disapproving look the King bestowed upon her as she took her seat. The Queen's forehead wrinkled in worry. Trinlys did not look up at all. How easy would it be to keep peace in the kingdom if no peace even existed in the family?

Only the young princess remained unaffected by the mood in the room. She gave Filibria a warm smile.

The mood did nothing to her appetite. After eating a few bites, Filibria resorted to pushing the food around on her plate. She gave up and rose from the table when the men finished their last customary toasts.

Filibria walked alone down the hallway, her head bowed. She almost bumped into the man blocking the passage.

"I'm sorry..." she began and looked up into the piercing eyes of the captain. "Excuse me."

A slice of a smile slit his face. "Filibria of Delvaria." He performed a bow and stepped aside. She hurried past, knowing he was watching her. Why was he on the royal private floor?

Filibria slipped into her room. How she wished she had her mother—or Malda—to talk to. She fingered the writing materials at her desk, composing a letter to her mother in her head.

How had her mother survived the first few months of her marriage? Though she had patiently led Filibria through the laws and regulations of a peace weaver, she had never talked in depth about her own experience. How had her mother made the marriage work? How could Filibria make her own marriage work?

"Who is Wrestan?" Filibria asked Mother Brylla when the woman arrived to tend the fire and prepare her bed. "He rode with us from Delvaria, and he sits at the high table. A strange position for his station."

Mother Brylla, in the middle of folding down the bedsheets, stopped. For a moment, a look of concern crossed her face before she smoothed it away.

"Why do you ask?"

"I met him in the passage after I left the Great Hall. I do not like his eyes, the way he looks at me." Her reason suddenly sounded childish.

"He holds no royal position, so he should have no access to this floor. Don't you worry about him and don't let his staring get to you. He is only trying to make you cower. He thinks he's above us all. He doesn't care that he's on nobody's good side except the King's."

Even if he did upset her, Filibria knew she should not let it show. It would do no good for the captain of the guard to know she was scared of him. Whoever wielded fear wielded power. But for some reason, she could not drop the subject. Whether she liked it or not, the captain had gotten under her skin.

"He seems to upset Trinlys. When Wrestan danced with me, Trinlys almost seemed angry."

Mother Brylla straightened, her comfortable figure tense all of a sudden. She shoved her glasses up her nose and squinted through them. "No doubt Trinlys was jealous. As I said, Wrestan does not make himself amiable, but it's nothing for you to worry about."

The woman's actions told her otherwise, Filibria decided. Mother Brylla did not settle back into easy conversation while she completed her tasks.

"You've been invited to the royal solar, haven't you?" Mother Brylla asked when she finished.

Filibria's heart sank. Her bed, freshly made, looked so inviting. She drew herself up, trying to summon the courage to be uncomfortable for an hour or so more. Her duty was to connect with her new family, to show them the human side of the kingdom they once hated.

The solar was small but cozy, decorated in bright colors and beautiful tapestries. The Queen and two of her maidens sat around the fire, talking and embroidering. At the Queen's feet perched the prince's sister on a small stool, working on her needlework. Trinlys himself lounged in front of the fire, his head on his dog's stomach. When Filibria entered, he sat up, pulling out a chair for her.

"Welcome," the Queen said.

"Thank you." Filibria sat and Trinlys flopped back down onto his dog. The silence settled again, cold and awkward. Filibria groped for a conversation starter, for anything, as the fidgeting and restlessness grew. She turned to the girl, about fourteen, several years younger than Filibria's own sister. Already she had been in Eirarin for two days but had not met the rest of Trinlys' family properly.

"We have not been properly introduced. What is your name?" Filibria gave her a warm smile, but the girl did not answer.

"Tiaeve," the Queen said. "She has been mute since birth."

"Oh. Sorry. I did not mean..."

"How could you know?" the Queen replied gently. "Both my children are quiet enough to be mute, but she understands you perfectly."

The princess smiled at Filibria.

"Tiaeve," Filibria repeated the name. How appropriate, for like the little tiaeve flowers, the princess was pale and gentle. Tiaeve only bloom for one day, but they could cover a whole meadow like snow.

This opened the door for conversation. Before Filibria had joined, the Queen had been asking her son more details about the wedding. Filibria watched him, trying to read his emotions while he described her home, her family, and the ceremony without many details or animation. How did he feel about the wedding? Did he want it? Had he prepared his whole life for marrying a peace weaver, like she had prepared to peace weave? He had at least remembered more of it than she could.

The talk turned to the coming tournament, but it did not linger on the subject long. It became apparent no one in the room was looking forward to it.

"It will be many days," the Queen told Filibria, "but you will not be required to attend them all. Just the first and last. It will be your duty to award the prizes."

Then the conversation died out, but not unpleasantly. The Queen and her daughter turned back to their needlework. Trinlys and his dog dozed. Filibria picked at the embroidery on her sleeve, wishing for the first time she had needlework to focus on too. While other girls sat with their needlework, she had trained for peace weaving, so her skills with the needle suffered.

Once or twice, Keayn let out a long shuddering sigh. Filibria wished she could do the same; the thought brought a smile to her lips.

"But of course!" The Queen dropped her needlework and looked at her son. "You two have not had a peaceful moment together since the wedding and here we are sitting around blocking any conversation. Come girls, we must retire and leave them in peace."

Filibria almost protested, but it was too late. Before she knew it, the women had left.

The silence in the room dropped to a heavier level. Now Trinlys was fully awake, staring at the ceiling quietly. Neither dared look at each other.

"I do not know what married people talk about," Trinlys admitted. "My parents rarely talk to each other."

"I do not know either." Filibria admitted.

"It was not thought essential in your training as a peace weaver?" he laughed. "Surely you must have trained frequently?"

"Every day for as long as I can remember," Filibria replied. "But marriage…" She let her voice trail off. "Is that something you can train for? My training taught me how to act a certain way, even when I did not feel it. How to read a room. Which chalice was used for which ceremony. Politics. A little history. How to be a queen. But…not how to be a wife."

Trinlys sat up so he could look at her better, eyes burning with interest. "I have always been intrigued by peace weavers. I never thought I would marry one."

"I never thought I would marry an Eirarin, peace weaver or not," Filibria confessed with a small laugh.

"I never thought I would get married at all, actually," Trinlys responded quietly. He stroked at his dog's fur, burying his fingers deep.

Filibria wanted to ask why, but the question felt too deep, too personal. She replayed every conversation she had overheard between lovers, trying to change the conversation. Her gaze wandered over the room and it settled on the Eirarin coat of arms, emblazoned over the fireplace. It was an uplifted hawk's talon, ready to strike unsuspecting prey. The prince noticed her studying it.

"The talon," he said. "Birds have always been honored in Eirarin. It was said our ancestor was a man wronged and driven from his town. He was a hunter and had with him only a bird, a dog, and a horse—the ancestor to the one that now belongs to you. He let the bird free and it came to rest on this hill. Gathering men to him—outlaws mostly—he built a fortress here. Later, as he grew rich from thieving, he built a permanent castle, and a town settled around it."

"It's not a pleasant heraldry," Filibria remarked.

"No. I have never liked it much. I prefer the Delvarian one more. It is deeper in meaning, more artistic."

Filibria closed her eyes, allowing the Delvarian heraldry—also a bird—to materialize. It was a dove, its wings outstretched, grasping an arrow.

"I do not know the tale behind it," she admitted.

"I do. The dove symbolizes peace and the arrow, war. Your kingdom prefers peace, but it will fight if need be. Your kingdom began when relatives of Lord Cpeordos were forced to flee east after the Great Slaughter. They wanted a peaceful kingdom above all else. Which is why it is fitting you should come here to keep peace."

"You know more about my kingdom than I do," Filibria laughed. The silence continued.

"Do you have only your sister, or more siblings?" Filibria asked.

"Only her. There were others, but they died when they were young."

"I am sorry."

"I do not remember them," the prince said. "How many siblings do you have?"

"Three. An older brother, a younger brother, and a younger sister."

"Do you miss them?"

Filibria thought about it. She had not been close to them for many years. Kial, her older brother, once her closest friend, had become obsessed with weapons and battle strategies, hardening him like a smith shaping a blade—and her younger siblings still enjoyed a life with no royal obligations. "No. I do not miss them. My family was never close."

Silence again. A log shifted in the fire, sending up sparks; they both twitched at the noise. The dog gave out another shuddering sigh and started to snore.

Filibria's mind ran through her parents' conversations. They always focused on matters of the kingdom, or remarks about weather and food. It did not matter. She was not here for small talk, she decided in frustration. If her new husband would make conversation hard, then so be it. She would not try either. She was here for peace, not for him.

"What do you like to do?"

Filibria startled at the prince's voice, an earnestness in his eyes when she looked at him. Maybe he was trying.

"I like to ride, play the harp..." Between her inability to use the needle and her devotion to peace weaving, she had never worked hard at most womanly tasks. It had never bothered her, not until now. Hopefully, her husband did not mind. Not that it mattered, she reminded herself again.

"I think we have a harp around here somewhere. No one in the castle has played it for years, though. As for riding, our stables are full of horses. We should ride together sometime. The forest is beautiful this time of year and I know many secret paths."

"I would like that," Filibria answered. "What do you like to do?'

"I study."

"Books?" When the question escaped, Filibria felt foolish.

"Yes, but also nature. I help train horses for the stables. I also like riding—and dancing."

"As you proved yesterday."

His face grew red. "Are you tired?" he asked when the conversation lagged once again. "I can't imagine you've recovered from the journey yet."

"You had to travel it twice," Filibria replied, dodging the question. Would he expect her to share his bed tonight since they at least knew each other a little better? If they were this awkward at conversation, how much more would they be sharing a bed? If she kept up the conversation, he might not ask again.

The prince shrugged. "I enjoyed it. Or would have, if my nerves had behaved." He made a weak attempt at a laugh.

"Have you been to Delvaria before?" Filibria asked.

"No. It would not have been appropriate given our"--he cleared his throat—"our previous relationship, but I have traveled elsewhere. What about you? Have you traveled far?"

"I had never left Delvaria before now," Filibria admitted.

The prince regarded her gravely. "Then this must be very different for you. Were you scared to leave?"

"A little. I was more scared to come to Eirarin."

"I can understand that. I had never heard anything good of your kingdom before, but I had heard of *you*." He smiled.

Filibria wondered what exactly he had heard, but did not ask. Instead, she admitted she had never heard of him before. "No one had. There were rumors you were not the true heir."

"Fake heir? Ha. I wish I were. Life would be easier...but here we are. And things will turn out well in the end, don't you think?"

Filibria ducked her head. Her hands fiddled with her hem, threatening to destroy the dainty embroidery. No, she did not think it would turn out fine. How could she? She was a stranger here in a strange land. Her life would never be the same again. When she looked up again, the prince was still posed, looking for an answer. Why did he care all of a sudden?

"We cannot look too far ahead."

"No, we can't," the prince sighed. "Are you tired? You do not have to stay here for my sake."

What could she say now? She wanted nothing more than to escape to the safety of her room and forget her troubles. But would she even be allowed to sleep in her own room tonight? Why could he not just clearly communicate his intentions and expectations? But how could she expect him to when she was too scared to even ask? Nevertheless, she could not keep it off forever.

"Yes. I could sleep now."

The prince doused the fire, darkening the room. Awkwardly, he offered her his arm. Filibria took it, allowing him to lead her down the hallway. The same uncomfortable apprehension from the night before clutched at her stomach.

When he stopped, they were in front of her room. He pushed her door open. Inside, a fire burned low, illuminating the vast canopied bed. It looked so warm—so inviting, so safe. The prince stalled in the doorway.

"Th-Though we are married, you may stay by yourself until you are ready," he said quickly. "No matter how long that takes."

Relief flooded through Filibria.

"Thank you."

"Goodnight, Filibria."

"Goodnight."

CHAPTER

Seven

THE NEXT DAY, FILIBRIA'S third in Eirarin, dawned sunny and beautiful, and when Mother Brylla woke her early, she knew the tournament was inevitable. The castle's courtyard swarmed with people from the outer towns and hamlets, excited for the day's events.

The commotion carried, muffled by the stone walls, as maids laced Filibria into a light blue dress, fastened only by a simple silver girdle.

"The whole kingdom has traveled to see the tournament—and you." Mother Brylla set a silver coronet on Filibria's head and viewed the results with satisfaction. "The royal family is waiting for you in the Great Hall."

Filibria and her new family traveled by wagon to the fields to the west of the castle. The land had been leveled and stands constructed. Colorful tents bloomed over the fields as far as the eye could see. Each occupant sat outside hawking their wares. Cocky young men strutted around, trailed by their squires, while highborn women and maids alike, dressed in their finest, fluttered here and there, laughing, talking, and flirting. Above everyone's heads waved the bright banners and pennons of each knight, declaring their loyalties; the most prominent colors were the gold and red of Eirarin.

Filibria took her place on the canopied royal dais between Tiaeve and Trinlys. From where they sat, they could see both ends of the lists. After the droning steward finished his speech of pomp and prose, praising the King, the new marriage, the knights, and the general prosperity of all, Tiaeve pulled out her needlework and ignored everything else. Trinlys dozed, but Filibria did her best to look interested. Only Jarin, who sat on a stool by Filibria's feet, watched with rapt attention.

The day was hot and loud. The lists strained to the max with people craning to catch a glimpse of the knights on the field or the foreign princess on the dais—the peace weaver.

Everywhere Filibria turned, she met eyes staring back at her, open and unabashed. She always averted her gaze first. The people of Eirarin were noisy and uncouth compared to the Delvarians. Eventually, Filibria kept her eyes to herself, avoiding anything beyond the lists. She could almost block out the people, but not the endless cacophony or the unbearable heat.

Her brother had loved tournaments growing up, competing in every one he could, but Filibria could not understand the thrill it gave the men. Neither, apparently, did her new husband, which gave her a strange sense of relief.

"You do not joust?" she asked him when they took a break from sitting.

Trinlys's face colored a little as he shook his head. "No. I...I am more of a scholar. I have never been good with a sword...or any weapon."

"I do not understand the glory men find in such brutality," Filibria confessed.

A look of relief crossed Trinlys's face, as if he had been nervous she would not accept his passive life. "Me neither. I much rather watch the people watching. You can learn so much about people that way."

The horn sounded, signaling the next match and putting an end to their conversation. Filibria silently followed the prince back to their seats.

The day dragged on as knight after knight saluted their King, mounted their horses, and charged each other. Fights broke out occasionally between the jousters on the field or the betters in the stands, but they were soon contained; even those fights failed to arouse Filibria's attention.

But when a small hand slipped into hers and squeezed it, Filibria's attention was captured. Tiaeve clutched Filibria's hand, her eyes shining and her needlework forgotten in her lap. Filibria followed her gaze to where a young man, barely into knighthood, was saluting the King.

"Cevren, knight of the Outer Vale," the herald announced. A wide smile bloomed on Tiaeve's face, even as it flushed a light shade of pink.

Filibria watched the girl, fascinated. Here was open, unashamed love. Tiaeve was unburdened by duty, free to feel however she wanted. For the first time in her life, Filibria felt jealous of such freedom...and sadness that she could not share that feeling of sweet freedom. Filibria did not like the dissatisfaction she felt; such feelings were dangerous.

The trumpets sounded and the opponent entered the lists. *Captain Wrestan.* His black hair flowed from under his helmet like raven wings. The golden talon of Eirarin gleamed on his armored chest. He would be fighting for the King. Wrestan bowed low in front of the royal box. A herald announced in a bored voice,

"Wrestan, captain of the guards of Eirarin."

The light in Tiaeve's eyes died. Her grip on Filibria's hand tightened. She did not let up her grip until the young knight was knocked from his saddle by a chest blow and had to be carried off the field. Filibria gave the princess's hand a small sympathetic squeeze.

Late in the day, when the field cleared and people went home for the night, Filibria noticed a little blue flower had mysteriously appeared in Tiaeve's hand. She recognized it from her bouquet—a dandlehock, the symbol of hopeful love.

The tournament lasted three days. As it progressed and each vale, settlement, and town's best challenged one another, it became clear Wrestan would be the winner. Though talented and even handsome, the crowds were silent after each victory. Filibria secured pleasure in the fact the kingdom disliked him as much as she did. The King made up for the silence though, cheering for Wrestan like the man was his own son. Filibria's dislike for him only deepened with each passing day. It hit rock bottom when she, the one they were honoring, had to present him with his winner's prize.

"Accept these gifts, brave knight of the kingdom," Filibria intoned, "may they serve you well." She kept her gaze down, avoiding his eyes. Wrestan bowed low, took her hand, and kissed it before she could pull it away. The look he gave her made her skin crawl.

"I did it for you, my princess. May I serve *you* well."

Only Filibria saw the lightning-quick smirk Wrestan shot Trinlys, but thankfully Trinlys did not take the bait. His face remained impassive as Wrestan swaggered off.

At last, the festivities ended and life returned to normal. The halls, courtyard, and town cleared of people. Filibria retreated back to the safety of her room. She had pushed off her grief for the festivities, but now, she felt empty and cold. Here, she did not have to watch her emotions. Here, she did not have to agonize over starting a conversation with Trinlys. Here, she was free from the stares of the people, but her serenity did not last long before Mother Brylla found her.

The woman took one look at Filibria curled up in the window and sighed.

"You won't get to know him if you avoid him."

"I know…I just…It's so hard to talk to him." When Filibria said it, a weight lifted off her heart. "One minute he is warm and talking, and the next he won't say anything. I was trained for politics, not a real relationship."

Brylla's face softened. "Did you ever consider he might be as scared and unprepared as you? Maybe you're as hot and cold as he is, so he feels just as uncomfortable as you do with him."

Filibria sighed. "I thought it would be easier than this. I just wish…I wish he would be happy with what we have now. Not something more real; I was not trained for real." Her training had taught her to put a face on everything. A face on herself as she passed the peace cup, a face on her marriage—to hide whatever true feelings actually existed. It was safest that way. Controlled, easily managed or manipulated.

Mother Brylla regarded her sadly. "I think you put too much pressure on yourself, dear. It's only been a couple days. You hardly know each other. Give it a bit of time. Love cannot be rushed."

Love? Did Brylla think her marriage was for love? True, it was her duty to love Trinlys for the sake of peace. But if she let her feelings take over, how would that affect the political side of the marriage? Or worse, what if the feelings never came at all?

"Will you at least come down to the kitchen so you aren't alone? I'll give you a bite to eat and something warm to drink before bed. It will do your heart good. We don't talk much while we work."

"He's down there, isn't he?"

Mother Brylla smiled. "Yes, but he's with his books. It won't hurt you to at least sit with him. Come on."

With a sigh, Filibria complied.

They followed a dark corridor at the bottom of the stairs. At the end of the corridor, an orange glow emanated under the door, almost as if they were approaching a dragon's lair.

In the warm light of the kitchen, women worked over tables and fires: kneading dough, chopping vegetables, seasoning meats for the coming meals. Trinlys was curled up on a bench by the fire, reading a book. He was so absorbed, he did not even look up when she entered.

"Go on then," Mother Brylla whispered, nudging Filibria.

"I don't want to disturb him."

"He needs disturbing. Go sit by him, and I'll bring you both something to eat."

When Filibria stood directly in front of Trinlys, he finally noticed. Without saying a word, he closed his book and straightened up so there was room for her on the bench. Filibria sat stiffly next to him.

"Did Mother Brylla put you up to this?" Trinlys asked, brow arched.

Filibria nodded, looking away as he chuckled. "I'm sorry...She didn't give me much of a choice."

"That's Brylla for you. I don't mind though."

He smiled, cheeks coloring with the hint of a blush. It warmed something within Filibria.

"Here you are then," Mother Brylla said. She brought them a wooden platter with thick slices of bread and a pot of honey. "Take yours first, Filibria, or Trinlys will eat all the honey. He's a bear when it comes to the stuff." She set the tray next to them and retreated.

"Here." Trinlys took a piece of bread, drizzled honey on it, and gave it to Filibria. When he drenched his own piece, Filibria laughed.

"No judging," he said, but he smiled.

"The kitchen has you spoiled."

"The kitchen raised me," Trinlys replied. He finished his bread, licking the last drops of honey off his fingers.

They sat side by side, watching the kitchen bustle about, saying nothing. But for the first time, it did not feel uncomfortable. The smell of wild honey and yeast permeated the warmth and laid heavy on Filibria's eyelids. Before she knew it, her head drooped, found a solid surface, and she was asleep. On Trinlys's shoulder.

Filibria woke with a start. A firm arm wrapped around her shoulders, holding her in place, but it quickly slipped free when it felt her stir.

As Filibria straightened, memories came rushing back. She was in the kitchen. With Trinlys. *Trinlys.* She had been sleeping against him. The fire had burned low since they were the only ones still in the kitchen.

"Sorry, I did not mean to fall asleep," she mumbled.

Trinlys smiled. "It happens, but you should probably go to bed. It is late."

Filibria stood up. Instead of following her, Trinlys opened his book again.

"Filibria?" he said when she reached the door. "I know we have both been busy these past couple of days. But we should...we should probably make an effort to spend time together."

Filibria studied his face; the earnestness in it scared her. "What do you propose?"

"What if we went riding tomorrow? After breakfast. Riding gets us away from all the crowds and people."

After how he had treated her during the bedding ceremony, she owed it to him to at least try to form more than a political bond. "I would like that."

"Tomorrow then," Trinlys said with a wide smile.

"I'm going riding this morning," Filibria told Mother Brylla as the maid picked out her clothes.

"Good. I'm glad."

Filibria was silent for a moment, fiddling with a question in her mind. Finally, she let it loose. "I can be a peace weaver, but I do not know how to be a wife. At least, not a real one. I was taught how to please a husband and act as a wife in public...but I don't know anything beyond that. My mother said if there was love, it would come naturally." It was not coming naturally though. "What does Trinlys expect of me?"

Mother Brylla sighed. "Not much, dearie. He's lived his whole life trying to live up to others' expectations. All he wants is someone to share his burdens and his happiness with; someone who cares about him."

She had two kingdoms to care about. How would she have time for a husband as well? "That is a lot to ask for."

"But nothing you cannot supply. He is not asking you to be his wife yet. He merely wants a friend."

A friend. Filibria knew she could manage that.

Mother Brylla stepped back to survey Filibria. Instead of the usual light dress, Filibria wore a long riding tunic, the skirt split down the middle for horseback riding. Mother Brylla tucked a strand of hair behind Filibria's ear.

"Trinlys needs you, Filibria. You were brought here to weave peace, but I think you will live here to love him." A horn echoed through the stone walls. "Go now, that was the breakfast horn."

Throughout breakfast, Filibria puzzled over Mother Brylla's words. She had not come to love. She had come to serve, to bind the kingdoms as one, politically. If she loved Trinlys, would she become too distracted? Maybe it was best to keep her heart out of it. Do her duty, be his wife, bring peace.

Trinlys caught Filibria in the hallway afterwards.

"I will take you to the stables when you are ready."

"I am ready now."

"Good." He almost ran through the narrow corridors and through the kitchen, his dog trotting silently behind him. As they passed through the bustling kitchen, the cooks and servants alike hailed Trinlys warmly, plying him with morsels. Mother Brylla winked at Filibria and handed a dripping piece of honeycomb to Trinlys.

Out in the courtyard, young children chased each other laughing while their mothers pumped water at the well and gossiped, and a few women hung the last of their laundry before the sun's rays intensified. Somewhere, deep within a hut, a blacksmith's hammer resounded steadily. Above everything arched a clear blue sky, and gentle winds picked at the pennons, tossing them lazily into the blue.

Trinlys paused in the courtyard to break the honeycomb in half. He offered one piece, the smaller piece, to Filibria. She sucked on it as they made their way towards the stable.

She and Trinlys ducked into the dark stables. Horses rested, stamping their hooves or swishing their tails occasionally. The smell of hay and manure, strong, but not unpleasant clung to everything. A fat kitten scurried out from one of the stalls, hissed at Trinlys, and disappeared into a pile of hay.

Just inside the stables, a twisted old man jumped up from his chair where he had been dozing to bow to Trinlys. Then he spied Filibria, and his shriveled face lit up into a gap-toothed smile.

"So you're the lass they've been talking about for nigh up to two months now. Trinlys is the only one who wouldn't say a word about ya. Nervous as a worm in a barrel full of fish, weren't ya?" He winked and Trinlys blushed. "You're lucky lass, to get a man such as Trinlys here. One of the best riders in all of the land."

"We will need our horses," Trinlys said, cutting off the praise before the man could say more.

"Of course, of course. This way." The man lurched along with a bad limp, likely the result of an accident involving horses. Though slow and forgetful at times, he stayed on at the royal stables because no other man in the land could match his care and attentiveness for horses. All this he revealed while he moved slowly past each stall, greeting each horse by name.

"Here we are," he said and stopped in front of a stall. Inside, Filibria's horse dozed.

"Let me show you Swift Foot," Trinlys said to Filibria. An eager twinkle gleamed in his eye.

The ostler clicked his tongue. "You know I can't let anyone near that beast."

Trinlys was not listening. He led Filibria to a stall at the end of the stables. Inside, a huge black stallion stamped its feet and snorted. Trinlys climbed up the gate and leaned over, scratching his fingers between the horse's ears.

"Fastest in the land. Bred from the sires in the north. His lineage is older than ours. Only my father may ride him and he would murder anyone else who dared." Trinlys jumped off the gate and dusted his hands off.

Outside, the ostler had already saddled Filibria's horse.

"You really got the finest for your wedding, lass," the ostler said. "She's precious. The King hardly gives away his royal horses, and the prince here trained this one just for you." He stroked the horse between her ears fondly. "You'll have to come up with a good name for her."

Filibria ran her fingers through the horse's mane. Now that she had had a chance to see King Dalen's character, the gift of so precious as a horse confused her. How could he give her such a gift when he did not even act like she was of any real value? Had it just been for show in her own kingdom? At least, they could not take the horse away from her. She was growing fond of it.

"You need a name," she said to the mare, running her fingers down the blaze on its forehead. She tried to think of a good name, but at that moment, Trinlys emerged from the stables, leading his own horse.

A stable boy held the reins while Trinlys helped Filibria into the saddle. When she had adjusted her skirts and got a firm hold of the reins, he mounted his own horse. The ostler watched them with a wide grin.

After thanking the old man, Trinlys and Filibria rode out of the courtyard, through the streets of the village, and out into the open fields. Trinlys's dog loped along at the horses' heels.

Trinlys took the lead, heading southeast through marshy bogland. Dotted across the fields were men and women at work cutting up the turf and stacking onto little carts.

"For fires," Trinlys explained. It saved them from cutting down the valuable trees to feed their fires. Beyond the fields, the hills rolled gently up into forests.

Filibria glanced over her shoulder at the royal city, perched like a stone wart on the green land, in stark contrast to the muddle of wooden homes spilling down the rest of the hill. They passed fields of grain, still green under the summer sun. In Delvaria, most laymen were shepherds and fields were overgrown with grass and sectioned off into stone walls to pen the sheep. In comparison, the fields of Eirarin stretched away to the forest with no visible boundaries.

Filibria relaxed in her saddle, taking a deep breath of the country air, thick with the rich smells of earth, growing things, and the unfamiliar tang of boglands. The world around her quivered with life and her blood sang in response. Without meaning to, she let a laugh escape her.

Trinlys turned back in his saddle with a confused look on his face, but Filibria only shook her head and he turned back to the land ahead.

They left the fields and came to a hollow between two wooded hills. Here were several barrows, the burial place of the Kings of Eirarin. Small flowers, different colors for each barrow, bloomed over the entire valley. Filibria wondered what each flower meant, but she was too shy to ask.

Delvaria had similar valleys. It was clear that both kingdoms had too many barrows for the years they had existed. Too many kings placed in early graves because of their shared hatred and greed. It shed a solemn light on the importance of Filibria's position; yet another grave reminder of what was at stake if she failed.

Beyond the mounds loomed a thick forest. Trinlys rode straight into it. He chose his way with confidence, though Filibria could see no path. Their destination was a pond in a small dingle. Trinlys brought his horse to a stop and dismounted. He helped Filibria from her saddle too.

While Trinlys tied their horses to a tree, Filibria settled at the pond's edge. She slipped off her shoes and sank her feet into the clear water. Silver fish flitted away from her, hiding away under the pink flowers floating on the surface.

Trinlys hesitated a moment with surprise, looking from Filibria's discarded shoes to her feet in the water. Then, without another thought, he pulled off his own boots and dropped down beside her. He cast a shy look in her direction but said nothing. The two of them sat side by side at the pool's edge, staring into the still water, until it was disrupted by Keayn jumping all the way in. Trinlys laughed.

"Is it like this in Delvaria?"

His voice startled her. "Like what?" Filibria asked.

Trinlys gestured to the surrounding trees. "So forested? I saw plenty of trees as we rode in, but beyond your capital, there were only mountains and plains."

"We have forests farther north, but not around the city," Filibria replied. "We only planted those forests so we could have our own wood and not rely on Eirarin. We do not use them for hunting or riding for fear we might kill the trees. When I rode with you, that was my first time riding in a forest."

"Where would you ride?"

"I was not allowed to ride much. What little I did was in a small field outside the town I was allowed to go with my maid, but my mother kept me busy in the castle most days." Filibria drew her knees up and hugged them close to her heart, as if they could dull the sudden ache there. He was only trying to get to know her, but it hurt to talk of her home.

"Here you may ride as much as you like, but just make sure someone else is with you, for safety and so you don't get lost. I will teach you the paths through the forest and soon you will know them as well as I do. And later, I will show you the harp. You said you liked to play, but I have had no time to fetch it for you."

"Thank you." Something stirred in her for this boy; it was not love though, more like pity. He wanted to make her feel happy, but his efforts were so...forced.

"Do you ride out here often?" Filibria asked.

Trinlys nodded.

"Alone?"

Again, he nodded. "I have brought Tiaeve out several times, but now she grows older and is expected to take on more duties. I like to be out here alone. It's peaceful." He blushed, realizing what he had just said. "But I like your company better," he added quickly.

"I suppose I will be taking on more duties too, though," Filibria said.

"Yes. You did not only marry me, you married all of Eirarin." The regret in his voice stung her. She tried to think of something soothing to say, but nothing came. A silence settled, leaving nothing but the gentle rustle of leaves, the quiet grazing of the horses, and the far away trickle of the stream feeding the pond. The sun poured over Filibria's face, making her drowsy. She realized after a while the awkwardness of their silence had melted away. It was pleasant, she decided and stole a glance at Trinlys's face. He stared into the pond as if he could see the bottom, lost deep in thought. What was he thinking about? Did he worry about their relationship like she did?

A dragonfly skimmed over the water's surface, breaking Trinlys's attention when it landed on Filibria's knee. He smiled and then looked up at her.

"We should probably return before we get missed."

Reluctance. She was reluctant to leave. It was a start at least. Without realizing it, she smiled.

"What?" Trinlys asked.

Filibria shook her head. "Nothing."

Impulsively, Trinlys bent down over the water and plucked one of the pink flowers from the surface, handing it to Filibria.

"What does this one symbolize?" she asked.

Trinlys drew the flower back sheepishly.

"Deceit," he laughed. "It was believed mystical women dressed like these flowers lured children and maids into the water with their beauty, but it's just a tale. The flower is beautiful...like you." He held it back out.

Warmth, like the sun filtering through the trees above, flooded through Filibria. She realized she was blushing.

"Let us hope I am also not deceitful." She held the flower to her nose, hiding her smile.

The dog chose that moment to leap, splashing into the pond. Trinlys whistled for her and she turned, eagerly swimming back towards them. When she clambered onto the bank, she shook her coat, sending water flying everywhere.

Trinlys laughed.

Filibria screamed.

"Do not mind her." Trinlys fondled the dog's wet head.

"I have never been fond of dogs," Filibria admitted.

"Well, you will grow to love Keayn. I am confident of it. She is one of the best dogs I have ever raised. Come now, I will help you into the saddle."

"Would you like to do this again tomorrow?" Trinlys asked on their ride back.

Filibria thought of the tranquil pond, of the quiet and the peace. Maybe there, away from the life of the castle, she would finally one day be able to open up to him. It was becoming clear that even if she did not like it, she would have to let her guard down around him.

"Yes."

Trinlys rewarded her with a smile and they parted ways at the top of the stairs once back in the castle. Filibria curled up in her refuge by the window. She stared out at the countryside, piecing together the past couple of days and sorting through the waves of feelings crashing through her.

Mother Brylla entered the room as the sun lit up the windowpanes like amber.

"I saw Trinlys earlier. He looked very happy." Mother Brylla chortled. She stopped when she saw the tears. Filibria turned her face back to the window, waiting for a rebuke, or a "none of that now." Instead, a soft warm embrace slipped around her, pulling her close.

"What is it, dear?"

"I miss home," Filibria choked out through a sob. The affection caught her off guard, making the tears flow harder.

"I know, dear. It's hard leaving all you've ever known." Several minutes passed as Mother Brylla just held Filibria. When Filibria finally emerged from the embrace, the woman set about wiping her tears.

"You're a brave lass, you know. And you've made so much progress here already. Now come, tell me about your day."

"It was...nice," Filibria hiccuped.

"Nice?"

Filibria sighed. "I don't know. We talked a little. We sat by the pond in silence. I don't know how to talk to him, Brylla. He's so...so quiet—almost dull." The words exploded from her and hung between the two women. Both were equally surprised by it. Mother Brylla recovered first.

"I doubt you're much more exciting," she said gently.

"But I am. I do things. I...I..." Filibria floundered for examples. What did she do? Peace was not much more than a title. "I have friends," she finished lamely.

"You think he is dull because you do not know him. Find out what excites him. That is my challenge for you, Filibria. Find out one new thing about your husband every day."

Filibria could only stare at Mother Brylla in despair.

"And in return, teach him one thing about you."

When Filibria went to dinner, the tight knot in her stomach kept her from eating much; guilt stabbed her every time she saw Trinlys. *Dull.* She had finally put words to how she felt about him. If Trinlys noticed she was off, he said nothing.

"I found the harp," Trinlys whispered halfway through the meal. "I thought...I thought you might play it for us tonight?"

Filibria's heart sank. Play it in front of his family? The harp was her escape. She rarely played it in front of anyone. "I would be honored," she whispered back.

Trinlys smiled proudly. "I think it's in tune."

As soon as she could, Filibria slipped away from the dining hall. She wanted to get to the harp first, to accustom herself with it before she made a fool of herself.

It waited in the middle of the solar for her. Filibria ran her hand over the dark polished wood, inlaid with silver. Who had once owned this beautiful instrument? What songs had it played? Filibria gently ran her fingers over the strings. Clear notes drifted out. Filibria sat and began a song, but happy memories of playing for Malda or her mother crowded her mind. Her song faltered.

"Beautiful."

Trinlys leaned against the doorframe, watching her. Filibria quickly erased the sadness from her face.

"Will you play another song for me?" he asked as he stepped in, settling down on a nearby stool.

She nodded, but before she could lift her fingers to the string, they were joined by a third person—the King. A noticeably anxious air immediately settled over Trinlys.

"You two are not allowed to ride alone," the King said flatly, refusing to look at them.

Trinlys straightened on his stool. "What do you mean?"

"I mean," the King said coolly, "when you ride, you must be escorted by a guard, no matter the distance."

"Are we prisoners in need of escorting?" Trinlys shot back.

"It is for everyone's safety. These lands are still wild. It would not do for something to befall the next heir—or his wife."

Trinlys struggled quietly on his stool, emotions flashing across his face as he battled each one, but he kept his mouth shut. Filibria sat at her harp, face burning. She wished she could disappear. The King did not trust her; that much was clear, though he refused to say it.

"I have made the ostler aware of my command, and he will see it is followed through."

If Trinlys wanted to argue further, there was no chance to, for the Queen and her daughter entered. If either of them felt the tension in the room, they said nothing.

"I heard you were to play for us," the Queen said merrily.

Filibria only nodded once. She plucked at a string, shattering the tension the King had created. Slowly, each note clear and sweet, she played, picking up the pace. The music put the room in a trance. Both Trinlys and the Queen wore smiles, their eyes lost in the music. Tiaeve leaned from her stool, watching Filibria's swift fingers. Their admiration melted away the memories that had made her sad, and Filibria played with ease. Only the King, sitting at the far end of the room, remained unaffected. When Filibria finally noticed his disinterest, her fingers slipped, tangled by her thoughts. It did not matter. It was not his duty to like her, but it was her duty to respect him. Peace depended on it. Her fingers steadied on the strings as the song swelled again.

When the door flew open, it killed the music.

"Wrestan!" the Queen rebuked, but the King silenced her with a wave of the hand. He nodded for Wrestan to speak.

Captain Wrestan bowed casually. "There is a matter requiring your attention, my King." He shot a glance at Filibria, though only anyone looking closely enough would have noticed it. Shivers ran through her body when his hungry eyes pierced her.

"I will go." The King gathered his robes about him and exited behind the man. With him went all the stiffness in the room. Trinlys stretched out with his dog on the hearth. Tiaeve crept closer to the harp. She touched a string and smiled at the sound.

"Can you sing as well?" the Queen asked Filibria.

"Yes." Filibria did not sing often, and rarely for an audience besides her family, but she knew the Queen was inviting her to. She could sing for them—her new family. Filibria moved her fingers lightly over the strings until they remembered a song, then she began to sing. It was a short song about a woman begging Nyair, Queen of the Sea, to give back her drowned lover. When Filibria finished, they all clapped.

"Beautiful," the Queen said at last, "it seems my son has done well. We have not had music in this room for many generations." She beamed at Trinlys until he blushed. "Come Tiaeve," the Queen said, "we will prepare for bed."

As the two bid goodnight and left, the unresolved tension from before returned.

"Your father does not trust me," Filibria murmured. "He barely likes me. I do not understand what I've done to earn such ire."

A cloud moved over Trinlys's face, but he kept his mouth closed.

"Why?" Filibria continued. "He chose this marriage, but he won't even look at me. And now he seeks to trap me in the castle. How does he expect me to make peace when he seems so cold all the time?"

"My father is..." Trinlys faltered into silence. "I do not know," he admitted at last. "He has always been this way and I struggle to understand him most of the time. Perhaps this ban on riding alone is only a trial for a short time. Surely, he will give you more freedom later. At least you are allowed to ride."

"He treats me as a prisoner! I left my home, everything I knew and I gained nothing here. I try to do my best to bind the kingdoms and for what?!" All of Filibria's frustration bubbled out before she could stop it. Her words came out more forceful than she meant. "I didn't want this." She pulled legs onto the stool and wrapped her arms around them, as if to hold back any other emotions that tried to slip out. She had already gone too far, revealed too much. Trinlys could not be trusted yet. If he ever repeated her words to his father, all peace and trust would be shattered. War would ensue.

"Do you think I wanted this either, Filibria? Do you think I was happy my father arranged this marriage for me?" He grew more animated while he talked, as if a dam inside had broken; his reserved self could not hold back the words.

"I was happy in the shadows. Forgotten. I could live my life as I pleased away from my father, but then I was dragged out into the light to marry you and I will never have peace again! You are not the only victim here." His pale face flushed red. The agitation in his normally calm eyes scared Filibria, melting away her anger.

"I'm sorry," Filibria said. "I wasn't angry at you. Only confused and scared."

With those words, Trinlys deflated.

"I'm sorry too, Filibria. You did not ask for this either. We are both scared and confused. The only thing we can do is make the best of it...together." He held out his hand. For an agonizing minute, his fingers reached through empty air, then Filibria took it.

"At least we have each other," Filibria said.

Trinlys smiled and squeezed her hand.

"We will do our best and fulfill our duties," Filibria murmured. "That's all we can do."

Trinlys propped himself up on one elbow to see Filibria better.

"Do you believe in love, Filibria?"

The abrupt question, especially after his outburst, took her aback.

"I..." Filibria thought back to the boys she had fancied in her girlhood. Had it been love? "I do not think we have a choice. We married out of obligation, not love."

"But do you think it is possible to find love? In books, characters find each other and fall in love. We were chosen for each other, forced together. Can love still come from it?"

"My mother always told me love is a choice you make," Filibria said quietly. "That even in marriages like this, you can choose love and make it work. You can find happiness."

"Choose," Trinlys echoed, tasting the word. "Yes. Our story is a backwards one. We married first and then hopefully one day, we find—or choose—love and happiness." He watched her so earnestly she had to turn away. "Will you choose love for this marriage? Will you choose to love me?"

"I don't even know you," Filibria murmured. She wanted nothing more than to run out the door and hide in her room. Where had this talkative side of Trinlys come from? It was so earnest, so painful. The space between them was suffocating; he felt so close.

"Not yet," he admitted, "and we must not rush it. Love can't be rushed, but do you think one day that you could?" His eyes burned with hope.

"Maybe one day."

Trinlys sat back, satisfied.

"Will you play for me again?" he asked.

She could do that. Filibria played as best she knew how while Trinlys lay back on the rug, his head against Keayn's stomach. Filibria watched him stare at the ceiling until his gaze unfocused and his mind wandered far from the room. *Dull.* No, not dull. He had feelings tangled deep underneath his passive face. He seemed such an empty, lonely soul, not like the boys she had known back in Delvaria. All they had rejoiced in were feats of strength, battles, and valor. Trinlys seemed deeper somehow. It would not be easy to sound the depths of his emotions.

The last notes of her song died away.

"I think I will sleep now," she said.

CHAPTER

Eight

WITHOUT THE GUESTS, THE castle felt empty and quiet, like a tomb. The King kept mostly to himself, seldom showing—not even for meals. It was a relief, in some ways. Filibria enjoyed the freedom of wandering the halls without the fear of bumping into hostile men, or being stared at while she ate. But, as Mother Brylla grimly promised, the castle did not always stay quiet. The King liked to surround himself with guests and soon another lord or knight would descend upon the castle, especially with the newly opened trade route bringing caravans past the capital down into Delvaria and vice versa.

And so, a week passed quietly and slowly. Filibria kept a low profile around the castle, only appearing at meals or in the family solar in the evenings. Other than that, it was hard to leave the safety of her room, where she could be herself.

As promised, the Queen attempted to teach Filibria how to weave. Filibria found herself on a bench in the Queen's chambers, before a very complicated-looking loom and skeins of colored thread.

The Queen patiently led Filibria through setting up the loom and the weaving.

"It is one of our most ancient arts," the Queen said proudly. She settled next to Filibria on the bench before the loom and demonstrated where Filibria's hands should go. After going through the motions several times, the Queen had Filibria try.

Dread filled Filibria. What if she failed? What if she disappointed her mother-in-law?

At the first thrust of the shuttle, a thread snapped.

"It will grow easier," the Queen encouraged. She deftly tied the thread back together. "It takes time, just like any skill."

More threads snapped and others twisted, breaking the pattern. Once, the shuttle fell out. Every time, the Queen swooped in to fix the problem and encourage Filibria on, but after a couple hours, even she had to admit it was beyond saving.

Filibria dropped the shuttle and leaned back. Every muscle in her back and arms cried out in protest. "I cannot do it. I have never been good with threads. I do not think I can weave."

"It's alright, dear. Not all women were meant to be weavers."

Filibria stared at the tangle of threads. She was the Princess of Eirarin and the whole country would know she could not weave like they did. *Weave*. In a way, she did weave...but what if she was no good at that either?

"Filibria? Are you feeling alright?"

"I need to rest, I think."

"Of course. Weaving can be tiring to the eyes and back at first. Oh, and I don't know if Brylla told you, but there is to be a feast tonight. You will be passing the cup for the first time in our halls."

Filibria's heart sank. "I will be there," she murmured. She thought back to her first time passing it in Delvaria with her family supporting her and her people cheering her on. This time, her second time doing it outside of training, would be different. Her new family and new people would be watching her, judging her. It would take so much more willpower to stay strong and not stumble.

"I will show you where the cups are," the Queen said.

Off the side of the banquet hall was a small room where the various platters, cutlery, and goblets were kept for quick access. Set apart from the rest, on a cloth of red velvet sat an assortment of chalices and smaller cups. Filibria had never seen so many in her life. It gave her a sense of relief; Eirarin did value the tradition.

The Queen stood by, watching closely while Filibria surveyed the collection. Filibria took up a beautiful glass chalice, worked with buds and vines. It collected the torchlight, tossing it off into shards against the wall every time she tilted the cup.

"It's beautiful," Filibria breathed.

"I'm glad you like it. Our best glassmaker crafted it. We thought only the best was fit to drink with when Delvaria visits."

Filibria's heart leapt in her chest. How proud her mother would be to see her carrying this chalice towards them to weave visible peace between the two families; it would be the highlight of her duties.

The next chalice was silver, still rich but simpler in design. Filibria picked it up, weighing in her hands. "I think we will use this one tonight," Filibria decided. "Rich enough for my first time passing it, but not too rich for the occasion."

The Queen clapped her hands. "Perfect. I am glad our collection pleases you." She took the cup from Filibria. It would be waiting for her when she entered the hall later that evening.

But as Filibria walked back to her room, she could not shake the vision of snarling threads that clung to her mind. She kept the memory of her failure and its symbolism to herself. It would not do to have anyone doubting her abilities or faith in herself.

That night, Filibria had still not shaken off the bad feeling and the thought of passing the cup for the first time only made it worse. What if she failed tonight? What if she dropped the cup? Or spilled it on someone?

A hush fell when she entered the Great Hall. Trinlys was already seated; his eyes met hers immediately and he drew her across the room, through the crowds of people. The heavy silver chalice awaited her on the table before her chair. The room held its breath.

"We have never had a peace weaver to grace these halls before." The Queen's words crashed over her as she slipped her hands around the cool silver of the cup. The words could be reassuring, or terrifying. What preconceived notions lay out there in the Hall? What if she was a disappointment?

Trinlys's hand snuck across the table and quickly touched hers. When she met his eyes, he was smiling proudly at her. But then, beyond him, she caught a glimpse of Wrestan's glaring face. Her fingers tightened on the chalice and resolve coursed through her. She would not falter; she would not fail—not tonight.

Taking a deep breath, she turned to face the room. The chalice, lifted above her head, glinted in the firelight. Her wrists throbbed with the quick beat of her heart. All eyes turned to the raised cup, to her.

"Let peace reign in these halls as long as the timbers stand straight and the foundations lay firm!" Her voice rang through the quiet, solemn and strong. For years, she had practiced these words with her mother, in her room, out over the rolling fields. But never had it sounded so formal, so awe-inspiring.

"May it be," the crowd intoned. But before she had even taken the cup up to the King, the raucous air had returned to the crowd. Filibria could only ignore it as she made her rounds.

After the King, she took the chalice to Trinlys. He could not stop smiling, even while he drank from it. His hands touched hers again and their warmth flowed through her.

Filibria tore herself from her husband and bore the chalice on to Wrestan.

"Thank you, peace weaver." Was his tone mocking her?

Filibria did not respond. Wrestan jerked the cup from her hands, almost spilling it; a spilled peace cup boded ill luck. His eyes glinted over the rim while he drank deep, watching her. An eternity passed before he surrendered it back to Filibria.

It took forever to make the rounds through the whole room. The men laughed and joked as they took the cup and drank from it. Crude jokes rippled out on breath heavy with alcohol as she passed. Hands pawed at her skirts, her bodice, her hair. The solemn air in the halls of Delvaria while the cup was passed did not exist here. Was peace only a joke to them? Did her sacred role mean nothing?

Filibria's hands and back ached when she finally set the empty chalice before the King.

"Peace has been woven and the bonds are strong," she intoned. The words felt hollow, like a lie. The King only nodded, but the Queen's smile brought warmth to Filibria. At least she had made someone proud.

From that day forward, Filibria slid thanklessly into her duties. She passed the cup at feasts and partings, dispensing gold after hunts or scrimmages. She learned the ranks of the knights around the castle and the chiefs in the surrounding dales. She kept a smile on her face for her kingdom, but she felt like nothing more than a symbol—an oddity from another land to be scrutinized. It was as if the kingdom was holding its breath, waiting for her to fail. Her role, instead of political, felt merely ceremonial. But she did not complain. Not even to Mother Brylla.

Despite her faithfulness, the King remained impassive towards her. Filibria liked her duties less than the King did. The men of Eirarin did not hold respect for peace weavers like the men of Delvaria did. And Wrestan only grew worse. Whenever she handed the cup to him, he made sure their hands touched. She always kept a smile on her face, was always strong and graceful. At times, it felt like she lived behind a hard, unchanging shell of herself as her real self slowly slipped away. In public, she smiled and laughed, always leaning towards Trinlys. She held his arm whenever they entered the dining hall. She stuck close to his side whenever there were eyes to observe them. To the outside world, she was the perfect wife. But to herself and others who knew her better, she was no better than a fraud. Away from the public, her arm slipped out of his, her gaze fell to the floor. Guilt that no feelings had yet formed for him ate her up. Yet the more she withdrew, the faster Trinlys seemed to fall for her. He sought her out, lavished her with attention, and always had time for her. Filibria began to spend more and more time in the safety of her room.

And so, days rolled into weeks and finally, a month passed. Filibria had been away from Delvaria for a month. A lifetime. She grew familiar with the castle and its grounds, but she was still distant to all but those closest to her, the women at least. With her duties at the forefront, she let everyone, including Trinlys, fall to the wayside.

She did continue to ride with him, despite the ever-present guard riding close behind them. They kept their conversation light and trivial, usually sprinkled with facts of the land or its history. Filibria knew she trusted him, but a wall still stood between them; a wall she had built long ago. To let it down would be to let emotions loose.

If Trinlys sensed the wall, he said nothing. He always made an effort to be by her side, even if there was no conversation between them. If nothing else, her husband was loyal, and Filibria found herself leaning into that with each passing day.

"In a week's time, it will be Taxing Day," Trinlys announced one day while they rode. "My presence will be required in the Great Hall. Will you join me? You do not have to if you do not want to, but I would enjoy your company."

"I suppose I must," Filibria replied. "It will be part of my duties."

A shadow crossed Trinlys' face. "I do not want to *make* you go with me."

"I do not mind," Filibria said.

Trinlys turned in his saddle to face her. "You put on a face around me, Filibria. It's the same one you use when you pass the cup. As if I am just another one of your peace-weaving duties—and I hate it. You promised that one day you would maybe find love for me. What happened? I'm tired of your charades." His eyes searched her. She had to turn away.

"I don't know how!" Filibria shot back, harder than she meant. Her defense was charged with guilt. "I have been trying, believe me, Trinlys, but I don't know how."

"I want something that is real." The pain choked his voice. "Not this."

"And I was trained for this," Filibria replied. "Not something real. I'm sorry."

They had entered the courtyard. Filibria slipped off her horse unaided. There was silence as Trinlys led the horses over to the waiting ostler. Filibria followed uncertainly, hoping the conversation was over.

It was not.

"Even if we only have a friendship under the guise of marriage," Trinlys said. "It will make me happier than knowing you are only obliging me because it is your duty."

Filibria hurried towards the castle, glad to be free of the guard. The last thing she needed was for a report of their conversation to reach the King's ears. She drew up inside the door to the kitchen and turned to Trinlys, who had kept close at her heel.

"What about children?" she challenged. "The marriage is not complete until there is an heir. If we are only friends, there will never be children. This marriage is for politics. Maybe instead of pining for something real, you should do your part and act as I have to."

She could see her words struck him deep.

"We have time for children," Trinlys said weakly. "I would rather have children born out of love than born out of duty." He reached for her hand resting on the doorframe, but then thought better of it. "I'm sorry, Filibria, but I can't live like this. You bring me joy when you ride with me and I know I have feelings for you.

But it stabs me in the heart every time, because I know you only see me as part of your duty. Please," he begged. "If you cannot do anything else, just be my friend."

"I do value your friendship, Trinlys...I do."

But Trinlys was already walking away down the hall.

Filibria stood helpless, watching him. She could pass all the cups she wanted in the Great Hall, but in terms of the union between her and Trinlys, it felt like the threads were only unraveling.

Nine

Filibria did not love him. The thought twisted at Trinlys's heart. To be fair though, why had he expected her to? Before this marriage, he had been a nobody, a forgotten son hidden away. He lived like a rat, always lurking in the shadows, scuttling down secret passageways away from eyes and ears, always hiding. He was scared of his father, scared of his role, and terrified to one day be king. Hardly the prince Filibria deserved.

Trinlys sighed. Filibria was so strong, so stoic as she stood in front of all and wove her peace with the cup. She never shirked from his father, never broke. She had left everything behind to come here; yet she bore the heartache—if there was any—with grace and beauty. And what had he done? Demanded her love? He did not deserve it, nor did he deserve her.

Trinlys pulled himself further into a ball on his bed, hugging his knees against the ache in his chest. Maybe it would be better if he no longer existed in her life, or even in this kingdom. What would his father care? He was only an anchor weighing the peace weaver down, begging for undeserved attention like a stray dog. Trinlys clutched his head, trying to grab ahold of the thoughts and quiet them.

He had to do something, go somewhere, move—before the thoughts overtook him. His feet led him along the dark servant's tunnel towards the kitchen, towards the haven that was Mother Brylla. She would comfort him like a mother until the storm inside had passed. She would keep him safe from himself. Never once had Mother Brylla scoffed at his fears or called him a child like his father had. Never once had Mother Brylla looked terrified and burst into tears like his mother. No. She held him, comforted him, listened to him, and, if he needed it, counseled him. Mother Brylla alone understood him and could handle him, even he could not handle himself.

Trinlys's footsteps faltered as a new thought entered the maelstrom in his head. How would Filibria treat him? Would he be too much for her? What if he dragged her into the confusion he lived in? If they ever got close enough…

His legs gave up and he sank onto the floor in the dark; his sobs echoed through the stone tunnel.

Trinlys did not know how long he had been there, but suddenly, the passage flooded with the warm glow of a candle. He shrunk against the wall. It would not do for a servant to see him like this.

The light reached him, throwing his shadow into the dark beyond.

"Trinlys?" It was Mother Brylla's warm, strong voice. "What are you doing here?"

He knew he did not need to answer, for Mother Brylla had already reached him. She held the candle up to his face, peering at him over the top of her glasses.

"Get up, dear. Let's get you to the kitchen."

In the kitchen, Mother Brylla seated him on a bench and brought him a blanket. While he curled up in it, she heated some milk, grating a bit of nutmeg into it and stirring in a generous amount of honey. The drink was a special recipe of hers. It never failed to calm his nerves, easing the tension in his shoulders.

Mother Brylla slipped the warm mug into Trinlys's hand, then she took a stool across from him and sat.

"Tell me what's wrong."

Trinlys took a sip of the warm milk. It flowed through him, filling him with warmth and the tiniest spark of hope.

"Filibria does not love me."

Mother Brylla pushed the glasses up her nose and sighed. "She has not been here long," Mother Brylla reminded him.

"She cares more about weaving peace than she cares about me. I know that is why she came here...but I thought somehow, maybe she would come to care for me."

Mother Brylla watched him talk, tapping the mug every now and again to remind him to drink while he poured out all his thoughts and feelings to her.

"Do you want counsel?"

Trinlys nodded miserably.

"Love her," Mother Brylla said.

"I do."

"Love is unconditional. It does not matter if she ever loves you back. Love her and be there for her. What she is doing is harder than you can ever imagine. Show her you support her no matter what. Though she may never love you back, she will treat you well. You both are a team together and you must support one another in this hard role you have both been given. Figure that out and then one day, the love may be mutual. Never give up on her, Trinlys." Mother Brylla took the empty mug away and took both of Trinlys's hands in hers. She stared solemnly over her glasses at him. "And Trinlys? Never give up on yourself. Do you hear me?" She squeezed his hands. "Never, ever, give up on yourself—for yourself, for me, for Filibria, but mostly for this kingdom. Never. We all need you more than you can know. I cannot bear to lose another son."

Her words sent warmth deeper than the drink through him. Trinlys nodded solemnly. He would not give up—for Mother Brylla. His eyes felt heavy; the drink had done its work. His head was quiet, save for one nagging thought.

Trinlys nodded. The drink had taken over. His eyes felt heavy. His head was quiet, save for one little nagging thought.

"What if she can't handle me?" he whispered. "She's stuck with me for the rest of our lives. What if I am too much for her?"

"You won't be—and I will teach her how to take care of you. Now, off to your bed before you keel over here. I will talk to Filibria. I am here for both of you."

A new thought cut through the growing fog in Trinlys's brain, causing him to frown. "What if she does not let me love her? She keeps pushing me away. I can't just force my love on her if she doesn't want it."

Mother Brylla slipped an arm around his drooping shoulders. "We can only take this one step at a time."

Trinlys nodded, leaning against her warm shoulder.

CHAPTER

Ten

"Still in your own room," Mother Brylla grumbled. She pulled open the blinds, letting in the late summer sun. Filibria sat up, rubbing at her puffy eyes. "I don't mean to hurry you, lass, but most new wives have a child on their lap before their first anniversary rolls around. You'll never start a family at this rate."

Mother Brylla's gentle encouragement had grown steadily into strong chiding such as this. Most of the time, Filibria could brush it off with the remark of, "There is still time." But not after last night.

Filibria pulled the covers over her face to block the light. "Not today, Brylla, please." The bed dipped as Mother Brylla sat down. She pulled the covers back from Filibria's face, noting the puffiness of Filibria's eyes.

"Are you alright, dear?"

"I don't know what I am doing anymore, Brylla. Even Trinlys is tired of me now. We fought."

Mother Brylla remained quiet.

"I suppose he's talked to you about it?" Filibria asked weakly.

"He has, but neither of you are wrong. You are both trying your hardest to do your best, the way you know how."

"He's content with a friendship," Filibria said, "it's what he asked for last night. I can give him that."

"A friendship won't result in children. If the King found out the marriage has not been consummated, he could annul it if it didn't please him."

"Would that be such a bad thing?" Filibria challenged. "The King doesn't seem to like me, after all. Maybe it would be best for all of us if I just returned to Delvaria."

Mother Brylla watched Filibria thoughtfully over the top of her glasses. "You know you can't return to your kingdom. It would result in war. Besides..." Mother Brylla's lips hovered open for a second and then she closed them and shook her head. At last, she sighed.

"Filibria?" The heaviness of the tone sent a chill through her. "I know how heavy this duty weighs on you so I have hesitated to say more to you about this kingdom...but you deserve to know. This kingdom is broken. It has been for generations. Each king cares only for himself and drives his land and his people into the ground. You cannot see it, for out of fear, our people put up a facade. But they are scared, poor, hungry, and tired. I do not know what purpose the King had for arranging your marriage. It goes against any principles he has. Honestly, it scares me. But if you pull through—if you stay, if you support Trinlys, give him the encouragement he needs—then one day, when the King passes, you will ascend to the throne with Trinlys at your side and Eirarin will finally be free. Trinlys will never be able to become king on his own. He needs someone to believe in him, to help strengthen his position as heir...someone who *cares*." Mother Brylla grabbed Filibria's hands, squeezing them tight. The old woman's eyes shone with tears behind her glasses. "You are our hope, Filibria. The first hope Eirarin has seen in years. You can't desert us now."

Filibria dropped her head, unable to meet the woman's eyes, heart beating with panic. This was more than she had signed up for; she had not been trained for this. This kingdom expected too much from her.

Mother Brylla watched Filibria, as if reading her face and a light dawned in her eyes. "You're scared of the emotions that might come with loving Trinlys?"

Finally, someone had said it. It was not until those words were spoken aloud that Filibria understood it herself.

"Yes," she said, startled. "I...I was trained not to show my emotions. I don't know what will happen if I do."

"Hmmm." Mother Brylla tapped a finger to her lips. "Come now." Mother Brylla rose suddenly from the bed. "Let's get you dressed. You do not have to do anything drastic today."

As Mother Brylla worked, her words echoed in Filibria's head. She had come to weave peace, not birth a new and better reign into existence. And why did the King want an alliance with Delvaria if it would only better Eirarin *after* his death? The questions swirled until she felt sick to her stomach—but they could not mask the dread of seeing Trinlys at breakfast.

"I'm not hungry," Filibria said when Mother Brylla tried to coax her down to the hall.

Mother Brylla planted her hands on her hips. "Well, you cannot stay in your room all day. If you want to avoid him, I know Tiaeve would be happy for a harp lesson."

"Thank you."

"Just for today though," Mother Brylla grunted.

Filibria fled to the safety of the princess's chambers with her harp. She stayed there for the rest of the day even though the looks Tiaeve gave Filibria confirmed the girl also knew of the turmoil; at least the mute princess could not offer unlooked-for advice and comfort.

When Trinlys did not show up for dinner, Filibria began to worry. Should she look for him? And say what? Mother Brylla would be keeping an eye on him, Filibria reassured herself as she fled to the refuge of her room again.

"Did you see Trinlys today?" Filibria asked Mother Brylla later while the maid readied her for bed.

"I have. All day, in fact. Tomorrow, Filibria, you are going to see him. You are going to talk. Both of you. Until you both reach an understanding with each other."

Filibria's stomach twisted, but she knew her fear would be no match for the sternness in Mother Brylla's voice.

"Alright," she murmured.

"Good. I will let Trinlys know. Now sleep. No overthinking."

The order held no sway over Filibria.

Mother Brylla arrived bright and early in Filibria's room the next morning to see that her orders were carried out.

"Trinlys wanted to ride today, but I forbade it. It would not do to have the escort overhear you. You two will be meeting in the garden."

Of all the places in the castle, the garden was one Filibria had not been to. Mother Brylla assured her it would be quiet and unwatched.

"He will be waiting for you so you had better hurry."

Despite Mother Brylla's coaxing and prodding, Filibria dragged her feet.

"I don't know what to say to him. I cannot be sorry for my words. I spoke the truth."

"You two are stuck together for the rest of your lives, so you have to come to some understanding. You have to find a balance between duty and love. It's not wrong to show some emotion, dear. It won't break anything."

"But love doesn't matter! Duty does. I came to this kingdom for duty, not love."

Mother Brylla pursed her lips. "Talk it out." She shoved Filibria through the open door, closing it behind her before Filibria could come up with another argument.

The garden was peaceful; too peaceful for the turmoil inside Filibria. Riding would have been better. She passed through an arch separating the herb and vegetable gardens from the ornamental flora. Here, large trees grew, such as willows that dropped over to shelter benches beneath their bows. Late-blooming roses rambled up the stone walls of the gardens, sweetening the air with their scent, and bees droned lazily as the wind sang softly through the leaves.

Trinlys paced near a bench, occasionally plucking buds of lavender and throwing them to the ground. He only stopped to run his hands through his already wild hair.

Filibria slowed as she approached him. When he finally noticed her, he jumped. His eyes were red and puffy, like hers had been. Surely, he could not have been crying? The thought bit at Filibria's heart. He did not deserve this.

"Princess Filibria." The formality in his tone tore through her heart.

"Prince Trinlys," she replied with as much stiffness. Through his eyes, she saw the pain it caused.

They stood facing each other. She could smell the crushed lavender emanating from his hands as time stood still. A bee drifted dangerously close, but neither moved to swat it away.

At last, Trinlys gestured to the bench behind him, and they both sat down on either end, as far from each other as possible. Filibria looked at him and then looked away; he did the same.

"Blasted Mother Brylla," Trinlys exploded. It was so unexpected, Filibria snorted, holding back a laugh.

"I don't know how you grew up with her," she said.

Trinlys sighed. "You have no idea. I've joked that she should overthrow my father and run the kingdom. Between the kitchen and the royal floor, she practically runs half the castle already. It would not take much for her to take control of the rest of it." His face paled at the treason of his words. He hurriedly checked the empty garden for listening ears.

Filibria laughed. "Put her in charge of the entire land of Mygin Formhain and she would have every kingdom in it living alongside each other in peace and harmony."

"I will admit, I am a better man because of her," Trinlys said. He sobered and met her eyes. "I apologize. I know how heavy your role must be, though I sometimes forget. It was unfair of me to ask you to abandon your duties for me. I was being selfish. I cannot demand love from you."

"I do enjoy being with you, Trinlys. I do—but I was trained so hard to do my duties: to pass the cup, to always comply with rules, to always smile. I was so busy learning to do things for others and give myself to others, I never learned to do anything else, to do anything for myself...to fall in love."

A pained look crossed Trinlys' face. "I don't think you learn to fall in love. It just... happens. And if it hasn't happened yet...maybe it never will."

"No...I—" She was lying to herself and to him. She *would* have time, but she did not have the will. She could not let herself.

"It's alright," he cut in. "Even if you never love me, I will enjoy being your husband, for you are at least my friend, and I enjoy your company. That is half my fear dispelled. I feared my future wife would be a monster I could not stand." He attempted a smile.

"I'm sorry, Trinlys."

"Don't be. Bring peace to this kingdom by passing the cup and reminding us that Delvaria has a face and is a neighbor, not an enemy. And one day, maybe there will be children. I will stand by your side no matter what. Now"—he stood up—"I think that was enough talking to satisfy Mother Brylla." A weak laugh cracked out of the mask on his face. "I won't keep you any longer."

Tightness squeezed Filibria's heart so hard that each beat was painful as she watched him walk away, shoulders slumped and head bowed. He did not deserve this hurt. Maybe she was a monster after all. Maybe being his friend, and taunting him with hopes of affections was crueler than pestering or ignoring him.

An overwhelming impulse to run after him and hug him took hold of her. From where, and why, she wasn't sure. He was so selfless with his love, but she hoarded hers, hiding behind her role.

What if she just let go?

What if she allowed herself to love him?

No. Emotions would only distract her from weaving peace between their two kingdoms. She was the face of Delvaria in this foreign kingdom, and she could not have her face turned by a man. She would do her duty; she would stand by Trinlys like he had promised to stand by her, urging him on to be a better king than his father. And if it hurt him, it would not matter, because it would be for Eirarin and Delvaria. Monarchs ought to always put their kingdoms first. It was the right thing to do.

She did not even notice the flower she had crushed in her hand. Her tense fingers relaxed, allowing the petals to fall to the ground. Filibria sighed, aching for the safety of her room.

When she arrived, Mother Brylla was waiting for her.

"Not now," Filibria groaned.

"I know how it went. I already talked with Trinlys."

"And?"

Mother Brylla sighed. "I cannot control your relationship. You talked and I am happy with that."

"Did Trinlys tell you how we also besmirched you?" Filibria grinned mischievously, ducking to avoid Mother Brylla's swat.

The woman straightened her apron, tension easing. "As long as you both can agree on something, I will happily take the brunt."

A week rolled by, and Taxing Day arrived. Despite the tinge it held because of their fight, Filibria waited with eager expectation. Every dale would turn up to pay their yearly taxes to the King. In Delvaria, it was a joyous time when people got together and saw long-lost friends. They would camp in the fields in their colorful tents, hawking wares from their regions, no doubt making double what they had come to pay. From the looks of the festive crowds filling the courtyard, Eirarins taxing was shaping up to have the same festive heart.

Yes, Filibria would have to pass the cup in the hall and perhaps sit in on the pledges each chief renewed as he paid his taxes, but when it was over, she hoped to be free to roam through the town and makeshift tent markets beyond.

"Can we go out into the fields this afternoon?" Filibria asked her husband the first chance she got.

Trinlys's face went pale. He swayed from one foot to another, rubbing his temple. Filibria had known him long enough for those actions to make her stomach sink; something was wrong.

"You are to stay in your room," Trinlys whispered.

"What?"

"I'm sorry, but it is the King's orders."

"Why? Should I not be in attendance as a peace weaver at least?"

"His reasoning is, these are his people, his affairs. There is no need for you to weave peace between Eirarins."

"It's tradition," she argued weakly. Most men in Delvaria did not feel comfortable doing things together until they had all drunk from the cup. It gave them a sense of visible unity. Apparently, Eirarin saw it differently. How long would it take Filbria to adjust to the idea?

"I've woven for them before. For every hunt," she continued. Why was she even talking? Who was she trying to convince? From the uncomfortable look on Trinlys's face, she knew he was thinking the same thing. Why would the King be so unreasonable? Then it struck her—so hard she took a physical step back.

"What is it?" Trinlys asked.

"He doesn't trust me. He doesn't want me seeing the strength—or weakness—of his people. He doesn't trust me."

Trinlys refused to meet her eyes.

"But why? I'm the peace weaver! Even if I wanted to, I could not run back to my own kingdom and report numbers. I'm trapped here! He treats me like a prisoner!"

"I'm sorry," Trinlys mumbled, "but there's nothing I can do. If it consoles you, he no longer wants me to attend either, so I am free to do whatever you like. Within the castle walls at least."

Filibria did not hear his words. "How am I supposed to weave peace if your father cannot even trust me?"

"I don't know." The defeat sounded so deep, so hollow in his voice. Without thinking, Filibria reached for his hand and squeezed it.

"I'm sorry, Trinlys. I know it's not your fault. I will keep to my room and stay out of trouble. My obligations are to your father...whether I like it or not." Those words clearly pained him. Her hand slipped from his, giving him no chance to speak as she turned and fled—from him, from the feelings threatening to bring tears.

Filibria had to content herself with watching the crowds mill about the courtyard below through her window. But even that, overshadowed by the King's order, spiked such unrest within her. Why did he not trust her? Anger ignited and started to burn. She needed to scream; she needed to throw something. Filibria scanned the room, looking for a sacrifice to hurl at the solid stone wall. Just when her eyes alighted on the empty chamber pot, a knock sounded on her door.

"Come in."

The door swung open hesitantly and Trinlys, dressed in drab clothes and a dull cloak, poked his head through. Seeing her alone, he slipped into the room and quietly closed the door behind him. His eyes glowed with a light she had never seen in him before: mischief.

"Quick. Put on your plainest clothes and let's go."

"Go where?"

"Into the fields, like you wanted—but be quick. We can't be seen leaving the castle."

Filibria hesitated, staring at him.

"*Hurry*," he hissed.

"I can't. What if we are caught?"

"I have never been caught before. I know secret ways out."

"But if we do get caught..." The King would be furious. Her commitment would be broken; all frail threads of trust would be completely severed. She would be disgraced, either thrown in the dungeon or sent packing back to her own kingdom.

"Do you want to go or not?"

She glanced at her husband, suddenly so boyish. His face flushed with excitement and the thrill of escape...and he was doing it for her. He was risking his own position for *her*.

"Yes."

She made him turn his back while she changed into the plainest dress she owned. Thankfully, she had an old cloak she used for riding, sun-bleached and mud stained. Mussing up her hair completed the look, or so she hoped.

When she finished, Trinlys grabbed her hand. "Let's go."

He led her down the stairs and into a narrow corridor, lit only by a single thin slit. When they passed by, Filibria peered through. It looked right into the Great Hall, which sat empty. The corridor was a servants' hall, Trinlys explained, and the slit served the purpose of keeping track of the meal courses to bring a new one in—or spying, the latter being the most popular use.

The small corridor led into the kitchen, where the remains of breakfast lay about the countertops and tables, along with the early preparations for lunch. All the servants, save Mother Brylla, were out. She merely glanced up as they passed through.

Trinlys took another little door leading into the servants' tunnel. Here, underground, were large stone chambers holding cured meats, cheeses, vegetables, and big barrels of wine and ale; the place smelled damp and cold.

"How do you know about all these places?" Filibria asked. She pinched her nose at a cave reeking of dried fish.

"By living unnoticed," Trinlys replied.

They reached a large wooden door and it swung outwards into sudden blinding daylight. Filibria took a deep breath of the fresh warm air. They stepped out of the root cellar at the edge of the inner castle walls. Jarin—her page—waited there for them. He hopped impatiently from one foot to the other.

"Get going now," Trinlys said to him, "but don't go too far ahead. Keep an eye out for any guards or castle staff and let us know."

Trinlys slipped a few coins into the boy's hand and he nodded, shooting off like an arrow.

Trinlys led Filibria through the cramped outer buildings to a small gate in the wall. Today, it stood wide open, allowing the servants easy access into the town below. Filibria paused in the doorway, and feeling her resistance, Trinlys turned back.

"I don't think I should go," Filibria said. "What if we get caught?"

"We won't. Please? If we do, I will take the blame."

He was doing this for her. But to be fair, he would be doing it without her too. Taking a deep breath, Filibria let Trinlys lead her through the door, into the town below.

It was the perfect day. Dazzling white clouds drifted over the open blue sky. Birds wheeled over the town. A soft breeze blew through the streets, rustling the colorful bunting strung between houses. Men, women, and children turned out in their brightest colors. They wove through the booths, like flowers following the river's current. As Filibria and Trinlys got caught up in the flow, Trinlys grabbed her hand and squeezed it.

Color burst from every corner, concealing the drab town. A thousand smells, from perfume to fresh bread, mingled in the light breeze. Hawkers shouted, musicians sang, people laughed, banners fluttered, and below it all rang the strong beat of feet carrying the people through a maze of streets. It was intoxicating, filling Filibria's head until she laughed. Trinlys stared at her, his smile so wide she thought it would stretch his face in half.

"What?" She laughed again.

"It's you," he said, his voice quiet with awe. "The real you. You're more beautiful than I imagined."

Filibria's face flamed with embarrassment, but also with guilt. Her mask had never faltered in his company. But out here, it slipped off easily. Out here, for the first time in her life, she was invisible to everyone. It was a wonderful feeling. No stares, no one moving quickly out of her way, no curtsies or bows. Her shoulders rubbed up against other people as they fought their way through the crowded town to the equally crowded fields beyond.

"I wish it could always be like this," Trinlys said and his face fell. "I wish this was our normal life." "It can be. Just for today."

Like the sun appearing out of the clouds, his smile returned. "Let's not waste a moment of it."

Trinlys led the way, slipping through the mass like a fish fighting the current. His eyes gleamed with excitement every time he turned back to check on her. This is where he belonged. In another life, what would he have been? A scholar? Or even a thief perhaps? His quick steps and knowledge of secret passages would have served him well in the latter. What would *she* have been? Filibria wondered. The thought had never crossed her mind before. From birth, she had always been destined to be a peace weaver. But what if fate had been different? She could not even imagine any other future, and the thought disturbed her. And that was when she bumped into Trinlys.

He stood in front of a bookstall. The owner knew him well and plied him with new books—all for a high price. They were, after all, rare. Trinlys sifted through the stacks, haggling and bargaining. He left with several books under his arm and an impish smile on his face.

"You will read them all one day," he promised Filibria, "I will teach you."

"No doubt the reason you bought them," Filibria teased. "You were thinking only of me."

"Of course."

Filibria laughed. "I have no use for reading."

"Please don't tell me you are like the rest of them"—he waved his hand towards the castle—"believing reading weakens your brain and should be left to numb-minded scholars."

Filibria paused, weighing the amount of jest against judgement in his tone. "I...I was never taught anything positive about it. I never even thought about the merits or harm of it."

"I will persuade you of its merits," Trinlys said, his tone suddenly earnest. "Reading opens worlds you never imagined."

"I have enough trouble fitting into this one."

"Sometimes," Trinlys said, "you can use other worlds to escape the world you are living in."

Filibria kept close to Trinlys as the crowds swelled around them. Several times, they almost parted, but Trinlys kept his hand firmly in hers. Jarin, giddy with excitement and loaded with coins, had abandoned them long ago.

Trinlys stopped at a booth and bought a white bun.

"Try it," he said.

Filibria took a bite of the steamed dough. Strawberry juices oozed out. Trinlys watched her face with eagerness.

"It is delicious."

Trinlys pulled her on to the next store and pressed her into trying a juice from ember leaves. The strange sour-sweet taste burned her throat going down. She made a face and handed the cup to Trinlys. He laughed and finished it off for her. In the streets, performers danced and played music. Trinlys stopped occasionally to watch. When one act finished, he threw a couple coins and dove back into the crowds. Filibria got caught up in his childlike delight. She found herself watching his face, waiting for his reaction to various things. Several times, their eyes met. Every time, he smiled and squeezed her hand.

They made an important stop at the honey stall. Like the bookstall, the owner was well acquainted with Trinlys, allowing Trinlys to sample every flavor he had.

"I did not know bees could make so many kinds," Filibria laughed as Trinlys let her try the last drop of a raspberry honey.

"Beekeepers put their hives around various different plants because the nectars will affect the taste of each batch of honey. Or" —he winked at the honey seller—"they mix different flavored syrups in their honey. It all tastes good."

Filibria made a face at him, but had to stop as Trinlys pressed a spoon of honey to her lips.

"Clover," he said as she tried it. It was good.

Trinlys finally parted from the stall with several jars and a very content smile.

In the town square, a band played under a shop's awning and the crowd had cleared to allow several couples to dance. More joined, forming a large circle.

"Shall we join?" Trinlys asked eagerly, but Filibria shook her head. She was too tired, Trinlys was carrying far too much, and even if she wanted to, dancing might draw unwanted attention to themselves. Trinlys contented himself by standing at the edge of the crowd, watching the laughing couples dance without a care in the world.

Suddenly, on the other side of the square, Filibria caught a glimpse of Wrestan. Too intent on pushing his way through the crowds, he had not noticed them yet, but Filibria did not want to risk it. She grabbed Trinlys's hand, pulling him into a doorway.

"Wrestan," she hissed.

Fear quickly replaced the confusion in Trinlys's eyes. Pressed up so close against him, Filibria could feel his heartbeat increase.

"We should go back," Filibria said.

"He won't recognize us immediately. Besides, it is a big town and the chances of bumping into him again are slim," Trinlys wheedled.

"If Wrestan catches us, I will be locked away in my room forever. Please? I am tired anyway."

"Alright."

Nevertheless, Trinlys's footsteps back towards the castle were slow. He lingered at several stalls. At one, he bought candy for Tiaeve; at another, a green and a sky blue ribbon.

"The color of your eyes," he said, presenting the green ribbon to Filibria.

Filibria smiled. "And the color of yours." She wound the ribbon through her fingers, clutching it tight.

Up the street, they were rejoined by Jarin. The boy's face was sticky with sweets, reminding Filibria of her own childhood fairs.

"I saw Wrestan," Jarin gasped.

"So did we. We are headed back now."

Thankfully, the courtyard was mostly empty when they crossed it. The chiefs were already inside, giving their pledges and taxes. Trinlys led Filibria back to the root cellar, then through the secret servants' passage. When they reached the small slit, Filibria paused to spy and a gasp escaped from her lips. Inside was a flood of jostling bodies, crowding every inch of the hall. They cleared before the dais occasionally like an ebbing wave, to let a new crowd of men approach the King. Out of the slit, she could hear a lot better.

"Twenty heads of cattle and a wagonload of grain when the harvest comes in from Balon Dale," the chieftain boomed proudly, "and five knights, two hundred bows, and a hundred spears." He drew his sword and laid it at the King's feet. King Dalen passed him a cup and he drank of it, holding it high. "Balon Dale pledges its undying allegiance to King Dalen and all of Eirarin." The hall cheered as the chieftain and his men were swallowed up in the next wave to reach the dais. Again, a chieftain pledged his taxes and then stated the amount of men under his command.

Filibria pulled back from the slit, frowning.

"Is it normal to pledge warriors on a Taxing Day? Usually that is only in times of war, with war pledges."

The concerned look on Trinlys's face picked up the pace of her heart. He stooped to look through the hole. When he turned back, he had paled.

"It is not usual," he admitted.

"Then why? I thought Eirarin was at peace?"

"That would explain why my father did not want you around." Trinlys clenched his fist. "Perhaps it's best if you return to your room. And Filibria? Say nothing of this to anyone. Please. Tomorrow, I will take you somewhere less dangerous. I should not have risked your safety."

"I enjoyed myself. It was the most fun I have had since arriving. Thank you."

Trinlys smiled, then his face started turning red, as though he were choking on unsaid words. "I...You...I know how things stand between us. But...but you make me want to be alive, Filibria." He then turned sharply and fled down the hall, as did she.

Filibria closed the door to her room, his words ringing in her head and stabbing at her heart. She sank down into the chair at the desk. If only she had been married to a normal prince; one who only demanded her body and then spent the rest of his time hunting and drinking with the rest of the castle. Filibria unwrapped the ribbon, feeling somewhat foolish for such a thought. It lay before her on the desk, more precious than any of Trinlys' other wedding gifts.

He had given it out of love, not obligation—but she had bought nothing for him. She balled the ribbon up and stuffed it out of sight in a drawer. She could not stand him. *No,* she could not stand herself.

Though it bothered her deeply, Filibria said nothing of what she had seen in the Great Hall to Mother Brylla. Though she trusted the woman, she did not want to betray Trinlys and their secret. Why would King Dalen have need of so many warriors? As far as she knew, he had no other enemies besides her home kingdom. And he had sworn peace.

"Did you enjoy the town?" Mother Brylla asked when she came to change Filibria for dinner.

"How did you...How did you know?"

Mother Brylla chuckled dryly. "I have eyes and ears everywhere, dear." She sobered. "But so does the King. What you did was foolish, not to mention dangerous."

"Trinlys knew I wanted to go out. I should have said no. It's my fault."

"That boy will do anything for you. He must understand he cannot drag another person into such consequences, especially someone as important as you."

Filibria fell back on her bed.

"I just want to be normal! Today, out there, no one stared at me. No one curtsied. I've never felt like that before. I felt free. Happy. I felt...I felt as though I could maybe love Trinlys. In here, I'm nothing but a prisoner. The King doesn't even trust me." She thought back to the war pledges. Now, she no longer trusted the King.

"You didn't come here to be normal, Filibria. Like it or not, what you do decides the fate of kingdoms. And that includes sneaking out, invisible or no. Now get up and let me dress you. You are passing the cup tonight."

Filibria groaned.

"I will admit," Mother Brylla said a couple minutes later in a softer tone, "I am glad you got to see the town. Even though the King will tax them dry these next couple of days, what you saw was the resilience of the people. Poor and beaten down, they still rally to enjoy themselves and share their skills. What you saw today was the heart of the kingdom, something King Dalen can never break."

"You should start a rebellion, with all the eyes and ears you have." Filibria laughed.

Mother Brylla swung her around so hard, Filibria almost fell.

"Never. Say. That. Again. Do you understand me? Those words are *treason*." Mother Brylla's voice trembled with anger and fear.

Filibria shrunk from her grip. "I'm sorry. I was only joking. I did not mean it."

"There are ears everywhere. Never trust anyone."

Mother Brylla finished Filibria's hair in silence. But when Filibria rose to leave, Mother Brylla pulled her close.

"You are my rebellion, Filibria. You are Eirarin's hope." Bumps rose over Filibria's flesh. The chill of Mother Brylla's words clung to her for the rest of the day.

Eleven

Filibria dutifully passed the cup throughout the hall before dinner, though her heart was not in it. What was the point? The men surrounding her had eagerly pledged their swords to their king. Intoxicating thoughts of war and bloodshed raced through their veins, even as they sipped peace from the cup in her hands. The bonds fell apart immediately after she wove them, like spiderwebs in a strong gale.

Filibria returned defeated to her seat beside Trinlys. He had said nothing all night, but sat pale and tight-lipped, staring far beyond the walls of the room, lost in another world. He was another bond lying unbound before her. She could not even weave her life with his, but maybe she could try—or pretend, at the very least.

Her hand slipped under the table and brushed Trinlys's, bringing him back to the room. He turned to her and smiled. The smile pierced her, piercing through the echo of Mother Brylla's words and lodging in her heart.

As the evening progressed and the rowdiness grew, Trinlys took Filibria's hand again, gesturing towards the door. She pulled back. What could he possibly want?

Trinlys leaned closer, "Let's go to the kitchen. I cannot stand all this noise."

Relief flowed through Filibria; she could do that with him.

They snuck out the back of the hall, and instead of taking her to the stairways, Trinlys led her to a small door. It led through a passage down to the kitchen. Another servants' passage, one used to bring food into the hall.

As they neared the kitchen, they heard raised voices arguing over something. Filibria slowed, but Trinlys pushed on through the door without hesitation.

The voices stopped when they entered. Mother Brylla and one of the other head cooks stood facing each other, their faces red. They both turned to look at the intruders.

Mother Brylla's face relaxed. "Trinlys! Filibria! Come in. Sit, sit. I will get you something to drink." She gave the cook a look signifying the end of the conversation. He bowed towards Trinlys and Filibria and left.

"Is everything alright?" Trinlys asked.

Mother Brylla let out a long breath.

"It's these feasts. Your father—the King—is running us into the ground. Not to mention depleting the entire countryside of food. The cook just told me the King plans to host a hunting party next week."

Trinlys groaned.

"But that's next week," Mother Brylla said, breaking into action, "and this is now. What can I get you two?"

"Peace and quiet," Trinlys replied.

"I can do better than that. I will get you some warm milk. Peace and quiet inside *and* out."

Filibria had never tried warm milk before—and never with nutmeg. It had an almost instant effect as drowsiness washed over her, and for the second time, she found herself asleep on Trinlys's shoulder.

The next morning, Filibria sat in the solar, gently guiding Tiaeve's fingers to each string of the harp; she had been teaching the princess for the past couple of weeks and the girl was proving to be a quick and clever student. Trinlys walked in and settled on a couch to listen for a while as he often did when they had lessons, but today he could not keep still.

"It's too good a day to waste in these gloomy halls," he said. "Come outside."

Filibria shook her head. "I don't want to ride today. The town is still too busy."

"Not riding. We will go to the garden. It will be winter all too soon. Come on. We will bring the harp. And you come with us, Tiaeve. It will be good to get our minds off the chaos of the past few days."

The two girls followed Trinlys, maneuvering the harp down the narrow twisting stairs and bypassing the Great Hall where the last of the chieftains lounged drunkenly. At last, they reached the ground floor and entered the high-walled garth on the south side of the castle.

The three walked past the garden beds to the trees as a gentle breeze blew. Birds sang their last songs of autumn in the boughs above as Filibria settled in the grass with the harp, beginning to play. To her surprise, Trinlys took his sister in his arms and began to dance. The sun lit up their faces as they swayed through the flowers, both laughing—so warm, so happy, so at peace. The elusive feelings swelled, filling Filibria until laughter bubbled forth and her cheeks ached from smiling.

When the song ended, Tiaeve reached for the harp. Trinlys bowed before Filibria as his sister struck the first chord.

"A dance, my lady?"

"No, you know I am too clumsy," she protested, but Trinlys had already drawn her into his arms.

"What do you do all day in your kingdom if you can't read or write or dance?" Trinlys laughed.

"Reading and writing are looked down upon and dancing is considered too frivolous. I only know some steps because my mother taught me the dances of her childhood kingdom. We spent our days doing more practical things," Filibria retorted.

Trinlys cocked an eyebrow, waiting for her to elaborate on her excuse.

"Like gardening, studying music, learning to play, and tending animals...like sheep. We did not dance on feast days like your kingdom does. We listened to bards while we played board games."

"What a practical, boring kingdom. I'm glad I rescued you from it when I did."

Filibria shrieked as he grabbed her waist, twirling her around in the air. He set her down, laughing. Tiaeve began a song, and Trinlys led Filibria through the steps, sure and gentle. In his arms, she forgot about her clumsy feet. His shimmering joy was contagious, his cheek full against hers from the wild smile they both shared.

The song ended, but Filibria stayed in Trinlys's arms, laughing as she caught her breath. Trinlys held her, suddenly stilling as he stared at her. Before she knew it, he ducked down and kissed her. Tiaeve giggled. Trinlys was blushing when he pulled away. Filibria could find no words. Even after he pulled away, she could still feel the kiss burning on her lips. She did not know what to do with herself, nor with him, and took a shy step backwards.

That was when they noticed a fourth person in their midst. The Queen sat alone in the shadow of the trees, watching them.

"Don't mind me," she said. "I saw you from my window and grew jealous, so I came to watch."

Trinlys held out a hand to his mother while Tiaeve started a song.

When they tired of dancing, the four of them lounged in the grass while Trinlys read to them. They did not stop until the sharp call of the trumpet for dinner reluctantly drew them back into the castle. On the way out of the garden, Tiaeve stopped to pick a flower. She gave it to Filibria with a wide smile. The stalk split, each stem supporting a small furled pink flower.

Trinlys noticed it and smiled.

"The sister flower," he said, "symbolizing the love of sisters."

An unexpected lump formed in Filibria's throat. She pulled the girl into a quick embrace, burying her face in Tiaeve's hair to hide any rogue tears. In one afternoon, it felt like the last chasm between her and this family had been bridged and she had walked across.

"Thank you, Tiaeve. It is a beautiful flower with an even more beautiful meaning."

"Did you enjoy that?" Trinlys asked Filibria on the stairs. Sunlight and laughter flushed his normally wan face; a bright spark gleamed in his eyes.

"Very much. Thank you."

They paused at the landing.

"Am I wrong in..."—Trinlys paused, searching her face—"in believing maybe your feelings might have changed...concerning me?"

Filibria panicked, even as a blush crept over her face. She ducked her head away from his searching eyes. She was not ready to admit the slow change in her heart. Not to him anyway, but she could not lie.

"You are not wrong to believe it," she admitted in a whisper.

Trinlys laughed; the most joyful and triumphant sound she had ever heard.

At dinner, the King announced his intentions to host a hunt. Remembering Mother Brylla's rant in the kitchen, a sober mood settled over Filibria. Even Trinlys, still glowing from her earlier words, now wore a grim expression.

Filibria and Trinlys escaped the hall soon after, retreating to the quiet safety of the solar; neither the Queen, nor Tiaeve, joined them.

"It won't be all bad," Trinlys mused out loud. "The hunt, I mean. It will give people a chance to gather to trade or sell. There might even be a bookseller or two." His eyes glinted.

"Are you not going out hunting with the men?" Filibria asked.

"No."

"Why not? I know you don't agree with it, but surely you will be expected to go."

Trinlys shrugged. "I do not care for such a sport. My father will go out with Wrestan at his side. All the men will boast and laugh and drink. They will be so loud, all the game for leagues around will be scared away. Then they will come back with their measly catch to boast and laugh and drink some more until they take leave of their senses. My father will not even notice my absence." Trinlys pulled out the chessboard and began arranging the pieces. They had taken to playing the game to fill the awkward silences still existing.

"Why Wrestan? You are his son, but instead, he ignores you and treats Wrestan like his heir."

Trinlys pursed his lips and moved his first piece. "I am glad my father ignores me."

"I just...I don't understand it. Any of it." Filibria stared off into the fire.

"It's your turn, Fili," Trinlys murmured.

A smile crept onto her face with the nickname. Few had used it for her before, but none of them sounded like Trinlys did when he said it. It made her feel warm inside.

"Fili?"

"Oh, sorry." Filibria moved her piece, but she was too distracted to put thought into it.

Trinlys quickly captured it. "When they go hunting, would you like to ride? We could slip out without a guard. No one would notice."

Filibria hesitated, torn. What if they *were* caught? But at the same time, running off alone with Trinlys sounded wonderful. This was exactly why she did not want the emotions in the first place! They would only get her into trouble.

"I'll make sure we don't get caught," he wheedled, as if reading her mind. "I know secret paths."

"I would like to ride," Filibria replied, though her better judgement screamed at her.

Trinlys clapped his hands. "Excellent! And sometime, maybe we could even take hawks out and hunt on our own. I have my own bird and we could train one for you. Do you know how to handle birds?"

"Yes. I had my own bird in Delvaria," Filibria said. "Her name was Inna."

"Do you still miss it?"

"Inna?"

"No, Delvaria," Trinlys said.

"Yes. It is a part of me. I do not think I will ever stop missing it. But if I left Eirarin to return, I would miss here too."

"Truly?"

The game was paused as Filibria mulled his question over. Though she would not miss the King or the castle, she would miss her room, her handmaidens, Mother Brylla, the Queen, Tiaeve, her horse, the long rides through the land, Jarin the quiet page...and Trinlys.

"Yes, truly. I would miss it...I'd miss you."

He smiled at this. "I would miss you too. Life has been different since you came, Filibria. I have hope now. Something to live for. I'm not just...a forgotten son. You've rekindled the fire in me I'd given up on." He reached out to take her hand but stopped. He contented himself with merely looking at her, trying to communicate his depth of earnestness.

The fire within her burned even brighter.

As Filibria watched him across the board game, the full meaning of her words to him struck her. He had changed her life so much, in the best way. She just had to find a way to fully express it to him.

CHAPTER

Twelve

Mother Brylla was in an especially good mood the next morning, humming while she filled the wash basin with fresh water. She threw open the curtains with a big smile on her face.

Filibria groaned at the sudden flood sunlight.

"You know, don't you?" Filibria asked, sitting up in bed.

Mother Brylla only chuckled.

"Is there anything Trinlys does not tell you?"

"If there was, I would not know, because he wouldn't have told me," Mother Brylla replied, ripping back the coverlet.

Over the next few days, the castle once more filled with men. Less than before, but still too many. Trinlys disappeared into the courtyard a couple times, returning hours later with armloads of books. He forbade Filibria from joining him, both because he did not want to draw his father's attention, but mostly because the crowds of men were wild and could not be trusted.

On the day of the hunt, horns sounded in the pre-dawn air. Filibria woke to the shouting and laughing of men in the courtyard, horses neighing, and dogs baying with excitement. A thick fog hung low over the castle.

She slipped out of bed, wrapping a blanket around her shoulders to ward off the chill as she walked to the window. Leaning against the glass, she saw thick swirls of motions, lit by ugly blobs of torchlight. It looked more like a mob than a hunting party. She shivered, despite the blanket hugging her body; it could not protect her from the unease heavy in the air.

Then they were gone, riding out through the sleeping town into the countryside. Peace and quiet reigned again.

By mid-morning, the mist had dispersed and the blue sky was accented with fluffy white clouds.

As Mother Brylla readied Filibria for the day, a timid knock thumped against the door. Not knowing who it could be, the older woman answered. Filibria stepped forward, peeking past. It was Trinlys. His eyes shifted to hers, face turning bright red as his eyes dipped down along her figure. Only then did Filibria remember her shift was somewhat see-through. Cheeks burning, she ducked out of sight.

"Would you...would Filibria still like to ride today? The weather is beautiful."

"I would," Filibria replied from behind the door.

"Have you no sense of decency, boy?" Mother Brylla shook her head. "She'll come out when she's ready. Scamper off now."

Blushing harder, Trinlys retreated as Mother Brylla closed it in his face.

"He *is* my husband," Filibria laughed.

"And he doesn't get any sneak peeks until you both start acting like it," Mother Brylla replied firmly.

"Did you know," Trinlys said as they rode knee to knee, "if you travel for a sennight west past Delvaria, you will come to the sea of Nyfen at the tip of the peninsula's cliffs? The water is a light green, the sands are sky blue, and the caves along the shore are of sapphire-colored stone. When the light reflects in them, it is a beautiful blue-green."

"My mother is from the southwest so I have heard of such a land, but I have never been," Filibria replied.

"Neither have I. I would like to, though. I have read about it plenty of times."

"I'm sure you have," Filibria teased.

"You could too. It wouldn't hurt."

"You know I cannot read, Trin." She liked how the nickname rolled off her tongue—and how he smiled every time she said it.

"And you know I want to teach you. I think you would learn fast. Please?"

Filibria shook her head in exasperation, though inside, she had already caved in. "You won't leave me in peace until I say yes."

"Then, will you?" he pleaded.

"Yes."

"Good, we can start after dinner if you want." Trinlys took the lead, halting their conversation for the time being. The trail narrowed, hemmed in on both sides by ancient trees. Then, after a mile or so, the trees fell away, leaving a clear circle of turf that bulged into a hill. In the very center of the hill, a spring bubbled up, before soaking away into the deep moss. Trinlys dismounted and turned his horse loose. It felt so nice to be free of a lurking guard; they could be themselves, go anywhere they wanted, talk about anything they wanted.

"This is a secret place," Trinlys said, helping Filibria from the saddle. "Only the woodcutters know of it, and they will not go near it, nor cut any of the trees. It is said to be a burial ground." They climbed to the top of the hill, and Trinlys fetched her water from the spring. It was sweet and icy cold. "The water is said to retain youth for the drinker, but I don't believe such things. I have drunk from it since I was a small boy, and it did not hinder my growth."

Filibria settled in the grass with her back to the cold stones of the spring. "You could almost live here," she said. Above them, the limbs of the trees tangled together, blocking out all but the faintest patches of light. No birds entered the quiet chamber. Only the quiet chuckle of the spring disturbed the deep silence.

"Yes, but no one does because of the graves. They are afraid of ghosts."

"Are you afraid of them?"

"No," Trinlys laughed. "The dead go to Eiefu, or they get lost in the Endless Ice. Why would they want to linger here?"

"Perhaps for the same reason you do, because it is beautiful."

"Then the ghosts and I are on agreeing terms and need not fear each other." Trinlys stretched out with his head propped against the stones and closed his eyes. With his thin fingers interlaced over his chest, he resembled a king, ready for burial.

Filibria looked down at him. The specks of light danced over his face, illuminating his fair skin. His eyes popped open, catching her stare. A warmth spread up Filibria's neck as she turned away to hide her blushed cheeks.

But then a noise pricked her attention. A horn, far off in the distance, and soon after came the distant baying of hounds.

Trinlys sat up. "The hunt is returning. We should go."

Filibria looked around her, taking in the cool, quiet green, filling up on the tranquility before she would have to return to the castle.

"I wish we could stay here forever," she whispered.

"Me too." Trinlys smiled at her. "We can always come back another day, if we have a chance to shake our guards off. This will be our secret place."

Filibria blushed all over again. "I would like that."

When they arrived back at the castle, they found the men had already entered the castle, leaving the stable hands to take care of the horses and the butchers to tend to the meat.

"They were successful. Father will be in a good mood." Trinlys led both horses towards the stables to unsaddle them himself while Filibria trailed after him. She watched him work, putting off the moment when she had to enter the castle again and put on the face of a peace weaver. If only she could just be Trinlys's wife. The intensity and suddenness of thought shocked her. It was the first time she had wished for a tangible life outside of being a peace weaver.

Trinlys wiped his face after putting away both saddles.

"We'll go through the kitchen," he said and led the way. The kitchen was a hive of activity, thick with the smell of roasting meats and herbs. Mother Brylla, her face flushed, flew here and there, giving orders. She nodded to Trinlys and Filibria.

"The King has ordered everything cooked up for a feast—and he wants it all finished before dinner even though they arrived back late," she said. "Each lord is to have his catch specially prepared." She huffed. "They will be so drunk they won't know one end of the deer from the other. Now hurry and get out from under our feet. Go change for the banquet."

Trinlys and Filibria slipped up the quiet steps. "Do you want to avoid the feast?" Trinlys asked. "We could eat in the kitchen." The idea tempted Filibria, but she reminded Trinlys of her peace-weaving duties.

His face fell. "I hate watching you serve those brutes," he said, "especially Wrestan. I know how he looks at you. I don't care for it."

"You know I have to do it," Filibria replied softly.

"All the same."

"Maybe there is time for a writing lesson before dinner?" Trinlys's face brightened at the suggestion. "I'll meet you in your room," Filibria promised.

In her own room, her chambermaids were tidying up. Despite Filibria's protests that the dress she wore was still clean, the handmaiden waiting on her insisted she change into a much lighter dress. Its sleeves, though long, were almost translucent. The bodice was loose, without the ribbing or stiff cloth to form it.

Filibria followed the hallway to the nearest of the towers, to Trinlys's room. Though she had explored most of the castle, she had yet to set foot in Trinlys's room since the bedding ceremony. No tapestries decorated the walls at this end of the castle. Only one torch, guttering to death, illuminated the dark passage. Filibria knocked on the door and instantly it opened. Trinlys took her arm and led her in.

Without the tension, Filibria was able to take in the details of his room. It was much larger than hers, but he had a much smaller window. To make up for the lack of light, he had candles on almost every spare surface. Books occupied almost one whole wall in rustic wooden shelving. Filibria ran her fingers over the spines. A warm, old, almost sad smell diffused from the books, wrapping the room in a friendly embrace.

"So many," Filibria marveled, making Trinlys laugh. "They must be worth a fortune."

"Indeed. To me, this room is more precious than even the treasury. A long time ago, it was once the library. My tutor lived here, but he was the only one who ever used it. I took over the room when my tutor passed."

"Were you close to your tutor?" Filibria asked, detecting a hint of sadness in his voice.

Trinlys stiffened slightly and scanned the room, as though he expected someone else to be hiding there.

"Yes. He was Mother Brylla's son."

"She had a son?"

"Yes," he murmured, "but never say anything to her, or to anyone. Ever. Understand?" The gravity in his voice sent gooseflesh down her arms. Before she could ask, Trinlys answered her question. "He fell from a tower one night while stargazing. People were led to believe it was suicide, but...He was very smart, questioning everything for himself, never taking answers without proof or logic.

Some of the servants whisper that he spoke his mind too loudly, and that's why he's gone." Trinlys ran his fingers over the spines of the books.

"Trinlys?"

He turned to face her.

"Is Mother Brylla in danger?"

"Everyone is in danger to a certain extent, but that is just how life is. But no, Mother Brylla is smart, smarter than her son. She knows to keep her eyes open and her mouth shut. She has survived a very long time after all. Come now, let's forget all of this and learn to read."

He moved to gather more pieces of parchment. How could he act as if living like that was normal? Why was everyone in danger? Was she in danger?

Trying to brush the thoughts away so she could savor the moment, Filibria moved past the books to look at the rest of the room. The other walls were bare of tapestry, covered only with plain dark paneling. Several deer heads and one boar's head decorated the walls. Trinlys's bed was larger than hers too. Memories came flooding back and she shied away from the bed to look at his desk. Parchments, scrolls, books, maps, and messy inkwells concealed it. Filibria picked up a map and studied it, though it made no sense to her.

"Do you wish you could travel more?" she asked, reaching for another map.

He chuckled ruefully. "Of course, but I am a peaceful prince of the East, Fili. Unless I ride to war, I have no reason to go anywhere. Going to fetch you was the first time I left this land in a long time. Here"—he pointed to the markings on the map, his fingers moving over the names—"this is the whole continent of Mygin Formhain." His finger landed on a small spot of land. "And this is Delvaria and Eirarin."

Filibria put her finger over her home kingdom. It swallowed up both kingdoms. They were so small, so insignificant, she thought.

"I did not realize Mygin Formhain was so big."

Trinlys laughed and pulled out another map. When he unrolled it, Filibria gasped. The surface was covered with blobs of land. He pointed to a small island, half the size of her hand.

"Here is Mygin Formhain in the world of Eldrim. Our kingdoms aren't even marked on it."

"The world is so big, and we are so small. It makes me feel..." She shivered.

Trinlys took her hand. "But every single struggle, every single person in this world got it to the place it is now. What you do matters. Study history and you will see. You never know what you put into motion with the simple everyday choices you make."

"That scares me even more than the size of the world," Filibria laughed.

Trinlys rolled up the map. "It excites me. Yet...yet I never do anything. I just sit here and dream—and read." He started clearing the desk off, brushing everything into a pile to one side. Trinlys pulled out a chair and chose a book.

"We will start with the simplest book I own," he said, placing the thick tome on the desk. He motioned for Filibria to sit down beside him, then he opened the book. "I will teach you to write and read at the same time." Choosing a fresh pen, he sharpened it and dipped it in an inkwell. They sat side by side, so close their hair mingled over the pages.

Patiently, Trinlys taught her the finer arts of holding the pen. Filibria paid more attention to his slender fingers, so confidently holding the pen, then the lines of ink on the paper. With a shake of her head, she brushed her thoughts away and concentrated on the letters.

"Here, you try."

When Filibria took the pen in her left hand, mimicking him, Trinlys laughed and moved it to her right one.

"Only a few people are left-handed. Did you know that it gives us an advantage when attacking up a spiral staircase? But I am not much help defending one from above." His face grew red with the sudden realization he was rambling. "Anyway, from what I've seen, I am sure you are right-handed. This will work better for you." His fingers folded around the pen in her right hand.

The pen still felt awkward in her clumsy fingers.

When Filibria could write the first five letters unaided, Trinlys turned back to the open book. Passion and happiness filled his voice as he sounded the letters for her. His smile was like a sunbeam when she slowly read out her first word. Caught up in the moment, he grabbed her hand.

"You did it Fili! You can read!"

"Only one word," she reminded him with a laugh. His excitement boiled back down to determination and he forged ahead with the next word.

"Try reading this," Trinlys said and gently took the pen from her. He wrote three short words then leaned back, watching her face with a shy eagerness.

"I...lo-love...you?" Filibria sounded out. The meaning of the words hit slower than the sounds. When they did, she gasped, making Trinlys laugh.

"Three words in a row," he crowed.

"You mean it?" She ran her fingers over the words, smudging the ink. "You mean these words?"

Trinlys put down the pen to take her hand. "Of course, Filibria, I love you. I do. And it does not matter if you ever love me back. I am here for you no matter what happens."

"But Trinlys, I—"

The words died in her throat as the door swung open. Jarin stood on the threshold. Only his erratic breathing filled the silence as he froze, eyes darting between the two of them. His already flushed face turned a shade deeper, like a freshly cooked beet.

"I-I'm sorry," he stuttered. "I've been looking all over for you, my lady. Where have you been all this time?"

"In my room. We were reading and writing," Trinlys replied, cleaning off the tip of the pen.

"Dinner has started. The King is calling for the peace weaver. He is getting very impatient, threatening to send guards to search for you."

Filibria jumped up from her seat. "We will be there promptly."

"He's very angry," Jarin warned, "and he knows you went riding today."

"We'll deal with that later. Run down to the hall, Jarin, and tell my mother we're coming," Trinlys said.

It was then Filibria noticed her hands, blotched black with ink. Even the hem of her sweeping sleeves had specks of black. She gave a cry of dismay.

"It won't wash off," Trinlys said. His own hands were almost clean, save for a small spot on the index finger of his right hand. "Only time can wear it off."

"But not before dinner."

"No. Change out of your dress. We can't do anything about the stains, unless you have gloves?"

She did not, and it would be unseemly to pass a cup in gloves anyway. She would have to bear the shame of her stained hands.

Trinlys waited outside her door while she changed into a fresh dress, then they sprinted to the dining hall.

Before they even reached it, they could hear the raucous laughter and boisterous voices within. Slowing before the door, Trinlys took her ink-stained hand and gripped it hard.

At first, no one noticed them enter, but when the King grew quiet, the silence spread around the room and every head turned towards them. The King's face was puffy and red with drink. He glared at Trinlys as Trinlys led Filibria up to the dais.

"Where have you been? Did you not heed the time? We have guests here and you arrive tardy and rumpled. We started the feast without the peace cup."

"I am sorry, Father." The golden chalice waited on the high table. Trinlys reluctantly let go of Filibria's hand so she could take it. Filibria slipped her fingers around the smooth, cold bowl and held it out to the King.

"Drink of the peace cup," she murmured, "and may the bond of peace in these halls be strong." The King stared at the cup but did not take it. Instead, he frowned.

"What is on your hands?" The Queen's eyes flickered from Filibria's hands to her husband's face, where a storm gathered.

Filibria lowered the cup, wanting nothing more than to hide her stained hands in her skirt.

"Ink, my lord," Filibria whispered.

"And why is there ink on your hand?"

"I have been teaching her to write," Trinlys responded. He ducked his head, as if expecting a rebuke—and he was right to, as it came swiftly.

"Write?" The King brought his fist down on the table. Filibria jumped and wine sloshed out of the peace cup, splashing like drops of blood onto the table. The King's face twisted white with fury. "And I suppose this explains your absence?! You are filling her head with your nonsense. You are useless, good for nothing! And now you try to influence her. She is a peace weaver and nothing more. If you kept your head out of your books and took notice of the world around you, perhaps you could gain a little sense. I rue the day I leave this kingdom and it falls into your fumbling hands." At first, the King kept his voice at a harsh whisper, but with each insult, his volume grew until it was a roar.

Everyone else in the room remained painfully quiet, each trying hard to show they were paying no mind to the conversation. Everyone, that is, except Wrestan; a sly smile crept over his face and remained for the rest of the evening.

"You are incompetent. Incompetent." With each syllable, the King drove his fist into the table. Platters rattled and goblets spilled. "A fool. Leave my sight now."

Trinlys rose, bowed, and walked from the room, leaving his plate full. Filibria ached to follow him, but she dared not. She could only stand there in fear, willing tears not to fall.

"And you," the King hissed at Filibria, "you were supposed to be here when the dinner horn sounded. I have guests from other lands. You kept them waiting. You bring disgrace to your kingdoms."

"I am sorry, my lord." When the King's anger had cooled a little, he took the cup from her and drank. Filibria carried the cup past Trinlys's empty seat, to Wrestan. As she held it out to him, he made sure his fingers brushed her stained hands. Her stomach twisted in disgust at the smile on his face. Why did he relish her discomfort? Why did he enjoy the heir's humiliation?

Filibria forced herself to carry the cup to the tables below. What was the use? All peace had left the cup. *She is a peace weaver and nothing more!* King Dalen kept her like some war slave put on display for his men instead of a sacred binder as she was intended to be. Filibria fought back her tears. She must be strong and cheerful, no matter what. When she finally returned the cup to the table, the Queen rewarded her with a sympathetic look. Filibria dropped into her seat and hid her hands under the table. Jarin did his best to coax her into eating.

Halfway through the meal, Wrestan tripped Jarin with his chair. Jarin and a full pitcher tumbled into the sodden rushes; wine splashed over Tiaeve's and Filibria's skirts. Jarin picked himself up, squeezing his eyes shut to will away the tears.

"Fool," Wrestan hissed, "you have soiled the ladies' dresses." Jarin glanced towards the King, who had not yet noticed. "Pig."

"Enough, Wrestan." Filibria's voice quavered with control. "Jarin, you are forgiven. Go back to the kitchen. I will manage on my own."

Jarin nodded, unable to stop the tears, and fled from the hall.

As soon as she could, Filibria left the banquet herself, hiding her wine-stained skirt. She paused in the hall leading to Trinlys's room, but she was the one who had disgraced him in front of his father. He would not want to see her, so she fled to the safety of her own room.

Filibria stood in front of her window, watching the hunters pour out of the castle and ride away again for a night hunt. The glass distorted the raucous laughter, the loud voices, and the horns. The King rode at the head of the party on his prized stallion. At his side rode Wrestan; the sight sickened her. She laid her head down on the windowsill and wept. She could do nothing right. Everyone she cared about she had hurt today. First, Trinlys and then Jarin.

Filibria did not want to attend the solar that evening, but she knew the King would not be there, and she wanted a chance to apologize to Trinlys. The Queen and Tiaeve sat silently working on their embroidery. They looked up when Filibria entered but did not speak. Trinlys was not there. After a brief time, Filibria excused herself on the pretense of tiredness.

She lay wide awake in her own bed. King Dalen truly hated his son; Filibria no longer doubted that. But all the same, it was her fault Trinlys had been hurt. She should at least beg forgiveness, even if he did not want to see her. Wrapping a mantle around herself, Filibria slipped from her room.

Filibria padded through the dark hallway. Instead of heading towards the east wing though, she took the stairs towards the kitchen. It was late, but Mother Brylla was still awake, preparing food for the next day.

She took one look at Filibria and enveloped her in a hug.

"I can't do it." Filibria sobbed. "I can't keep peace and love him too. It's too much. I end up failing at both."

"Hush, child. Hush. Here, let me make you some nutmeg milk." She settled Filibria on the bench and set about preparing the milk. When she finished, she handed two mugs to Filibria.

"Go to him, child. I know you want to, I can read it in your eyes. You need him and he needs you."

"Thank you."

Filibria carefully carried the mugs up the stairs to the east wing. The torches glowed deep red as they burned out for the night. Laughter and song wafted up from the hall below, where some men still feasted. Filibria reached the large door to Trinlys's chamber and lifted the latch. It swung inward without a noise. The prince stood by the window, silhouetted against the moonlight. He turned when the door opened. Something fell to the floor, skittering across the stones as Trinlys kicked it into the shadows, all before Filibria had a chance to see what it was.

"Trinlys?"

"Filibria!" Trinlys crossed the room. "Why have you come? Could you not sleep?"

"No. I came because I knew you would not be able to sleep." She handed him the mug. "I am sorry for what happened today."

"Thank you." He took it and put it on his desk, already forgotten. He turned back to her. "I am sorry you had to witness my father's anger. I am used to it by now, but he had no right to get angry at you." Trinlys reached out for her but drew his arms back with uncertainty. "My father meant nothing by it. He only had too much to drink."

"Do not try to soothe me with lies, Trin. I know true anger when I see it. And I know a hurt heart when I see one too." Filibria moved closer to him and leaned against him. "I am sorry." Haltingly, he began to stroke her hair. "Though he may have said them with full consciousness, your father's words were false. You are none of those things." She could barely make out his features in the darkness. What little light there was gleamed on the tears rolling down his face. She reached up and brushed them away with her stained fingers. He caught her hand and held it tight.

"He hates me," Trinlys murmured. "And he hates you. I am afraid for you, Fili. You should have never come here. I don't know why he arranged for this marriage in the first place. If he knew how much happiness a wife—you—has brought me, he never would have arranged it. He has some deeper purpose, but I cannot figure it out."

Filibria did not hear his last words. She hugged him. "Trinlys, Prince of Eirarin, I have chosen to love you. I love you, Trinlys. I know now. I do." Filibria stretched up and kissed him, tasting salt.

Trinlys hugged her tighter.

Filibria spent the night in his chambers, comforting him to sleep. Her only regret was that Keayn insisted on sleeping at the end of the bed, almost crushing her toes.

When she protested, Trinlys laughed. "You get me, you get the dog." And it was settled.

CHAPTER

Thirteen

FILIBRIA WOKE FIRST THE next morning. She lay still so she would not wake Trinlys. Morning light bathed his face. Gone were the normal lines of worry on his forehead, replaced by the faintest of smiles. Filibria tucked her hand under her to resist the urge to trace the outline of his face.

A light knock came on the door, then it creaked open. Like a child caught in the act, Filibria sat up hurriedly, pulling the sheets around her. Mother Brylla stuck her head around the door with a smile.

"I'll leave you two be this morning. Just let me know when you want dressed—and you can have breakfast in the kitchen if you want."

Filibria fumbled through a nod.

When the door closed, Filibria slipped out of bed and padded to the window. The world was covered in heavy grey rain; it only amplified the cozy room behind her. As Filibria went back to bed, a glint on the floor caught her eye.

A dagger lay on the floor just beneath the bed. She remembered the strange clatter the night before. Fear gripped her heart. What did it mean? Quickly, Filibria picked up the dagger like she would a dead mouse and placed it in one of the desk drawers. Then she scampered back to bed. She would do her best to forget about it.

Filibria settled back against the pillows to watch Trinlys until he woke. The King could not part them now; nothing could part them now. She was his forever, and he hers. The feeling burned warm and bright, keeping the chill from the window at bay. But then the memory of the dagger stabbed at her heart. Should she ask Trinlys about it? Did she want to know? She decided she did not.

Trinlys's eyes fluttered open. He blinked like an owl as he took in his surroundings. His brows scrunched as his bleary gaze focused on Filibria, but then his eyes lit up and he smiled sleepily.

"Good morning," Filibria said. "Mother Brylla said if you want breakfast, we can get it in the kitchen." Trinlys nodded and buried his face back into the pillows.

Filibria only laughed.

Eventually, Trinlys rolled around to look at her again. He just stared up at her, slowly running his fingers through her hair tumbling around the pillows.

"What will you do today?" he asked finally.

"Well, we can't go riding. It's raining." Filibria wrinkled her nose. That meant the King and his men would not be hunting. Instead, they would be cooped up in the hall all day. Words and ale would flow; fights would break out. They would have to do their best to avoid the rest of the castle today, Filibria decided. "I don't know. I was wondering if...if—"

"I could teach you to read?" he whispered.

"Yes, just reading though. Do you want breakfast? I could have Jarin get us something."

A gleam entered Trinlys's eyes. "Do you know what I do want?" He snaked an arm around Filibria's waist, pulling her laughing and blushing to him.

In the end, they did not read. When they finally left the bed, it was only to move to the window to watch the lightning and rain. Neither talked, but the silence was not awkward or uncomfortable. Even without words, they were communicating.

Filibria leaned her head against the window. Every so often, she glanced up at Trinlys's face, finding he was deep in thought.

"Do you think..." she began hesitantly. He smiled down at her, giving her courage. "Do you think you could write a letter for me?"

"To whom?"

"My family."

Trinlys took her hand. "Do you still miss them?"

The tenderness in his voice was too much. It almost felt like she was betraying him by still mentioning them. The dam broke, and her tears flowed.

"I'm sorry," she said as he pulled her close. "I didn't think I would miss them this much." He led her to the desk and sat her down, consoling without any judgement.

"I can write what you want to say. Anything, even if it's only a little." Now that she had a way to write it, Filibria could think of nothing to say. After a while, Trinlys put down the pen. "Maybe later. Do you want to tell me about them?"

Filibria poured out her memories of growing up in Delvaria as the hours slowly passed. Of the feast days, the field days when they went out to help harvest or shear sheep, antics with Malda or her siblings when she was too young to start training. Tears came, but so did laughter and smiles. Trinlys held her through it all, attentive and gentle. Filibria finished with her mother's tentative suggestion of visits, but Trinlys only shook his head.

"It would take a lot to reconcile the countries. Years maybe. The trade routes have only just opened and there is still tension and grumblings."

"But I can try to reconcile," she whispered. "I will try my hardest."

He smiled at her. "I believe you will and I will help you. I would like to meet your family properly."

"I would like for them to meet you too."

A warning horn sounded for dinner, making Trinlys blanche.

"I guess I have to get ready." Filibria reluctantly moved out of his arms. She had enjoyed the day wearing only her shift, free of laces and stiff skirts.

"I will see you down there," Trinlys whispered.

Mother Brylla awaited Filibria in her room. A warm fire blazed bright, fighting off the chill as the storm continued.

"I'm proud of you, Filibria," Mother Brylla said with a smile. "You have come so far."

Filibria ducked to hide her blushing face. "Thank you."

"I'll be expecting news of a wee one soon," Mother Brylla teased, only deepening Filibria's blush further, but then Mother Brylla sobered. "You do his heart good. I'm glad you've finally accepted him."

"But I am the one who got him in trouble yesterday."

"No. His father would have found something else to accuse him of. Do not blame yourself."

"Why does he hate Trinlys so much?" Filibria asked, fiddling with the edge of her sleeve.

"It is not my place to say...but it was nothing you did, you understand?"

Filibria nodded. She thought of the dagger she had found. Mother Brylla might have answers, but she did not want to know—not yet.

"There you go," Mother Brylla said. "You're finished. Hurry on down to the hall now."

"Thank you."

The King was not present at dinner and for that, Filibria was glad. Wrestan was, though, and his eyes followed her, like a hawk watching a mouse. Filibria chose to ignore him; not even his stares could penetrate the lightness and joy in her heart. She belonged fully to Trinlys now. To her relief, Jarin waited in his usual spot behind her chair, ready to serve her. She gave him a small smile and he returned it.

Trinlys arrived when the servants entered with the first course. His face lightened at the sight of his father's empty chair and his hand brushed Filibria's neck as he sat down. She gave him a smile.

They sat in their places long enough to be polite before scampering back to Trinlys's room.

Soon after, Tiaeve found them and brought the harp into the room. The two girls took turns playing and singing. Afterwards, Trinlys helped Filibria read a few lines out of a book. Tiaeve, who had been his pupil longer, was further advanced, but the two girls still turned it into a competition, Tiaeve moving her fingers silently across the words to indicate her place and pace.

Tiaeve retired to bed, and Filibria returned to her room long enough to have Mother Brylla help her undress.

Filibria wrapped a robe around her shift and padded back down the hall to Trinlys's room. Up ahead, she saw a person too tall to be Jarin. With a sinking heart, she realized it was Wrestan. She put her head down to pass him.

"Good evening, Princess."

"Good evening," she replied curtly. When she glanced up to acknowledge him, she saw him glance down the hall towards Trinlys's room and then frown deeply at her. Filibria picked up her pace, fleeing to safety. Was Wrestan spying on her?

She said nothing of it to Trinlys; now they both had their secrets.

Mother Brylla kept Filibria company one rainy afternoon a couple weeks later. Trinlys had gone on a rare errand to another vale, something to do with horses, and Filibria had been forbidden to accompany him. To keep her mind off the injustice, Mother Brylla coaxed her away to her cozy room. They did not talk much. Mother Brylla mended some of Filibria's dresses while Filibria read one of Trinlys's new books. Under Trinlys's careful tutelage the past couple of weeks, her reading skills had increased rapidly. She had almost finished half the books on his shelves and now eagerly joined him in the wait for new ones.

Filibria lowered her book as a nagging question consumed her attention. She had not been able to drop the question since it had first formed there. Without meaning to, she opened her mouth and asked:

"What happened to your son?"

The needle dropped from Mother Brylla's fingers, but she swooped to pick it up, pricking herself.

"Who told you I had a son?"

"Trinlys. He said your son was a scholar."

"Yes. He was." Mother Brylla watched the jewel of blood grow on her fingertip. She kept her emotions hooded behind her passive face. "He was; now he is gone. He spoke too loudly and held opinions people did not like—but he did not hate his life. He did not fall on accident." She sucked the blood away and turned back to her work.

"I'm sorry," Filibria said.

Mother Brylla only nodded.

Knowing Mother Brylla would say no more, Filibria picked her book up. What kingdom of secrets had she so blindly walked into? Nevertheless, this kingdom felt like home more and more, she reflected, unable to concentrate on the words in front of her. She had fulfilled her duties and grown closer to her new family—all except the King, of course.

Though Filibria still missed Delvaria, she found the ache had dulled into sweet memory. She would still lapse into those memories at times, but her new home was here now, with Trinlys. She sent occasional letters to Delvaria, but she never heard back. Now she sent letters more out of habit than hope.

And Filibria had begun to sing, not just when she was asked to. She sang while she walked or rode with Trinlys. She hummed when she played chess. She did not realize the change herself until Trinlys mentioned it.

"It means you are happy. You are a songbird who no longer feels caged," he had said. Though she had never associated her singing with her happiness, it was true. Life in the castle could still be strained, but when she was alone with Trinlys or Tiaeve, she could be herself. She could keep peace and she could love, finding her place in life. She had become a part of this castle, of the royal family. She was needed.

So, the seasons passed slowly, and each season brought a new, unexpected joy. Feasts, hunts, and dances rolled by one after another as important guests came and went. Sometimes Filibria and Trinlys joined in the festivities, other times, they actively avoided them. Outside, in the world, fields were furrowed, green grain tossed in the breezes only to stiffen to yellow in the harsh northern wind. The new trade route through Delvaria flourished and the gold flowing into Eirarin began to show both in the town and in the castle. New, expensive tapestries and golden braziers appeared on walls in the Great Hall. Bright pennants colored the city too, and the marketplace overflowed.

Trinlys and Filibria were content with their life. Others, however, were not so.

Trinlys and Filibria rode into the courtyard, flushed with exercise and laughing. Trinlys swung down from his horse to help his wife down. Neither had noticed Wrestan yet. Trinlys took the reins of the horses while Filibria headed for the kitchen. Trinlys nearly knocked into Wrestan. He recoiled and nodded stiffly.

"Good day." Wrestan glared. When the prince was out of sight, he marched into the castle, barging into the King's chamber without knocking. The King sat at his desk, rubbing his temples while the steward leaned over his shoulder, reading off papers and adding numbers.

"Taxes," King Dalen growled. "They will be as rich as us in no time." He looked up from the accounting.

"You are dismissed," Wrestan told the man. The steward glanced at the King for confirmation and Dalen gave him a nod. The man hurriedly gathered his papers, exiting without another word.

"Sit down," King Dalen said, but Wrestan remained standing, pacing the room.

"How long is this to continue?" Wrestan demanded.

"How long is *what* to continue?" The question stopped Wrestan in the middle of the room and he turned to face the King, his face red.

"What? You ask *what*? Them! Trinlys and his witch. She has been living here for months and you have done nothing. They are as thick as thieves. They even favor each other now. Yet you do nothing."

Dalen calmly tented his fingers. He stared over their tips at the captain of the guards, who had resumed pacing. "Patience, Wrestan. Kingdoms are not built in a day."

"What about months? And what if they have a child?"

"A child is the easiest to dispose of. Trust me, Wrestan. It was in our plans all along. The less you know of them, the better. But the time is coming. I already have my men moving. The first steps have been taken."

"You keep me in the dark so you can wield power over me."

"You think I fear you?"

"You fear everyone," Wrestan spat.

King Dalen stared levelly at the man, but neither blinked. Neither looked away.

"You are dismissed," King Dalen ordered coldly. Wrestan stood a moment longer, as if defying the King's order, then he retreated, slamming the chamber door behind him. What he could do with the King's power!

From then on, Wrestan kept clear of Trinlys and Filibria—at least when they were together. As often as he could, he would somehow appear in Filibria's way. He would say nothing. A quick look, evil or greedy would do. He knew it unnerved her; he could smell her fear.

On the last day of harvest, a messenger finally came from Delvaria.

Filibria and Trinlys were out in the garden. Filibria sat against a tree with Trinlys's head in her lap. She read to him from one of the books they had recently acquired. The air was balmy and heavy with the smell of ripe fruit and cut grain. Lazy bees bumbled about and in the tree above, birds sang their last songs.

Trinlys played with Filibria's hair while she read, enjoying the vibrations of her voice from her stomach. "Your hair is like honey." He passed a strand across his nose. "Especially when the light hits it."

A giggle escaped Filibria. She tried to smother it with mock seriousness. "You're not paying attention. After everything I've endured to learn how to read, you just want to play with my hair."

"Your voice is soothing like honey, too. I'm falling asleep." His eyes twinkled and he scrunched his nose at her, ducking to avoid her playful swat.

"You're just hungry."

"I wouldn't be opposed to a snack, but I'm too comfortable." He wound her hair between his fingers. The day was perfect, Filibria decided, and she picked the text back up. Even as she read, she etched the sounds, the sights, the smells, and the feel of Trinlys relaxed against her, into her memory. Her smile tripped up the flow of words and she laughed.

"What is it?" Trinlys asked.

"Nothing, I just love you." She touched the tip of his nose.

Trinlys reached up to caress her face, but his hand froze inches from it as Jarin burst into the clearing; the mood popped like a bubble.

"An emissary...arrived this morning...from Delvaria, my princess," the page boy said between breaths. "He demands to speak with you...and the King. Mother Brylla says to hurry and change. You must not keep him waiting any longer."

The book fell from Filibria's hand, hitting Trinlys on the forehead. His pain went unheeded as Filibria stared at the boy. His words slowly sunk in. Delvaria. Her home. A message. She jumped up, spilling Trinlys from her lap. He sat up, rubbing his forehead.

"And to think I was the sole object of your love only moments before," he said, but smiled. "Go, Fili. Run. I will meet you in the hall."

Filibria quivered for a second, torn between her husband and the hall, but then she turned and ran out of the garden, Jarin close on her heels.

In her room, Filibria found her maids waiting to help her into a new dress.

"Hold still," Mother Brylla chided for the second time, "or this will take longer."

"News, Brylla," Filibria whispered, "from my family." She hardly believed the words leaving her mouth. In her impatience, she tried to assist Mother Brylla with the laces, but her hands shook so much she only succeeded in tangling them.

Mother Brylla gave Filibria a tolerating smile and moved her hands back down to her side.

"Yes, now hold still."

As soon as Mother Brylla released her, Filibria lifted her skirts and ran down the stairs to the Great Hall.

She slowed just outside the doors to compose herself. It would not do to show her excitement. The tension hit her like a blast of foul air when she stepped inside.

A lone young man, dressed in Delvarian colors, paced before the throne where King Dalen sat. Several of the King's attendants stood about, watching the man warily. Among them was Trinlys. Filibria searched the messenger's face, but she did not recognize him. Nevertheless, he was a fellow countryman and it heartened her to see him. His face lit up in relief at the sight of her.

"Greetings, Princess Filibria." He bowed.

"Welcome. You bring word from my father?"

"No."

"Before he speaks his message," the King cut in coldly, "it is customary to drink of the peace cup." Filibria noticed with a burning shame the goblet the steward held out to her. It was a glass goblet, shimmering with the red wine within. Glass stood for fragile trust, held securely and passed securely from kingdom to kingdom.

Filibria lifted the heavy chalice. She held it out to the emissary. "Drink of the peace cup and let it strengthen the bonds between our kingdoms." Her hands shook with excitement, spilling the wine a little. She blanched, mouth dry.

He took it, watching her over its rim. Even as he held her gaze, he released his grip. The goblet fell to the floor, shattering. Wine splashed up Filibria's dress, soaking her skirt like blood. A gasp rippled through the room. Filibria's heart stopped.

"That is my message to Eirarin from the Kingdom of Delvaria. Long live King Kial."

CHAPTER

Fourteen

THE HALL BUZZED WITH noise and confusion. Or maybe it was just Filibria's head. She clutched it between her hands, willing herself not to shake. All the words blended into clattering noise. Kial was king? Was her father dead? Peace broken? What had happened? She forced her way through the tangle of thoughts back into the light of clarity. King Dalen was shouting from the dais he had mounted when the chalice shattered, Trinlys was trying to reach her through the crowd of soldiers who had appeared between her and the emissary. Nothing made sense. But it had to; this is what she was trained for.

"Enough!" Her hands fell to her side, voice rising over the confusion. Everyone fell quiet.

"What is the meaning of this?" Filibria demanded, glaring at the emissary.

"Your father is dead."

The shock hit her, but she deflected it, standing strong. "So this is how you react? By smashing goblets against the floor?"

"There is no peace, my lady. Your father, the King of Delvaria, was murdered. The murderer was caught and identified. He was from Eirarin."

The roar of protest rose in the hall, but the emissary ignored it and continued speaking to Filibria.

"Your brother, now the new King of Delvaria, sent me to tell you of your father's death. Your brother also commands you return."

Silence. This shock penetrated Filibria and she was vaguely aware of Trinlys opening his mouth to protest.

"I can't," she said. Her quiet tone somehow carried through the chaos.

"You have no choice," the emissary replied. "It is the King's order. He will not have you stay here as possible leverage while a death goes unpaid."

King Dalen descended from the dais, pushing Filibria aside to stand eye to eye with the messenger. His body quivered with barely contained anger. The guards around the room all took a step forward, their hands on their weapons.

"Your accusations are false," King Dalen growled, his voice low. "You accuse a kingdom tied in peace of murder. It is a ruse. A lie! And then you demand your peace weaver back." He spat at the man's feet. "It looks to me like your king wants a war, like *he* wants to break the bonds."

"He wants justice, and he will not bind himself to a lying, murderous kingdom. The peace weaver must return home. Later, if negotiations are settled, she may return and the peace will be restored."

"I will not leave." Filibria's voice was brittle, threatening to break, but she clenched her fist and looked the men in the eyes. "What peace would exist if I left Eirarin? I am not under my brother's rule. I am bound to my husband and as long as the bond stands, I will serve him above all others, even my brother. I will stay."

"How do you intend to keep peace," the emissary hissed, "in a kingdom bent on war and destruction? Better to forgo peace now than for Delvaria to lose you. For your death would only add to the strife. Do not be foolish. Come home."

Filibria drew herself up and met the emissary's determined eyes with determination of her own.

"I will not leave. I will hold peace for however long I must. Now go. You have my answer. Give it to my brother along with congratulations upon his ascension and condolences for our father's death," Filibria's voice wavered, but her expression remained stalwart. "If my brother knows what is wise, he will try to keep peace on his own end and not send emissaries who break peace cups. You are dismissed."

The emissary bowed stiffly and strode from the room. Silence hung heavy for a long time after.

"Everyone leave," King Dalen said at last. "I will call a council. They will not go unpunished for their accusations."

"Wait...No, I can help you," Filibria pleaded.

"Filibria, return to your room."

"But this is my duty! To keep peace. I can help."

"To your room. Now!" The King's eyes burned, but Filibria did not allow the anger to reach her. She stood her ground.

Trinlys gently took her arm and led her out of the Great Hall. She walked with him in a daze up the stairs back to her room. Once inside, he let go of her and Filibria sank to the floor.

"I don't understand."

"I know," Trinlys murmured. "I know."

"Why won't your father let me help? If I don't help, everything will go up in flames." Tears pooled in her eyes until her vision was as blurred as her mind.

"Filibria"—he took her face in both of his hands—"do you think that they would lie about your father's death to cause trouble?"

Filibria thought for a moment. Her father never would; after all, her father had married her off for peace. But her brother?

"I don't know," she whispered. But if not Eirarin, then who? Her brother was ambitious, but he would not have murdered their father himself. Maybe she could get answers. Maybe she could fix this from the other side.

"I need paper. I need to write a letter."

Trinlys supported her over to the desk, cradling her like she would break if he let go.

For hours, Filibria labored over the perfect letter. When it was done, she stood.

"I must take this to the emissary and explain the situation as best I can."

"Wait." Trinlys grabbed her arm. "You cannot go. What if my father catches you? I will take it."

"No. I have to reason with him. Please, Trinlys, it's my only hope."

Trinlys watched her face. "Alright, but I will take you there."

They snuck out of her room and Trinlys led her through his maze of secret passages until they came to the lower levels where guests stayed. To Filibria's despair, a guard stood in front of the emissary's door.

"Calun," Trinlys whispered from around the corner where they hid. The guard looked up, surprised to hear his name from the shadows.

"Do you know him?" Filibria hissed.

Trinlys only smiled, whispering for the guard again. "Calun!"

"Trinlys?"

As it turned out, the guard knew Trinlys well and when Trinlys explained the situation, he unlocked the door for him without hesitation. Filibria stood next to Trinlys, clutching his arm, her heart beating hard as sweat rolled down her face the entire time the two men talked.

The emissary was pacing his room when they opened the door. He jumped to attention at the sight of Filibria.

"Quickly," Filibria said, shoving the letter into his hands, "take this to my brother. Tell him not to act so rash. Tell him Eirarin is my home now. I will not leave. He must do everything he can to stop the war. Even if it means forgiving Eirarin of murder. I explain it all in the letter, but in case you can't get it to him, tell him all that. And...and tell my mother that I have found love"—she looked over at Trinlys with a smile—"and that I am safe here."

The emissary looked from her to the letter, completely at a loss of words. Finally, he bowed his head.

"Personally, I do not agree with the choice you have made, but I am at your service and will do as you request."

"Thank you. And do not worry for me."

Though she wanted to stay and pry him for news of her home, she knew the longer she and Trinlys stayed, the more dangerous it would be, no matter how many guards her husband knew.

When she left the room, the world felt a little less chaotic, a little less dark. She had done her duty. And she was staying. Filibria linked her arm through Trinlys's. He pulled her close, resting his head on hers.

"Do you know all the guards on such a personal level?" she teased.

Trinlys laughed. "No. You were lucky. Calun grew up with me. His mother works in the kitchen under Brylla. He sometimes borrows books for me."

A small shudder ran through Filibria when she thought what would have happened if they had not known the guard. The foolishness of trying to get a letter to the emissary settled in. What was she thinking? She had put Trinlys in danger—and herself. The last thing she needed was to anger King Dalen more. But then she had also not expected a guard at the door at all.

"What's wrong?" Trinlys whispered.

Filibria shook her head. "I just don't understand it all. I don't understand my brother. Or your father." Suddenly weary, she leaned heavily against him. Trinlys stopped in the hall and scooped her up in his arms. Despite her shrill, laughing protests, he carried her back to her room.

"Don't think about it now," he whispered, setting her down in her bed. "Forget it all for now. You've done what you could and I admire you for that."

He buried his head into her neck, and then his body started to shake with sobs.

"Trinlys?"

"I thought I would lose you today, Filibria. I thought I would lose you...and I still might."

Filibria pulled away so she could see his face, taking it in her hands and staring into his eyes.

"Why would I leave you? I love you."

"You have all the right to. I know how much you miss your family."

"No. I would never leave you. *Never.* I love my family, but you come first. Always. You are my new family. As long as I can fight back, I will not leave. I promise." She stroked his hair until the tears stopped.

"And yet," Trinlys said quietly, "half of me wants you to leave. To be safe. It's selfish of me for you to stay here in danger."

"I'm not in danger. Am I?"

"If the rumors the emissary brought today are true, then my father is not to be trusted. And he holds no love for you already. I see it in his eyes."

"But why would the rumors be true?"

"Why?" Trinlys looked down at her. "You know why. Delvaria is a small kingdom, but it is the link from Eirarin to the sea. If Eirarin controlled your kingdom, they would not have to pay tolls or taxes. They would be able to export cloth out of Mygin Formahain for the first time in decades. Your father was powerful and strong, able to keep Delvaria together, to defend it, even if he must use those he loves most to secure its peace and safety."

"He did not love me anymore."

"Yes, he did. You were his prize, Fili. I saw the pain in his eyes when he joined our hands. He was giving up his greatest treasure to ensure peace. But with your father dead, Delvaria is in danger. My father deeply wants your kingdom, more than he wants peace."

"Then why did he propose and welcome this peace tie?" Filibria argued.

"That is what I cannot figure out. Can your brother keep Delvaria as safe as your father did?"

"Perhaps. He is as strong as my father, stronger even in arms. He will defend Delvaria."

"What about peace though? Can your brother keep it?" Her brother had loved war and had spent hours training while neglecting his lessons in diplomacy. It had been a strain of strife between him and his father, who believed a king should be well-rounded in all subjects. Her brother would welcome a war so he could prove his worth in his new position.

"No, he cannot easily keep peace. That is why I am here." She would not see both houses she loved slaughter each other; she must be strong.

But how long could she keep peace? How long would it be before she snapped?

CHAPTER

Fifteen

FILIBRIA JERKED AWAKE WITH a cry, her heart thudding loudly in the dark. The unattended fire was only a bed of glowing embers, allowing a chill to seep into the room. Outside, an eerie wind beat against the window as Filibria lifted Trinlys's arm off her and sat up.

"What is it?" Trinlys stirred beside her, rubbing the sleep from his eyes. He sat up and put an arm around her quaking shoulders again, stroking her loose hair.

Filibria only shook her head.

"A bad dream?"

Filibria nodded. It had started with the thud of feet, like an army, which had turned into the thump of a weaving shuttle, then the snarled threads resurfaced. Only one thread had remained on the loom. In the end, the thread had snapped. In the darkness, in Trinlys's arms, the dream dissolved, but the horror remained.

Trinlys did not ask for details. He only pulled her closer.

"Shh." Trinlys eased her back down beside him, still embracing her. "Sleep. It was only a dream. It will be morning soon."

When Filibria closed her eyes, the snarl of threads from her dream appeared again, taunting her. *"Not all women were cut out to be weavers."*

The emissary left the next day, without Filibria, and the tension he brought stayed, seeping into every crack. King Dalen closeted himself away with his advisors and Wrestan. Despite Filibria's insistence that she needed to be part of the council, he only ignored her.

Everyone in the castle, except those closest to her, started to give Filibria a wide berth, regarding her with wariness or curiosity. The trust she had slowly built up began to crumble around her day by day.

"I do not understand why," Filibria lamented. She sat in the kitchen after hours, wrapped in Trinlys's arms. Mother Brylla worked alone by the fire, preparing bread for the next day.

"Someone spread strong rumors—mostly false—around the castle. I do not know who, but I have refuted them, dear. As far as I know, they have not spread beyond the walls and will not. Do not fret."

Filibria wanted to ask more, but she knew Mother Brylla was protecting both her and the person spreading the rumors. She could rest easy, though; Mother Brylla was a force to be reckoned with. Things would be forced to return to normal, and Filibria could focus on the more important matters at hand.

She sighed, leaning more of her weight against Trinlys. "I just wish I could help, that I could give advice. That is the reason I am here, but the King brushes me off." Trinlys's arms tightened around her. "I just feel so useless."

"Worrying over it won't help. Off to bed with you both now. Get some rest." Mother Brylla threw a towel over her bread dough and brushed her hands off.

Trinlys and Filibria reluctantly left the warmth of the kitchen and headed upstairs. When they passed the King's chambers, light still slipped under the door, along with the sounds of shouting, then there was a loud wail. Filibria paused in front of the door, but Trinlys slipped his hand into hers and pulled her past it.

The next day, rumors rippled through the castle. King Dalen had proposed another peace marriage between the kingdoms.

"He has gone mad," Filibria cried when Trinlys grimly told her the news. "Who would he marry off and to whom in my kingdom?"

Trinlys took her hands, as if to steady her for what he knew was coming. "Tiaeve. To your brother."

Filibria's face drained of all its color. "No. No. She is too young. Not to my brother. No."

"Go find my mother, Fili. She has not stopped crying since she heard the news. You will know best how to comfort her."

The Queen wept in her room, surrounded by her handmaidens, while Tiaeve sat pale and wide-eyed at her mother's feet.

"She is too young," the Queen wailed. "I could not change his mind. What is the purpose of it? We already have you, Filibria! But he would not answer me." She took a breath to continue another round of weeping. "She is too young to bear children—and she will never be able to speak up for herself. She cannot fight for peace like you, Filibria."

Filibria could say nothing to comfort her because she spoke the truth. Filibria thought of Tiaeve in her own room in Delvaria, as scared and alone as Filibria had been in Eirarin. She saw the girl trying to placate Filibria's volatile brother, but she would not hold up as Filibria had. The princess had no training. She could not even say the oaths aloud. Tiaeve would be crushed and broken like the flower she was.

Filibria sat with the Queen, holding her hand and muttering words of comfort, but there was nothing she could truly do for the situation. It was all her fault. She had failed.

"We can only hope my brother will not accept the proposal. After all, I am already here. Another tie is unnecessary, and the princess is not trained at all." The words fell flat and hollow in the room.

As soon as she could, Filibria escaped to the safety of her room. She locked the door and sank to the floor, her nightmare rushing back to her. Her composure melted into body-racking tears she could not stop. Her father was dead and King Dalen did not deem her tie strong enough. Now he was going to sacrifice his own daughter to the cold duty of peace weaving.

Filibria hid her face, wet with tears, in her hands. She had failed. "Not all women were cut out to be weavers," the Queen had said. Tiaeve definitely was not.

Someone knocked on the door.

"Go away."

"Fili, let me in."

Filibria opened the door and Trinlys stepped in, welcoming her into his arms as he tucked her head against his chest. She closed her eyes and focused on his breathing. They were in rhythm, though his heart beat harder than hers; his eyes were red too.

"I failed," she sobbed.

"Shh. No, you didn't." His grip around her tightened, but his whole body shook slightly.

"And now we are going to lose Tiaeve."

"Shh."

That night, they snuck down to the kitchen together. They would not be able to sleep without Mother Brylla's soothing beverage to calm their thoughts. Thankfully, no one was in the kitchen but Mother Brylla. The red firelight illuminated the tight line of her mouth and her flared nostrils as she punched bread dough into submission; the table shook in protest with each blow.

She looked up as Filibria and Trinlys entered. Her eyes, which had been hidden from the light, glittered with tears. She brushed them away, smearing flour across her damp cheeks.

"What can I do for you?"

"We thought you might make us a cup of milk," Trinlys replied timidly.

"I can do that." She dusted off her hands and set about pouring and heating the milk. No one spoke as she did. An eternity passed before she handed them each a warm mug. They quietly thanked her. Trinlys headed out of the kitchen, but Filibria paused in the door and looked back to Mother Brylla, who had resumed pummeling the dough.

"Who looks after you?"

Mother Brylla paused. "What?"

Filibria asked again, "Who is it that looks after you?"

"No one. I don't need anyone to. Now don't worry about me. Drink your drink and go to sleep."

Filibria nodded solemnly and closed the kitchen door behind her as the thumping resumed. The sound grew muffled as she mounted the stairs. Mother Brylla had the same strength as her mother—broken many times but always forged again stronger than ever. They both stood tall in the fiercest gales, alone, while other trees fell around them.

"Where has your mind wandered?" Trinlys cut in through her thoughts as she slipped into bed.

"Away." She snuggled up against him, savoring the heat and warm smell of honey emanating from his skin. "But I am here with you now. I am here for you."

Trinlys kissed the top of her head; it sent the same warmth through her as the milk did.

"And I am here for you—always," he whispered.

Filibria smiled drowsily and Trinlys caught her cup before it could fall from her relaxing hands as sleep overtook her.

Filibria and Tiaeve sat in the garden in a daze, the harp silent between them. Filibria had done her best to impart the basics of Tiaeve's new role to the young princess. Overwhelmed by the amount Tiaeve would be incapable of carrying out, Filibria fell silent. Years of careful training could not be condensed into the quickly passing week. There was nothing to keep the grimness of the situation at bay anymore. The Queen had stayed locked away in her chambers for the entire week. Mother Brylla kept mostly to her kitchen; a rare temper escaped her from time to time, scaring everyone who faced it. Everyone tiptoed around the royals as if the princess were dead.

The garden gate squeaked and both girls looked up as Trinlys entered, face grim.

"The messenger has returned," he croaked.

Tiaeve burst into tears and Filibria gathered her into her arms, holding her close. Trinlys joined them to deepen the blanket of protection around his sister, but soon they would be able to do nothing for her. She would be alone in Delvaria.

King Kial had gladly accepted the proposal of an Eirarin bride.

Filibria's head swirled with thoughts. Did her brother see his proposed bride as ransom for the safety of Filibria in Eirarin? Maybe if Filibria had returned willingly to Delvaria, this could have all been avoided—but then she would have had to leave Trinlys. Was she selfish? Did she value her comfort over Tiaeve's safety?

A tear escaped her eye, then another, until a small river flowed down her cheeks. Trinlys's arms folded around her, pulling her close to give comfort she did not deserve. A small hand slipped then into hers; the gentle movement stung her.

"I should have tried harder," Filibria sobbed.

"Shh. You did the best you could, Fili. Do not blame yourself for my father's madness." Trinlys nuzzled her head under his chin, refusing to listen to any of her excuses.

King Kial would start preparations for the wedding right away, so Tiaeve was to prepare for her journey in the next couple of days and King Dalen arranged everything personally.

Trinlys offered to escort his sister, but King Dalen declined the offer; she would go alone with a retinue of guards.

King Dalen threw a feast in honor of the arranged marriage. While the ale flowed and the crowds grew merry, the royal family sat silent and stone faced on the dais. The Queen and her daughter's puffy faces betrayed the tears they'd shed. None of them ate. No food would fit past the lumps in their throats.

"It is a mockery," Trinlys exhaled between his teeth as his father raised yet another goblet of wine in a toast to peace.

When the King looked towards his family, they refused to raise their glasses.

"Do you not care for the future of this kingdom?" King Dalen challenged.

No one replied.

"Do you not care for peace?"

"You already have a peace weaver, yet you scorn her," the Queen said. Her tone betrayed unsteady anger.

The King's face turned red. "She has failed."

"That is because you would not let her help you. This is all your own doing! Tiaeve has not even trained! She knows nothing. How will she accomplish what Filibria was trained for?"

"Desperate times call for desperate measures. Our daughter will learn. As for Filibria, Delvaria demanded she return to them, a sign that she failed," King Dalen replied. "I had to strengthen the ties and so I did what I must."

"They asked her to return, yet she stayed and you did not honor her decision. You did not accept her help or counsel, even when she offered it!"

The rest of the room slowly fell silent as the King and Queen's voices rose.

"Hold your tongue, woman, and stay out of this."

"You ignore my daughter-in-law, scorn my son, and now you send *my* daughter away. Too long I have suffered silently, I will not hold my tongue now."

Swiftly, the King struck. The slap reverberated through the dead silence of the hall and the Queen gasped, holding her face that rapidly grew red. The King held his ground, glaring at her. Without a word in retaliation, the Queen rose and dismissed herself, eyes wet and aflame.

Filibria realized she had been crushing Trinlys's hand throughout the encounter. She let go with an apology, noticing then the anger burning deep in his eyes as he looked towards his father.

As if nothing had happened, the King raised his goblet and cheered to a toast of prosperity. The volume and merriment rose to a deafening pitch.

"I cannot stand this," Filibria whispered, "I'm going outside to get a breath of fresh air."

Trinlys squeezed her hand. "Be careful—and come back soon. I will be here waiting for you."

"Don't...do anything rash," she said. She could see his hand clenched white under the table.

Trinlys promised not to.

Filibria hurried down the steps towards the garden. The heat of the hall and the King's anger flushed her skin. Her lungs cried out for the cool night air. She needed to breathe. She needed to scream.

As she walked down the spiraling stairs, Filibria ran her fingers over the cool stones, trying to cool the tempest in her head.

Murmurs on the steps below broke through her concentration. She slowed until she reached the last bend. No one ever used the stairs beside occasional servants, herself, Trinlys, Tiaeve, and the Queen to get to the garden. She leaned forward and pressed herself against the stone to listen. Two men were talking, but too quietly for her to hear everything. She caught the word "ambush" and "kill everyone else." Gold coins clinked, then feet started up the stairs. Filibria turned and fled back up the stairs, holding her breath as her skirts rustled around her. She reached an alcove and pressed her body into it. Wrestan passed so close that he brushed her sleeve, but he did not seem to see her. Filibria waited until she could no longer smell his cloying scent before she came out of hiding and scurried down the stairs. She took the passageway past the garden and out into the courtyard, hoping to see the other man, but the courtyard was empty. Only the ostler sat hunched on a bench outside the stables.

"Did you see anyone pass this way?" she asked him.

"Aye, a young guard."

"Thank you."

"What's wrong, me lady?" the ostler asked, peering at her closer.

She shook her head. "Nothing."

A lie. Wrestan was surely up to something.

Filibria slipped silently beside Trinlys again. His food still lay uneaten before him. The men still yelled and drank on the floor below the dais. Filibria rested her head in her hands, replaying what she had heard. What could she do? Something was going to happen. Who could she tell? Anyone she told, she would only be dragging into danger alongside her. She looked to her right, past Trinlys, where Wrestan sat drinking and laughing as if nothing had happened.

Filibria tugged on Trinlys's arm. "I need to talk to you alone."

Out in the corridor, she explained what she had heard. Trinlys listened patiently, his brow pulled into a concerned frown.

"You have no proof Wrestan is planning anything," Trinlys whispered. Even though they were alone, they kept their voices low.

"Something is going to happen. I know it, but I don't know how to stop it."

Trinlys wrapped his arms around her. "You are not responsible for everything and everyone. I know you feel like you have failed, but you are putting too much pressure on yourself, love. If you mention what you heard, you will only cause more anger and trouble. Keep it to yourself."

Filibria surrendered, sinking deeper into his embrace. Without even being aware of it, she began to cry. The pain and dread of the past couple of days caught up with her. Trinlys swept her into his arms, holding her close to his chest, and carried her away to the safety of his room.

The loss of Tiaeve plainly showed in Trinlys. He kept to his room and only Mother Brylla and Filibria saw him. Filibria wept for him because she could not fully comfort him. Had her siblings wept for her? She doubted it. After Tiaeve's departure, a grey cloud settled over the castle and everyone in it...except for the King—and Wrestan.

Filibria slipped into the comfort of Trinlys's room. His head was bent over his desk, his entire body focused on the book in front of him. When Filibria touched him, he jumped and looked up.

"Fili!"

She slid her arms around him, resting her chin on his shoulder; his warmth made her body relax.

"What are you reading?"

Trinlys flipped the book so she could see the front page and she frowned as she read the words. "A Guide to Warfare and Leadership?" Her voice did not even try to mask her concern. "That is not your normal sort of read."

Trinlys slid his hand over hers and squeezed it. "Better to be prepared for anything these days."

"You think there will be war?" Filibria pulled back from him, tension returning to her body.

Trinlys read her face as she struggled and reeled her back into an embrace. "I realized recently that I know nothing of war, nothing of leadership. I only stay in the shadows and watch as the world moves around me. I even hide in your shadow. But if I wish to be king one day, I need to know every aspect of leading—both war and peace. And I have you for peace, so I do not need to read any books on it." He squeezed her waist, smiling when Filibria relaxed against him.

"You will make a wise king," Filibria said, kissing the top of his head.

"And you...you will make a beautiful, gentle, wise queen."

The next day, as the King continued to feast on the prospect of stronger ties with Delvaria, a ragged man burst into the hall, falling to his knees at the foot of the dais. He was beaten, bruised, and covered with dried blood. What could be seen of his clothing marked him a man of Eirarin, one of the King's guards, sent to escort the princess. The King jumped up from his seat, knocking over his goblet of wine. It spread unnoticed over the table and puddled red, seeping into wood and onto stone.

"What news! What news of my daughter?"

The man bowed his head. "Her cavalcade was attacked. It was an ambush. We fought back, but they were too strong. Everyone but I died. The princess...the princess fell too." He held out a twisted coronet, last seen on the head of the princess.

The King took it from him with trembling hands. "Who did this?"

"Men in the livery of Delvaria. It was dark and we were outnumbered."

The King stumbled back, almost crushing the golden band and gasped. "There will be war," he growled.

In a daze, Filibria looked around the room. The Queen was white, ready to faint and Trinlys's face had drained of color. But on Wrestan's face rested a slice of a smile.

The whispers.

The coins.

The word "ambush."

Wrestan had arranged it. It was as if someone had twisted a dagger into Filibria's gut and she gasped audibly.

"Filibria? What is it?" Trinlys asked, leaning close to her.

She only shook her head, tears blurring her vision. She needed to leave. She needed the safety of her own room.

Trinlys made to follow her when she rose, but she gestured for him to stay seated. She needed to be alone.

In her room, she sank to the floor and screamed. She could have done something. She could have saved Tiaeve if only she had said something. Instead, she had said nothing and now everyone she loved was in danger. What motive did Wrestan have for murdering the princess? Did the King know of the plan? Filibria jumped up and began to pace the room. How would her brother react to the false accusations of murder? Would he wage war? Both monarchs were too stubborn to back down from their threats. There would be no wergild for wrongs done as long as each denied their guilt. She *had* failed. Filibria covered her face and slid to the floor once more, curling up around the pain deep inside her. She would sleep in her own room tonight; she did not deserve Trinlys's comforting arms.

So deep in her grief was Filibria, she did not hear the key turn in her lock or the heavy footsteps pad away down the hall.

In the town, the bells tolled. The noise drove into Filibria's head, beating against her skull. The color bleached from the world, replaced with black.

The Princess of Eirarin was dead and Eirarin wanted blood.

A life for a life.

After Trinlys had comforted his mother and left, the Queen decided to stand up to her husband. She slipped into his chambers where he sat working. He did not even bother to look up at her.

"The death of your daughter has unsettled you. Reconsider your rash actions. Release Filibria."

"Unsettled me? It is an act of war and that girl—who claims to be a peace weaver—defends her brother! How can I know she can be trusted?"

"*Filibria*. Her name is *Filibria*. You arranged for this marriage, but you seem to hate her, scorning her every intent. You did nothing to welcome her. Your distrust of her is blatantly evident, but that is because you do not know her. I know her and she can be trusted. This is her home now. She has told me herself."

"More of her lies."

The Queen gripped the back of a chair until her knuckles turned white. "At least let her free. You treat her like a prisoner. If word of her treatment reaches her brother, he will act."

"Let him act. I do not fear his puny country."

"What sane reason do you have for keeping her locked up? You are angry and once it abates, you must let her out."

"Let her out? She will stay in there and rot. I will not risk my country for the sake of one foreign woman."

"She is no longer foreign. And what of your son? She is his wife!"

"He is in league with her. They ride for hours on end. Who is to say they do not meet with someone from Delvaria?"

"Trinlys is loyal to Eirarin—you know that—and he loves his wife."

King Dalen's head shot up. "Loves? What does he—or you for that matter—know of love? Love is for tales and legends. I did not unite those two so they could love each other. I united them—"

"To strengthen two kingdoms," the Queen broke in coldly, "and now you try to break those ties."

"She is not to be let out. Now leave my sight. I have more pressing matters to deal with."

"For too long I have sat by in the shadows and let you push us around, Dalen. I will not stand for it."

At her tone, the King looked up for the first time. His face was ugly as he tried to hide his astonishment.

"Are you threatening me, woman?" he growled.

"Only warning you. Goodnight."

The Queen held her head high as she turned and departed. Only when she was in her own room did she allow her strength to dissolve into tears.

"Send me Captain Wrestan," King Dalen barked to a nearby servant.

Wrestan strode into the room minutes later. After directing a casual bow in the King's direction, he settled into a chair. "Your plan is coming together?"

"For now, she stays isolated in her room," King Dalen said.

"But you can't keep her locked away forever."

"No. It seems even my own Queen has turned against me. We have another problem. It seems my son actually loves this girl from Delvaria and she returns his affections."

"I warned you of that."

"I did not think it possible," King Dalen mused.

"What is love when it encounters power?" Wrestan asked, "Broken love causes heartache. Heartache weakens strength. She will be pliable, clay in your hands. You can use it as leverage against her."

CHAPTER

Sixteen

A KEY JIGGLED IN the lock, after which the door creaked open enough to let Mother Brylla in. Still Filibria slept on, tired out by grief and confusion.

Mother Brylla watched the girl sleep for a while. When Filibria showed no signs of waking, Brylla began to put the room in order. She tidied the papers on the desk, picking any with writing on them out; a few of these she burned.

"Mother Brylla?" Filibria pulled herself up in the sea of pillows. As she realized the space beside her was empty, the details of the night before came flooding back. "Why did you not wake me to get ready?"

Mother Brylla paused, lips pressed in a thin line. Filibria knew her well enough to read the old woman and her heart sank.

"What has happened now?"

"You are forbidden from leaving your room. The King had your door locked last night."

"What? Why?"

"He does not trust you."

Filibria leapt out of her bed. "There has been a misunderstanding. I have to talk to him. I know he is unreasonable, but this is madness."

"No, Filibria." Mother Brylla caught her arm, pulling her back from the door. "You cannot go out and the King cannot be reasoned with. Not yet. You must wait for him to calm down and come to his senses. Anything you do now will only make the situation worse. We need to keep you safe and staying out of sight will do the trick."

Filibria's shoulders drooped, defeated.

"But what about Trinlys? Can I see him?"

Mother Brylla was silent again. "He does not know yet," she admitted finally, "but I will talk to him so he does not do anything rash either. He is forbidden from seeing you."

"He is my husband!"

"Filibria, listen to me. How you act now is crucial. You mustn't do anything to further anger the King."

Filibria pulled away and sank back on the edge of her bed. "What have I done to deserve any of this? Why does he fight my every move? What do I do now?" Her eyes filled with tears as she pleaded with the maid.

"You must be strong. No matter what happens, do not give up hope. And know that you do not fight alone." Mother Brylla squeezed her shoulder. "I will do everything I can to figure out the situation and think of a way to get you out of all this."

"I just want Trinlys."

"I know. I know. I am going to fetch your breakfast, I will be back soon."

Filibria crumpled against the window. Nothing made sense anymore. Just as her life stabilized, it suddenly came crashing down around her in chaos and confusion. She was a prisoner, not a peace weaver.

The key turned in the lock, but instead of opening the door, the person knocked. Filibria stood, wary of whoever was behind it; Mother Brylla never knocked.

"Come in." The door swung open and a young man slipped in. He quickly closed the door behind him then he straightened, remembering himself, and bowed. Filibria took a step back. He was the messenger who had survived the ambush.

"What are you doing here? How did you get the key?"

"Mother Brylla gave it to me. Listen, the stable master told me to come here. He told me to tell you the truth."

"Wrestan had Tiaeve killed, didn't he?"

The messenger shook his head. "Not Wrestan. He was only the messenger. It was the King."

Filibria's eyes widened. "King Dalen? But why?"

"He loves neither of his children," the man whispered. His eyes were wide and he fidgeted with the hem of his tunic as he spoke. "As to exactly why, I do not know—except that perhaps he wished to stir up more strife between the kingdoms."

"But she was his own daughter!" Filibria's mind could not get past that fact.

"Yes. My lady, if he killed his own daughter, what of his son? Think. Trinlys's life is in danger. He serves only as a hindrance because of you. The stable master sent me to you. To warn you of the danger."

"But Trinlys is the only heir left! The King cannot get rid of him."

The messenger pursed his lips. "Never underestimate the King, do you understand?"

"What of me?" Filibria whispered.

"You are a pawn in the King's hand. I do not know your place in all this, but it is not by Trinlys's side. The King only used him to gain you through marriage. You must warn Trinlys. Tell him what I told you."

"I cannot get to him. You must tell him."

"He would not believe me. He does not think his father would ever go that far. Besides, I wouldn't be able to get near him without drawing attention to myself."

"Yet you come to me?"

"I have friends, and no one is guarding you—not yet—but I must not stay long." Seizing her hand, he kissed it and was gone in the blink of an eye.

Filibria stumbled back, overwhelmed by the man's words. She needed to tell someone. She needed to see Trinlys, to make sure he was safe. She needed to warn him, but how? And what if he did not believe her? And why would the King want to get rid of him? Who would replace him? Filibria resumed pacing.

Soon after, the door creaked softly, opening just enough to allow Mother Brylla to slip in with a tray of food.

"I don't know what to do!" Filibria cried out.

Mother Brylla set the food down on the nightstand and then lowered herself onto the edge of the bed where Filibria sat. She slipped an arm around Filibria's shoulder.

"I know dear. Everything is moving too fast. The King does not want us to keep up."

"I'm so confused." Filibria buried her head into Mother Brylla's shoulder. "Help me. How do I keep peace? I passed the cup in the hall, I tried to stand up to the King. But this, all of this..." She waved her hand around the room as if the threat was tangible. "I was not trained for. I don't even know where to start or what to do."

"We have to take this one step at a time. And right now, from your room, you cannot do much, but keep your head up—and be sure to eat." Mother Brylla pointed to the tray.

Filibria sighed and bravely took a bite, but she could hardly swallow it past the lump in her throat.

"Write him," Mother Brylla said suddenly.

"What?"

Mother Brylla pushed the glasses up her nose to stare at Filibria. "Write Trinlys a letter. You cannot see him, but you can write him and I will take it to him for you."

"No. I can't put you in danger like that. And if it was found out..."

Mother Brylla took Filibria's hands. "Filibria, this kingdom is riddled with wrongs and you two are the only ones who can do anything about them. The King knows this and that is why he is keeping you apart. If I am the first to die in a revolution, then so be it. It is a sacrifice I am willing to make."

Filibria snatched her hands out of Mother Brylla's and stood up.

"Wait...Hold on...No revolution is happening. Slow down." She began to pace the room. "You were talking about a letter. I'm not...Trinlys is not...There is no revolution. I am a peace weaver!"

"There comes a time when you have to draw a line between love and duty. Now is that time. Will you let the King push you around and lock you away while he drives your kingdoms to the brink of war? Or will you fight back as much as you are able?"

Filibria sank down on the bench by the window, put her head in her hands, and groaned loudly. Everything was escalating so fast. Mother Brylla was watching her. A strange light burned in the old woman's eyes; it slowly died at the sight of the confusion and fear in Filibria's face.

"I'm sorry, I know it's so much and you have only just stepped into this strife. It has been my life and I am all too ready for it to change. Write Trinlys if you want to. And know if you need anything, I will give it to you or get it for you. I will risk even my life to keep you two safe."

"Thank you."

"And make sure you finish your breakfast." Mother Brylla slipped back out of the room.

Filibria was too upset to eat anything more. She missed the comforting presence of Trinlys. How little time it had taken her to get so used to him always being near. Her thoughts strayed to the paper on her desk. What could she write to him? Would it only put him in danger too? And was it worth the risk to Mother Brylla's safety? When would all of this end? How would it end?

The day crawled past. Mother Brylla returned faithfully throughout the day to check on Filibria or bring her a meal. As the sun set, she returned one last time to get Filibria ready for bed. After she left, a red glow, too intense to be the dying sun, flared outside. The strange light drew Filibria out of bed to the window.

In the courtyard, a fire burned. A pyre. Filibria pressed her face against the cold glass. She could see three figures standing solemnly in front of the fire: the King, the Queen, and the Prince.

The King had denied her the simple comfort of attending her sister-in-law's funeral, Filibria realized. Instead, she was shut away as a fugitive. Her basic duties were stripped away. Peace continued to unravel and she was not even there to make a futile attempt to grasp the edges and rebind it.

Mother Brylla found Filibria fast asleep on the floor when she walked in the next morning. She woke her up and berated Filibria for sleeping on the floor when she had a perfectly good bed, but her heart was not it. Her face was grave. She took Filibria's hands in hers.

"Whatever that guard told you yesterday, keep it to yourself. He was found dead in his bed this morning. Poison. The King claims the guilt of surviving the ambush was too much for him." Filibria's hands started to shake.

"Lies."

"Shh. I can only accept what the King says. He was the stable master's son. The poor man's broken." Mother Brylla set Filibria's breakfast down and helped Filibria change into a new dress. Not that it mattered anymore. Filibria had nowhere to go.

The King had made it clear that nothing stood in his way. Someone had died to give information to Filibria. Her body felt strangely numb as Mother Brylla slid the dress over her head and began to lace it.

What now? Who all was in danger? Who all needed to know what she knew? One thing was for sure; she had to warn her husband.

"Wait," Filibria said just before Mother Brylla left. She turned and scribbled a note onto a piece of paper. "Can you give this to Trinlys?"

"Of course." Mother Brylla slipped the paper down the front of her bodice, her eyes glowing.

"I'm not starting a revolution," Filibria warned. "I'm just making sure Trinlys stays safe."

"I will make sure it gets to him."

"Thank you."

Filibria had kept the message short and as cryptic as she could. It said only: *All lies. Trust no one.*

Filibria was hungry, but as she surveyed the breakfast tray, she remembered the messenger. What if her own food was poisoned? What if the King wanted her silenced more than he wanted her for his secret reasons? Filibria picked at the food to give it the appearance of being eaten then pushed the tray away.

Filibria could not focus the rest of the day. She drifted from bed to books, to the window, and all over again. The books reminded her of Trinlys, which sent her into fresh tears. The harp had been moved into the room, but Filibria would not play it. Visions of Tiaeve, happy and alive, laughing as she plucked the notes, surfaced every time Filibria looked at it. She pushed it into a corner and concealed it with a robe. When Mother Brylla came with her midday meal, Filibria jumped.

"What's gotten into you girl?" Mother Brylla set the tray down. She picked up the breakfast tray and frowned.

"Did you give the paper to Trin?"

"I did."

"Did he give you anything for me?" Mother Brylla pulled a book out of her apron and gave it to Filibria. The book was familiar and well-read, one of Trinlys's favorite.

"He said you might want something to read while you are confined," Mother Brylla said. Filibria wanted to search for the message in the book, but she forced herself to wait until Mother Brylla had left.

"You didn't eat much breakfast, dearie. Are you ill?"

"No. I did not feel hungry." Filibria's stomach growled at the new platter of food, betraying her. "What if it's poisoned?" Filibria whispered.

"Oh, dearie, of course not. This came straight up from the kitchen. No one in the kitchen would poison you. Eat up." Mother Brylla stood in the room, making sure Filibria ate a few bites, then she left.

As soon as the door locked, Filibria shook the book. A single small slip of paper floated to the floor and she snatched it up.

You are in danger too. Do not take risks. I love you.

She did not need to be told any of it, but she read the little message over again before she forced herself to burn it. Filibria sat down at the desk to write another note of her own.

Life is nothing to him unless it serves a purpose. I do not know what to do. I'm confused and scared.

Even though she knew Trinlys could do nothing for her, admitting her fears felt good. She only wished he could have been there in person to comfort her. Her hands were sweating as she slipped the letter into a book.

After delivering dinner, Mother Brylla put the book Filibria gave her in her apron pocket, left the room, and locked the door behind her. When she turned around, Wrestan was standing in the passage, watching her. The key slipped out of her hand and she bent down, pocketing it away again.

"What did the girl give you?"

"Nothing. I brought her dinner, as I always do. Since she is a prisoner now."

"She gave you something. I know she did. I have been watching you. Now you will take that something to Trinlys. They are communicating."

Mother Brylla shook her head. "No. How could they be? The King directly forbids me from letting them communicate in any way." The book's weight dragged on her apron. Surely, Wrestan could see it. His eyes were on her, so cold and piercing. He was a captain of the guards, not one of the royal family. He had no right to be on this floor of the castle.

"Give the book to me."

"The book. Oh, yes. Trinlys did give a book to Filibria to read, but I forgot to deliver it." She turned back as if to return to Filibria's room, but Wrestan's strong hand landed on her shoulder.

"Give me the book."

Mother Brylla slipped her hand into the apron, grasped the book by the spine, and pulled it out sidewise. It stuck in her pocket, and she shook it until it popped free.

Wrestan then snatched the book from her trembling hands with more force than was necessary.

Seventeen

MOTHER BRYLLA STOOD FROZEN as Wrestan shook the book. Nothing fell out and he began riffling through the pages, searching for something: underlined words, torn pages, anything. His illiteracy seemingly frustrated his efforts, his face turning red. Finally, he grabbed a handful of pages and tore them out of the book. He threw it all at Mother Brylla, knocking the glasses off her face; and they hit the floor with a resounding crack.

Mother Brylla gasped.

"No more books," Wrestan growled. "If this happens again, I *will* tell the King." He stormed off down the hall, shoving past her.

Mother Brylla stood still long enough to calm down before she gathered up the pages and book, stuffing them into her pocket. She picked up the remains of her glasses; their frames were twisted and small glass shards littered the floor. Anger welled up from deep in her stomach as she hurried to Trinlys's room.

"You're pale, Brylla. And where are your glasses?"

Mother Brylla only handed him the book and its loose pages.

Trinlys blanched, gathering it into his arms like a broken child. "What happened? Filibria! Is Filibria safe?"

"Filibria is fine, yes. Wrestan took the book and accused me of smuggling notes. He damaged it, and my glasses…but I'm no worse for the wear, dear. It could have been much worse."

"I'm so sorry. I told you it was too dangerous for you to do this. I don't want you to do it anymore."

"Hush." Mother Brylla pulled the small slip of paper out of her apron pocket where it had fallen. "He said you cannot trade books anymore. Stay away from Wrestan. He is dangerous."

Trinlys unfolded the paper and scanned it, then he threw it into the fire. Mother Brylla watched his face.

"He's going to make me take a side. Her or my kingdom. I don't know what to do," Trinlys whispered.

"Choose her. The kingdom will follow you."

Trinlys picked at his fingers. "I don't know how to fight."

"When the time comes, you will. Your heart will teach you. But for now, give her a reply."

Trinlys shook his head. "I'm not putting you in danger."

"I have already been in danger. I sat by the side and watched as he crushed the only love I had. You and Filibria are my new love and I will not stand by quietly this time. I will do whatever it takes to free you and keep you safe. You know that."

Trinlys looked at her and nodded solemnly. Behind the determination in Brylla's eyes, he saw the worn years of sadness and defeat. Heat surged through his veins; maybe he *could* fight back.

Wrestan watched Mother Brylla like a hawk as she walked past him on her way to Filibria's room again. His eyes were on her, judging her apron pocket. When she met his eyes, she nearly lost her poise, but he had no power on this floor, she reminded herself. She was only doing her sworn duty: looking after the needs of the prince and the princess. Nevertheless, Mother Brylla slipped quickly into Filibria's room, away from Wrestan's prying eyes.

Filibria was terrified when Mother Brylla whirled into the room, slamming the door behind her.

"Your glasses!"

"I know. I know. Wrestan is to blame, but don't worry, I got the message to Trinlys, and he wrote back. I stored it where Wrestan wouldn't dare look." Triumphantly, she pulled a long letter from the front of her bodice.

Filibria gasped.

"I've locked the door," Brylla said. "Read it and then write back. Answer everything. He needs to know."

Dear Fili,

Tell me the truth, all of it. Your hints are driving me mad. Father shows no sign of ever letting you out. He has sent messengers to Delvaria, but they have not returned. He has grown quiet and suspicious and locks himself away for hours with Wrestan. He no longer even looks at me. I am scared by it. Mother is too.

What purpose do you think the King has for you? For me?

Love forever,

Trinlys

Filibria mulled over the letter. Then, picking up her pen, she wrote down everything she knew or suspected. She did not know what the King planned for her, but if he did not hesitate to kill his own daughter to further his plot, he would not hesitate to go to any lengths to accomplish whatever he was aiming for. Trinlys would be safest away from the castle. And although Filibria would love to leave with him, it would only plunge both kingdoms into deeper chaos. Plus, she was still locked away.

Filibria tossed her pen aside in frustration. She could not stay trapped in this room forever. Delvaria was relying on her to keep the peace. Was there nothing she could do? She touched her letter to Trinlys; she could write. She could send the truth to her brother, tell him of King Dalen's madness and cravings for war. But would he believe her?

"Why do you keep your plans secret? Am I not part of this too?" Wrestan snapped. He paced in front of the King's desk, occasionally kicking at the leg of a chair. King Dalen ran his fingers over the rim of his goblet and flicked the wine droplets into the fire. He studied his wine-stained fingers, relishing Wrestan's irritation. "You fear me," Wrestan hissed. "You are scared I will overthrow you."

King Dalen laughed. "I didn't know it was a secret. You take after your father, so why should I trust you?"

Wrestan glared at the King. "But at least tell me what comes next."

"We have Delvaria on the brink of war and we have its princess locked away. Everything marches along according to plan. All we must do is get rid of Trinlys and clear the path to the throne."

"Yes, but how? How? You know how long I have been waiting to walk that path and yet you have never cleared it for me!"

"An ambush while he rides, perhaps. We cannot do anything while he is in the castle. It has to be secret. Subtle."

"He has not ridden in days." Wrestan smashed his fist on the desk. "He stays in his room or down in the kitchen surrounded by his fawning servants. What about poison?"

"No. That would arouse too much suspicion. The staff love him too much. We must not get rid of him too soon—not yet. Let us engage in war, and when we know we are successful, something will happen to him."

"Yet we must not wait too long, my King. He has a quick mind. It would not do to have him catch on to anything. He must not suspect us."

"As long as he stays angered over Filibria's confinement, I do not think he has time to worry about anything else."

"Do not underestimate him," Wrestan growled.

"Do not doubt me," King Dalen returned.

"That stubborn, pigheaded…" Filibria kicked her bedpost, grunting at the sudden pain as Mother Brylla stood patiently behind her.

"He says he won't leave you here."

Filibria whirled around. "He knows I can't leave! But if he plans on staying…Well, surely King Dalen can't kill him. Trin is his last living heir."

"Not his last."

Filibria gave her a strange look. "Whatever do you mean? Trinlys said…"

Mother Brylla took a deep breath. "Wrestan is the King's bastard son."

The words hit Filibria with the force of an arrow. She sank down onto the edge of her bed. *Of course.* Suddenly, everything clicked into place; everything made sense. Trinlys was in danger.

A new thought rose hot in Filibria's heart. "Why did you not tell me this all sooner?"

"What would it have done?" Mother Brylla replied. "We are powerless either way. I did not want you to worry over Trinlys more than you already were."

"Then why tell me now? Oh, I don't know. I don't know anything." Filibria covered her face. "I just wish I could see him. I just wish everything was normal. I wish no one was in danger."

"We all do. One day, it will be normal again. I promise."

"How?"

Mother Brylla pursed her lips. "Evil never triumphs, but you will have to learn to fight back and take a stand when the time is right. I do not know if Trinlys is safe or not, but I have always feared for him. It is his purpose for you—which I cannot see yet—that scares me the most."

"He killed his own daughter. He will stop at nothing," Filibria said hollowly.

"Exactly. He kills whoever he must to keep his secrets close and his plans in motion." Anger and sadness edged Mother Brylla's voice.

"What can we do about it?"

"We must stay diligent. We must try to keep up with the King's plans, and we must not be rash."

During those days, Filibria composed several letters to her brother, but she destroyed each when she was through. Her supplies were running low, but somehow, she could not think of the right words. If the letter ended up in the wrong hands before it reached her brother...

Finally, late one night, she finished the perfect draft. Now she had to get it safely to her brother. She hid the letter where she was sure no one would ever find it as she thought of a safe way to get it into her brother's hands. Mother Brylla would be able to help her find someone trustworthy. Cradling that comforting thought, Filibria fell asleep.

In the morning, when the door to Filibria's room opened, a new chambermaid stepped in. The girl was about her own age, but Filibria had never seen her before. Her heart dropped.

"Is Mother Brylla ill?"

The chambermaid did not answer. She set down the breakfast tray and swept back the curtains. "You can dress yourself," she said as she went to Filibria's desk and began gathering the papers.

Filibria sat up in bed. "What are you doing?"

"Removing your writing supplies, as the King commanded."

Cold chills traveled through Filibria. How much did the King know? "W-Wait."

It was no use. The woman crumpled up her last pieces of parchment and pens, tossing them into the fire. She dumped the ink in after it; colored flames jumped up the chimney. The woman gathered up the few books on Filibria's desk and moved towards the fire.

"Not the books too!"

The girl ignored her and tossed them in. Flames curled up around the pages and devoured them.

Filibria watched the devastation. She held her composure until the chambermaid left, locking the door behind her. Then Filibria buried her head into her pillow and wept.

Had Mother Brylla been found out?

Had the King done anything to her?

It was all her fault. She had endangered Mother Brylla and Trinlys by insisting Trinlys knew the truth. Now she was lost, completely alone, and drifting in overwhelming helplessness, locked away from the world. She could not even write anymore. Outside, wars were starting and plots were hatching, but in her room, she was living through timeless days. Worse, without Mother Brylla, the letter to her brother would never reach Delvaria.

Eighteen

WRESTAN BOWED TO THE King as the door closed behind him. "You summoned me?"

"Yes, sit down."

King Dalen poured goblets of wine for himself and Wrestan. As usual, King Dalen's gaze unfocused as they settled into their chairs, and he went silent for a long time, scowling into the flames. A log popped in the fire. Wrestan twitched. Instead of waiting for the King to speak first, Wrestan leaned forward in his chair.

"They've been sending messages," Wrestan said. "Filibria's serving woman was responsible. I had her replaced."

King Dalen took a sip of wine and swallowed it slowly. "Messages? How much has she told Trinlys?"

"We were unable to capture any of the letters. I told you not to underestimate him."

King Dalen rapped his fingers on the table while Wrestan kept talking.

"We have removed all her ink and paper, but you cannot keep her locked away forever. If word got out to Delvaria…"

"A risk we must take."

"How long are you going to keep her locked away? What if she tries to escape? We can't put guards in front of her room because you're afraid of the servants talking, but they are already whispering—and you don't guard Trinlys either. I am telling you, you are underestimating him. All of this is taking too long. I don't like it."

"We will wait until Trinlys is dead," King Dalen interrupted, "then she goes free. The grief of Trinlys will have been too much for her. It will turn her mind. She will blame me for Tiaeve's death, but no one will believe her."

"When will we take care of Trinlys?" Wrestan growled. "Soon?"

"I did not call you here to discuss that. Right now, I have more important news. A messenger has arrived from Delvaria."

Wrestan's eyes gleamed. He leaned forward. "And?"

King Dalen smiled and took a sip of his wine. "King Kial is angry at us. Of course, he accuses us of lies. You were right, Filibria did send him a letter explaining Eirarin's innocence in her father's death—as if she knew anything of the matter. But King Kial ratted her out to us because he does not believe her. He accuses me of dictating the letter, making her write lies. The letter aided us. He is more thickheaded than I believed. We only have to wait and he will bring about his own undoing."

Wrestan bowed. "I will obey your every word. Only command my hand and show me my place."

"Good. You will ride at the head of my armies. Make a name for yourself as brave and daring and the people will love you. Show up and you—my true son—will be victorious. Go now, I hear my wife approaching. We will talk more later."

"Wait." Wrestan paused at the door. "What if they have a child?"

"Why do you think I separated them, you fool?" King Dalen snarled. Wrestan bowed again and fled from the room.

A light rap sounded at Filibria's door. Keys rattled in the lock, but the door did not open. Curious, Filibria slipped out of her bed, lit a lamp, and opened the door a crack to peek through.

"Who's there?" The hallway was dark.

Something furry slipped past her legs when she opened the door wider.

"Keayn."

"Shh," Trinlys said, following his dog into the room. He caught hold of Filibria's wrist and pulled closed the door. Filibria had not seen him in over a month. He looked thinner and haggard. Before she could ask questions, Trinlys swept her up into his arms. She could feel his heart beating rapidly. Warmth enveloped her, setting a fire in her heart. She wanted to never leave his warm, strong embrace.

"What are you doing here?" she whispered. "If they find us...How did you find the key? Trinlys, you can't do this...We'll..."

"Shh. No one will find us. My father is too scared to place guards in front of your door. That would not look good if he was keeping his own son and daughter-in-law captive. Besides, almost all the staff in this castle are on our side, so there is no one who will tell him. We are safe, I promise." He ran his fingers lightly over her face, as if memorizing the lines. "I have missed you, Fili. I cannot tell you how much."

"Has Delvaria sent any more word?" Filibria asked.

"Not that I know of, but my father has been locked away for many days and will say nothing to us. I have been discouraged from riding, so I spend most of my days in my room."

"Trinlys, you have to leave the castle." Filibria squeezed his arm. "It is not safe for you here. Your father hates you and does not want you around. I'm afraid he is going to do something to you like he did to Tiaeve."

Trinlys took her hand. "I'm not going without you, Fili. I would not leave you here alone."

"You know I cannot leave. If I leave, your father will blame it on Delvaria and there will be war. I must stay here. You do not. Besides, if you go..." Filibria opened her drawer and pulled out the letter to her brother. Trinlys scanned it before he met her gaze, fear burning in his eyes.

"If someone found this in your room..."

"I know, but I have not found a messenger for it. You must take it to my brother. Between my letter and your words, he should believe us—and he will protect you."

Trinlys shook his head and returned the letter to the drawer. "My place is in Eirarin, beside you, Fili. Do not worry about me. I will watch my back. I am safe here."

He tucked her hair behind her ear, and she reached up to catch his hand. It was shaking; he was lying.

Trinlys led her towards the bed. "Let us forget all of this for now. Tonight, it is just you and me, safe in your room. Undisturbed."

Filibria willingly complied.

In the morning, before dawn broke, Trinlys slipped out of bed. He stood a moment, watching Filibria sleep. A ray of sunlight fell over her face, illuminating her golden hair. He wanted to kiss her, but he could not risk waking her. He snuck to her drawer and removed the letter, slipping it down the front of his shirt. It could not be found in her room. Who knew what his father would do to her. The letter needed to be destroyed or taken to her brother as she wished, but he could not deliver it. Not as the heir. He did not trust Filibria's brother.

Trinlys slipped back to his own chambers where his pack full of provisions and a cloak waited. With a heavy heart, he gathered them up and slipped through the secret passages in the dark castle. Mother Brylla was the only one in the kitchen. She gave Trinlys a nod when he cut through. Soon after, Trinlys passed by the stables.

Though he would love the speed of a horse, he would not be able to get his horse through the secret side gate—and a horse would be harder to hide. Trinlys squeezed through the side door into the meadow on the far side of town. Once outside the town, he started running.

Someone hammered on Filibria's door. Her eyes flew open. *Trinlys!* She reached out, but the bed was empty. He was gone. Heaving a sigh of relief, she rolled out of bed and opened the door. Jarin looked past her into the room. His face was white.

"Is Trinlys here?"

Her heart stopped. They had been found out.

"No."

"He is missing," Jarin cried.

"What do you mean?"

"He did not show up for breakfast. When we were sent to his room, we found it empty and undisturbed. His horse is still in the stable. The King commanded me to search your room."

"He is not here, I assure you." Filibria was already pulling on a cloak. She started to slip past Jarin, but he blocked her.

"Where do you think you are going?"

Filibria hovered in the doorway, torn between her desire and fear of what the consequences would be for her and others if she stepped out of her room. "I want to search Trinlys's room."

Conflict passed over Jarin's face. "You are still confined to your room."

Against her better judgement, Filibria's desire won over. "Please? I will return immediately."

Jarin weakened. "Alright, but hurry back to your room. I will get in trouble if they find you."

"I will, thank you." Filibria hurried past him down the hall. The door to Trinlys's room stood open and she ran in. His cloak was gone, so were some of his books. Surely there was a clue as to where he had gone.

"He is gone."

Filibria whirled around.

The Queen stood in the doorway; her face was pale and tear-stained, but lit with a small, brave smile. "He left, Filibria, for his own safety."

"But last night he told me he was not going to leave. Nothing I could say would change his mind."

The Queen's head jerked up. "Last night?"

"He...He came into my room."

The Queen clasped her hand. "It was a foolish thing, yet I am glad. I am sure it broke his heart to be unable to tell you where he was going, but it was safest for you if you suspected nothing." The Queen reached out and touched Filibria's face. "You must be strong. More than ever, we need your binding. I will do all in my power to keep you safe. Go now before someone besides me finds you."

Filibria hurried back to her room where Jarin was still waiting and he quickly locked her back in again.

A noise down in the courtyard caught her attention. Through the blurry glass, she saw a dark lump of waiting horses, then men arrived to choose their mounts. One man wore a blazing red cloak. Dogs streamed out of the kennel and ran to their masters. The men laughed and joked like they were riding out on a hunt. A horn blew. The men thundered through the gate and out into the wild. They were hunting. They were hunting for Trinlys.

Filibria curled up in her bed and cried. Trinlys was gone. He was alone and being hunted like a stag. Would he be safe? Where could he have gone? Her thoughts rambled over all the conversations they'd had. Perhaps he had gone to the sea and sailed to another land. Perhaps...she fell asleep.

In the middle of the night, Filibria bolted upright out of her sleep. Her eyes were puffy and her pillow still damp, but her head was clear. Trinlys had fled to the ancient burial ground, at least until the hunt for him had died down. *Of course.* She sank back onto her pillows, her heart now lighter. Perhaps she could go to him sometimes if she were ever let out.

The next day, her wish was answered. Even better, when the door opened, Mother Brylla entered. Filibria flew out of bed to hug her.

Tears rolled down her face as she sobbed. "I thought you had been caught."

"No, dearie." Mother Brylla hugged her tightly, patting her on the head. "Wrestan suspected me, but he had no proof to accuse me. He had me replaced for a time. I have been safe in the kitchen." Her face was grave, and her eyes betrayed her recent tears. "The King sent me up from the kitchens to serve you again. Quickly, dress. The King summons you. There is something you must know." Mother Brylla looked at Filibria and opened her mouth, but then she shut it resignedly. She pulled out Filibria's dresses and chose a deep blue dress—almost black.

Filibria watched warily as Mother Brylla helped her into the gown. "What happened?" Filibria asked.

Mother Brylla only shook her head.

Fear tied a tight knot inside Filibria's stomach.

Jarin was waiting outside her door; he too, wore a solemn air.

By the time Filibria reached the King's private solar off the Great Hall, she had prepared herself for the worst, everything from Trinlys getting caught to war declared on Delvaria.

Nineteen

THE DOOR WAS OPEN when Filibria reached the King's chamber, but that made it no more inviting. Low light from the fire filled the room with deceptive shadows, and a cloying scent hung in the air, like death—what she imagined a beast's lair smelled of.

When Filibria's eyes adjusted, she saw the Queen and Wrestan were also in the room. Wrestan locked in on her face, his eyes narrowing like a hawk sighting its prey. Filibria ignored him and turned to the Queen, seeing immediately the Queen's tear-stained face. Like Filibria, she also wore black, but she held her head high, her back straight. Filibria's heart dropped, causing her to hesitate in the doorway. Someone had died...again.

"Come in," the King said, beckoning to the only free chair.

It sat next to Wrestan. Filibria moved to it and sat, hiding her reluctance. Her father-in-law wasted no time in getting to the point. When he announced the news, his voice was flat and even.

"Trinlys is dead."

It did not register at first, then it was as if he had punched her.

"No!" Filibria gasped for air, gagging in the sweet smell. The room blurred. Filibria dug her fingernails into the arms of the chair, trying to keep her head clear. The hunting party had been successful; the King had found and killed Trinlys. Filibria searched her father-in-law's face. His sorrow looked sincere, though she knew better than to believe it. The Queen began another round of weeping. Wrestan sat back in his chair, his legs and arms crossed, showing no emotion.

"It is not true," Filibria whispered.

King Dalen narrowed his eyes. "I ordered my men to scour the countryside yesterday. They found his body floating in a river far from here. My guess was that he drowned his grief."

"He wouldn't have," Filibria protested.

"No? Well, you have not known him long. He was a troubled boy, haunted always by a burden of never being good enough. And he has never had his full senses, not since birth."

"Lies. You made him feel unworthy—and he could read."

"Exactly, but he could never lead the country, or a war and he knew that. It bore heavy on him. Nonetheless, his passing is untimely and grievous, especially so soon after the murder of our daughter."

Filibria bit her lower lip. She could not bear the pained look in the King's eyes—a mockery of a father's love. She glanced at the Queen; the grief she wore was real. Anger built up in Filibria's chest. How could she allow this to go on? First, Tiaeve, and now Trinlys...while the King went free, blameless.

She stood. "It was not a search party," Filibria stated. "It was a hunting party. You hunted down your own son and killed him. Just as you killed your daughter."

The air was sucked out of the room as the Queen gasped.

For the longest time, the King stared at her. The tendons in his neck twitched and his fist clenched, but then he let out a laugh, low and cruel. "What proof do you have? Your job is to keep peace, not spread rumors. My son is dead by his own hand. You are too overcome by grief to think properly. No one will believe you. Sit down, girl, and listen to me."

Filibria collapsed onto the chair, finding no more strength to fight back.

King Dalen stood up and began to pace behind his desk. He tented his fingers, watching his wife and Filibria over the tops of them.

"As you know, Delvaria blamed us for the death of your father. Then, when I tried to reconcile what we had not done, they killed my daughter. They are bent on having war with us. Though I do not trust you, your job as a peace weaver remains." King Dalen reached out and gripped Filibria's arm; his nails dug into her skin. "You can still help us! Just as you have so adamantly desired!"

Filibria tried to pull her arm free, but he tightened his grip.

"Because of the instability of my kingdom, I have been forced to quickly choose another heir to take my son's place. I have appointed Wrestan to be next in line for the throne."

Wrestan. Just as Mother Brylla had predicted. Filibria stole a look at Wrestan. His gaze was trained on the King's face, drinking in his words. Sensing her own glance, his head turned slightly towards her so that their eyes met for a second. Quickly, she looked away.

The King still droned on, his words thick with lies. "I have no closer relations and I trust Wrestan like my own son." The Queen gripped the arms of her chair tighter at the last phrase and Wrestan glared at his father. King Dalen ignored them both. Why was he lying about Wrestan? What did he have to lose by claiming him as his own son? The more the King hid his intentions beneath layers of lies, the more fear filled Filibria.

"Wrestan has followed my every order since he came into his position. He will be the King Eirarin needs." He stopped to make sure she was listening. "As for you, Filibria, a widow now, you have no ties to the throne anymore. To be effective in keeping peace, you will be expected to marry the new heir and thus secure once more the peace binding."

She blanched, the last piece falling into place. But why Wrestan? What would her marriage to him give King Dalen? Surely he was not that invested in peace, not after everything he had done. So then why? The fog of the unknown settled around her heart, chilling it.

"I will not marry Wrestan," Filibria replied with as much steel as she could. She ripped her arm free from the King, biting back pain when his nails left angry red lines across her skin.

The King's demeanor hardened. "You must. As your father-in-law and as your King, I command you." The King's voice dropped to a threatening growl, causing Filibria's defiance to flag, but the revolting thought of marrying Wrestan kept her resolve strong.

"I was sworn to marry the King's son, but now he is dead. I will return to my family as my brother requested. I have no more ties here. It is written that if a marriage fails, the peace weaver may return to her own kingdom." She willed her voice to sound stronger than she felt. "I *will* return to Delvaria."

King Dalen's eyes narrowed. "You will do no such thing. Your task was to marry my son to keep the peace. You were to bind the kingdoms and royal families. My son is dead, but your duty remains. More than ever, we need a tie between the two kingdoms. You *will* marry Wrestan. I will not have you running back to Delvaria only to reveal you are carrying the heir to the throne."

Filibria sank back into her chair. "There will be war because you provoked my brother!"

"Because he murdered my daughter." The King's voice was so low the hairs on Filibria's arms stood up.

Lies; every single word was a lie. Filibria watched his eyes, so filled with determination and anger. How was he so twisted? What was his end goal? His insanity scared her. Everything about him scared her. She fought her way through her thoughts and the hammering of her heart. There had to be an escape—a way out.

The Queen sat silent in her chair, her eyes wide with fear as she looked from her husband to her daughter-in-law.

"There must be another way," Filibria pleaded. "At least let me talk to my brother and let me try to prevent war. If you allow me, then I will marry whomever I wish. I promise." Her plea fell on deaf ears.

"You will marry Wrestan. That is final. Delvaria, until this has been settled, is the enemy and will be treated as such. No messages will be sent to them, unless it comes from my hand. From now on, you are no longer confined to your room, but you are forbidden to leave the castle. And if you cause any problems or try to leave, I will be forced to lock you away somewhere more secure."

Filibria fought to keep her mind clear from the anger and fear clawing at her, breathing in deep despite the sickening smell. She had to buy time. Who knew what it would do for her, but she knew she could not marry Wrestan. Not now, nor ever.

"At least let me observe the proper month of mourning for my dead husband," Filibria begged. "Then I will consent to your wishes."

The King paused, his eyes narrowing in contemplation.

The Queen swallowed hard, finally speaking up. "Do this one thing for her at least, Dalen. You also know the law states she must wait at least three months before remarrying to make sure she is not carrying an heir. You have just told her her husband is dead and now you are forcing her to marry another man!"

"She herself says she is not carrying an heir. She has been alone for a month already. I will give her two more months."

A wave of relief washed over Filibria; that was more than she could have hoped for. For the first time since stepping in the room, Filibria felt like she could breathe again.

"Thank you."

"Go back to your room, girl. And I am sorry about the death of your husband and how it has affected your mind. We will still care for you, though you might rant and rail against us. It must be hard for you, but the kingdom calls for a new heir. Sometimes diplomacy must come above family and love."

Filibria wanted to cover her ears and block out the sickening lies the King spewed.

"In these times more than ever, we have need of a peace weaver. For the sake of Delvaria and Eirarin, you must stay and weave your peace, even if you are grieving. We honor your sacrifice." King Dalen's voice dropped to a sickly sweet tone, making Filibria's blood boil. Now it was her turn to clench her fist to hold back her rage. He was using her, but why? To elevate Wrestan's status beyond his illegitimacy? It all made her sick. If she did not the leave the room, she would forget herself and do something rash. Her rage boiled too close to the surface.

Filibria got up from her chair, knocking it over in her haste to leave.

Her room, for a whole month had been like a prison, but now it felt like a refuge. Filibria buried herself in her bed and wept. Trinlys was dead and she had to marry Wrestan. Two months. It would pass all too quickly, and until then, she would have to bear Wrestan's smug looks. She would have to find a way to live without Trinlys.

On the day after the news, the King held a funeral for Trinlys. Filibria, as Trinlys's widow, played a crucial role in the proceedings, but she was only a face. A face concealed beneath a black veil.

Trinlys's body had been brought back from the river, but the river had taken its toll on the body and the King declared the remains shut up in a coffin. That night, the coffin was born with great ceremony through crowds of wailing women to the center of the courtyard where the pyre waited. Wrestan, arrayed in red, led the way. At the pyre, he stepped aside to let the men pace the coffin upon the fuel. Next came the steward, carrying a torch, which he handed to the King. King Dalen stepped forward and said a few words—all lies—then touched the torch against the pyre. With a whoosh of air, flames shot up. Through Filibria's veil, the flames ascending into the dark were grainy, unreal. The smell of smoke and oil-drenched wood permeated the air, suffocating her. She watched the coffin collapse in on itself, sending sparks dancing up towards the stars as the wailing rose in the courtyard and from the city streets below. It was all unreal. She felt nothing. Something in Filibria's heart did not believe Trinlys was dead. Maybe it was hope or maybe only delayed grief and denial.

Filibria glanced over at the Queen. Though tears, amber in the firelight, streaked down her face, her eyes were calm. She looked at peace. It was then that the Queen looked her way. She gave Filibria a fleeting smile and turned her attention back to the fire. The Queen was not mourning; she knew something.

Filibria felt the eerie, sickening presence of someone come up beside her. Without looking, she knew it was Wrestan.

"A tragedy," he breathed, shaking his head. "I am here for you, in anyway that you need, dear." His hand groped for hers, but she snatched her hand away and folded it out of reach across her chest.

"I will never marry you," she hissed.

"I am a very persuasive man. And, surely, you would not want to upset the peace of your kingdoms?"

Filibria did not answer. She left the pyre and returned to the safety of her room.

That was the last time Filibria was allowed to set foot outside the castle.

Filibria spent more time in the Queen's company after Trinlys's funeral. The Queen had taken the death of her children hard, and Filibria seemed to be the only joy in her life now. Though Filibria was empty of music, she played the harp to entertain her mother-in-law. They kept their conversation light, never talking of the King or what exactly they both knew of his plots. As much as Filibria wanted to confide in her, she could not risk the Queen's safety in any way. Her mother-in-law was all that remained of the loving family Filibria had come to enjoy. Instead, Filibria took her questions and concerns to Mother Brylla.

"Why must I marry Wrestan? Why does the King want it so bad? Surely the trade routes are not that important to him?" Filibria flopped back on her bed, staring at the ceiling as if the answers were written there.

"I don't know, dear." Mother Brylla bustled around the room. "Control? Keeping a closer eye on you? Elevating Wrestan to a proper place in society? Or maybe truly keeping peace with Delvaria? Who can understand the mind of that

King." She stopped out of habit to check her surroundings, even though they were locked safely away in Filibria's room.

"It troubles me. I cannot put my finger on whatever purpose he has for me, but I know it is not a good one."

"I know, dear."

From time to time, Filibria remembered her letter. She had forgotten about it during the past few days, but now she was free to send it. Yet what did it matter anymore? It was doubtful it would stop a war and it could do nothing to bring Trinlys back.

Filibria spent much of her time in the kitchen. Though her presence stirred up painful memories of Trinlys for the servants and cooks, she needed them and found they needed her too. They regaled her with stories of Trinlys as a boy. Her visits were always filled with tears, but the tears healed, opening the way for laughter once again. Mother Brylla loved to dredge up the old stories of Trinlys's misdeeds, making everyone laugh until they cried. Mother Brylla was Filibria's anchor in a dark storm and her constant companion in the waves of tears.

The kitchen staff did their best to keep her updated on the world outside. Filibria learned King Dalen had sent threats of war to Delvaria and that King Kial had responded with hostility. But then, King Dalen, in noble hopes of restoring peace, had rescinded his threats, informing Delvaria of Filibria's impending marriage to Wrestan. Her brother had yet to respond, which troubled her. Filibria knew he would not agree, but there was nothing he could do about it.

"He has appointed Captain Wrestan to be his heir because he now has no others—and you have agreed to marry Wrestan to keep peace! How noble of you," a kitchen maid gushed one morning. "You continue to keep peace for us, even in your grief."

Mother Brylla watched over the head of the animated maid assessing Filibria as the words hit her like stones. Filibria looked up to meet her worried eyes and tried to give her a weak smile.

Filibria hugged her knees up to her chest on the kitchen bench, bracing against the waves of sadness crashing into her. She missed Trinlys. Should she cling to the hope he was still alive? If Trinlys ever set foot in the castle again, he would upset everything. Surely King Dalen would murder him. If Trinlys was even still alive…The true evil and twistedness of King Dalen sank in. He had his kingdom believing he was the benevolent hero, making noble sacrifices. It made Filibria sick, physically and viscerally nauseous.

Before it could register, her stomach suddenly heaved its contents out onto the floor of the kitchen. The gossip went silent as all eyes turned to her.

"Poison," someone whispered.

Filibria stared in dismay at the mess.

Mother Brylla shushed the whispers and stepped through the crowd, quickly taking control of the situation. Maids fell in to help clean up while Mother Brylla supported Filibria out of the room.

Once in her own room, Filibria vomited again.

"Do you think it's poison?" she heaved.

Mother Brylla looked grave. "No poison would have touched anything you ate. I only serve you food I have prepared, and no one else in the kitchen has malicious intentions towards you." Mother Brylla helped Filibria out of her dress and into a soft nightgown, though it was way too early in the day for that. "Rest now. I will keep an eye on you. I will call for the physician if the need arises."

"Thank you."

Mother Brylla pulled back the coverlet and Filibria crawled into bed. Nausea still clung to her stomach, but worry clutched harder.

"Mother Brylla?"

Mother Brylla turned in the doorway. "Yes?"

"I miss him so much. It's so hard to be brave without him."

"I know dear. I know. Rest now. I will check up on you soon."

"Thank you." A single hot tear rolled down Filibria's face onto the pillow.

"Good morning, Filibria. How are you feeling?"

Filibria groaned from the depths of her pillow.

Mother Brylla pulled the curtains open after putting a tray of food on her nightstand. "I checked on you all last night, but you slept fine and did not seem to wake. Sit up now and have a bite to eat."

The meal did not look appetizing, but at Mother Brylla's insistence, Filibria took a couple of bites.

"I can't marry Wrestan," Filibria said, "I can't even stand to see him anymore." She ran her fingers over the embroidery on the coverlet. "I'm beginning to think it would be better if I was dead...then I would be out of the King's hands. I know that he killed Tiaeve and he wants to silence me for it, but he cannot get rid of me because he still has need of me.

"I'm not a pawn, Brylla. I'm tired of being used to bind and break kingdoms. I just wanted to live the rest of my life with Trinlys."

Mother Brylla sat on the edge of the bed and stared at Filibria, her face grim. "Listen, Filibria, death may look like the easier way out, but it is not. You are more use here on this earth than in Eiefu. Never choose that solution. Never. There is always another way out."

"What way? I can see nothing." Filibria threw up her hands in despair, almost upsetting the breakfast tray.

"It will come," Mother Brylla replied. "But don't ever let me hear you talk like that again. I promise to do what I can to help you. You are not alone. The castle staff stands behind you and we *will* keep you safe." Mother Brylla smiled.

A lump formed in Filibria's throat. "I can't ask it of you, Brylla. You have already risked so much. And I can't ask it of the others either."

"I'm not waiting for your permission, Filibria. Neither are they. We support you and protect you because we know it is what is right. We care about Eirarin—but more than that, we love you. And we love Trinlys. We will fight for you if it comes down to it."

Despite having more allies to think over the matter, weeks slipped by, and they could deliver no solution. Filibria decided she needed to write another letter to her brother, one that explained everything up to date. But when she went to her hiding place, it was missing. Fear clutched her, chest tight. It had been found!

Filibria worried over the missing letter over the next few days, but then she discovered something that overshadowed her worry; something that would change her entire life.

CHAPTER

Twenty

"I am with child," Filibria stated.

The words physically dropped the Queen into her chair.

"Are you sure?" The Queen gripped the arms of her chair, knuckles already white, as she leaned forward. The hope in her eyes bit deep into Filibria's heart.

Filibria nodded numbly.

"You are saved!" The Queen jumped up to embrace her.

"No. You do not understand." Filibria fought free to look the Queen in the eyes. "The baby will be killed when it is born."

"What? Nonsense. You carry the heir, the rightful heir to the throne of Eirarin. This would remove Wrestan from his inheritance. Even if there is war and both kings fall, you hold the heir to both kingdoms. You save them both."

Both kingdoms. Like a rock dropping, it hit Filibria and suddenly it all made sense. Of course, she had been a fool. She was the key to both kingdoms. If King Dalen controlled her through Wrestan and killed her brother and siblings, she would be Queen of Delvaria. Filibria gripped the Queen's chair at the weight of the realization: King Dalen wanted both kingdoms. It had been his plan all along.

"Filibria? Filibria? Sit down. You have gone so pale. Sit." The Queen helped Filibria into her seat. "What is it?"

"The baby is a threat. Not a blessing. The King wants Wrestan to be king. Of both kingdoms. I can't...I can't marry him. I cannot." Filibria stood again, trying to steady her breathing. "I can't."

The Queen's face went through pages of expressions. "Of course," she said sadly, "it all makes sense. My children were never enough for him and now they are gone, leaving the path clear for Wrestan. No doubt all part of his plot. He has always favored Wrestan, for he loved Wrestan's mother. Never me. He will do anything to make Wrestan his rightful heir. I was foolish to ever hope otherwise." The Queen sank into a melancholy mood.

"What am I to do then?" Filibria cried. "The baby will keep me from marriage until it is born, but after that..."

"You should leave," the Queen said suddenly. She gripped Filibria's hand. "You should stop my husband's plans. You should go to Trinlys. Find him. Escape."

"You..." Filibria's voice came out in a hoarse whisper. "You think he's alive?"

"Of course." The Queen almost laughed. "He knew he was in danger. He ran away. You need to go to him."

"Did he tell you this?"

The Queen hesitated. "I have my sources that saw him leave. He said nothing about you joining him, but I know he would want it. He would want to know you were safe."

"I cannot," Filibria said. "If the King claimed I was dead too, that would further anger my brother and push both kingdoms into war. I must stay and keep peace. I cannot abandon the kingdoms." Not even for the sake of her husband.

"There will be war either way, Filibria. My husband will see to it. For once, choose your heart over your duties. And then, in time, you might make peace. But without you, peace is impossible. Without you, King Dalen's plans will be foiled. Get away from him before he can use you further."

Filibria hesitated, torn.

"Go to Trinlys," the Queen repeated. "First and foremost, you are his wife. How happy he will be when he hears the news."

"Will you come with me? You are not safe here either."

The Queen shook her head. "I cannot leave my husband. He may not listen to me, but I will do what I can to stop his madness. He will not hurt me. Go and pack now. I will make arrangements for your escape. You must take a horse, for you should not be traveling on foot in your condition. And Filibria?" She caught Filibria just as the girl was about to turn for the door. "Flee to Delvaria. You should be safe with your brother. Perhaps...Perhaps there you can bring peace as you were meant to—but you must find safety first. Safety for you and... for your child."

Filibria came back and hugged her mother-in-law; both fought back tears. "I will try to fix all of this in Delvaria. My brother should understand."

"Good. Now go. I will do what I can for you, Eirarin, and Trinlys. I will say you have locked yourself in your room and will see no one, but I do not know how long they will believe it. Go, Filibria. Be careful." The Queen kissed her daughter-in-law's forehead. "Be brave."

As soon as Filibria stepped through the door to her room, she sensed something was wrong. She smelled the air, thick with a sickly smell. Then she saw him: Wrestan, standing at the window with his back to her, hands behind his back. His fingers played with a naked dagger. Beside him, her writing desk lay ransacked. The drawers lay in splintered fragments on the stone floor.

"Good," he said without turning. "I thought you had flown the nest already. We were not too late."

Filibria stumbled back into the hall, slammed the door closed, and began to run; she nearly knocked into Jarin.

"What is it?" he asked and then the door opened again. Wrestan burst into the hallway. "Run, my lady!"

Filibria looked back just in time to see Jarin barre into Wrestan, tripping him up, but he was no match for the bigger man. A sickening thud echoed through the corridor and then the sound of running feet.

Filibria reached the stairs. Behind her, she could hear Wrestan shouting and blowing his horn. Guards pounded down the steps above her head. She burst through the bustling kitchen, upsetting a crate of chickens. Cooks and fowl alike began squawking at her, but she was already in the courtyard. She flung herself through the stable door, where the ostler was napping in a chair. She startled him awake.

"Lass, what's got ahold of you?"

"A horse!" she gasped. "I need a horse!"

"Just a moment," the ostler said, rising from his chair. He moved around slowly, choosing a saddle.

"No time," Filibria said, grabbing his hand. "I must flee, now. Forget the saddle." She could hear pounding feet in the courtyard. The ostler looked surprised. His stiffness fell away in an instant.

"Well then," he said, gesturing to a grey horse. "She's ready. No, wait." He hobbled farther into the stables, opened a stall door, and a huge black horse thundered forward, nostrils flared. *Swift Foot.* Filibria shied away from the beast.

"Take him. No one will be able to keep up with you. Come." The ostler helped Filibria onto the horse's back and gave it a good smack on the rear. The stallion roared out of the stables, Filibria clinging to its mane for dear life. She was riding hard through the palace gates, before the first of the men even reached the stables.

"After her!" Wrestan screamed.

"She's riding the King's horse!" one soldier yelled and Wrestan and his men stormed the stables.

"Horses, man, now!" he shouted. He kicked at the ostler who had settled back into his chair.

"Well," said the ostler, slowing. "They'll take a while to saddle and bridle. These hands aren't what they used to be." He picked up the saddle he had chosen for

Filibria and moved along the line of stalls, looking into each as if his choice of horse mattered.

"Hurry!" Wrestan shouted.

"You can't put the wrong saddle on the wrong horse, you see," the man said, "it will chafe them."

"Forget chafing. Just saddle them!"

By the time all the men were mounted and riding, Filibria was deep into the countryside. As soon as she could, she lost herself in the forest. She reached a small dingle far off the regular hunting path and urged Swift Foot to stop there, hiding from the hunt. Though she heard horns and shouting throughout the day, no one came near her hiding place. Several times, dogs barked or howled to one another, but then they went silent. Still, no one found her. Fear crawled over Filibria. At any moment, she expected a wet muzzle to appear through the bushes. Only after Filibria heard them move further west, did she dare move on, mounting Swift Foot and blindly guiding the stallion through the forest that darkened with the fast approach of night and a storm.

Wrestan was in a black mood, storming into the King's chamber sopping wet. King Dalen sat at his desk, dictating a letter to his scribe. Outside, the rain howled and beat at the windows. The King looked up and read Wrestan's face, immediately dismissing the scribe.

Wrestan's clothes still bore marks from the long day of searching for the princess. He had come directly from the stables to the King's chamber.

"She has escaped then?" King Dalen asked.

"I am led to believe your Queen orchestrated it. Where else would Filibria have gone if she left her chambers?"

"Why did you not act sooner?"

"She ran from me. She slipped through the kitchen and out to the stables before anyone could catch her." Wrestan shifted uncomfortably. "She stole Swift Foot."

"What?!" King Dalen shoved his chair back and stood up. Wrestan took a step back. "How?"

"I do not know. She was riding it from the stables last we saw her. The ostler claimed he was asleep when she came in."

"And you could not catch her? She is only a girl raised in a castle. Not a trained knight."

Wrestan pulled himself to his full height and stood a moment in silence, slowly breathing. His fists clenched at his side and the muscles in his jaw bunched. "The page boy was protecting her. He tripped me, letting her escape."

King Dalen clenched his fist. "He will be taken care of. You mean to tell me that you were bested by a boy?"

"On top of that," Wrestan hissed, "she is riding the fastest horse—your horse—in the kingdom. She will be impossible to catch."

"That alone is enough for the death penalty. You must find her."

"She will not escape. I promise you that."

"You had better. If she reaches Delvaria..."

"You might ask your wife where she is," Wrestan snapped. "I have little doubt Filibria and her have been conspiring together. You were a fool to let the girl out of her room. First, your son slips between your fingers and now her. It seems you do not have control over the situation like you promised."

King Dalen glared. "You are the one who was responsible for hunting them down."

"You set your plans and suddenly they flee like birds, leaving no trace. It is not my fault they have disappeared. It was your responsibility to make sure they did not escape in the first place."

"Are you accusing me, Wrestan?"

"I thought you had everything under control, that is all. Forgive me if I expected too much of you. They are out there, running loose over the country with vital information, no doubt both headed towards Delvaria. They keep slipping through your careless fingers."

"Well, somehow she knows or suspects that I was responsible for my daughter's death. And you were the only one who knew outside of the guards, who all died. I'm not the only one who is being careless."

Wrestan glared at him.

King Dalen relented with a sigh. "We have both made mistakes. When I asked for her hand for my son, it seems I bargained for too much." He then scowled. "This was supposed to be easy, but the girl has made allies. Steward!" The door opened. "Send my wife in." Without hesitation, the man bowed and hurried away down the hall as King Dalen sat back in his chair. "The Queen knows too much. She will be the first silenced. As a lesson to the others."

"Are you suggesting..." Wrestan said, voice wavering slightly.

"If she had stayed where she was supposed to and kept her head out of politics, she would have been safe. This is getting too messy. We have to take more drastic measures to make sure everything remains contained."

"But she is the Queen! You are going too far."

"She is heavy with grief, having lost all she had in so short a time. I tried to stop her," King Dalen thought aloud, "but it was in vain. I reached her too late." Wrestan had moved over to the window. He watched the storm lash against the glass.

"At least with this storm, the girl cannot travel far. She will be tired. She will make mistakes. We should find marks in the mud tomorrow."

"See to it you do."

Wrestan moved towards the door, but the King beckoned him back.

"Stay."

At that moment, the steward returned with the Queen. She was wrapped in her mantle and her hair hung free of ornaments. At the sight of Wrestan, she drew back.

"What is the meaning of this? Why have you called me while I was preparing for bed?"

With a nod, King Dalen dismissed the steward. In one stride, he reached his wife. "Do you know where Filibria is?"

"You did not find her?"

"No. You know where she is?"

The Queen tossed her head. "Out in the countryside, is she not? You are hunting down the Princess of Delvaria like you would a hart? What if word reached her brother's ears? You have driven her from her home. After sending our daughter off to die and chasing our son from his house to drown his grief, you think she would want to stay? She has no ties here."

"If her brother heard, there would be war," King Dalen replied calmly. "I could not have planned it better myself, but the vixen must be returned. She has yet to play a vital part in all this. Where is she?"

"I do not know."

"Then where is Trinlys?" he hissed.

The Queen tried to back up towards the door, but Dalen grabbed her wrist and leaned in. She clenched her jaw at the stench of his breath. "He is dead, as you have said. Is he not?"

"Is he? Do you know where he is?"

Something cold and barely perceptible touched the Queen's throat. She swallowed. "Kill me and add it to your list of murders," she whispered. "I would rather die a thousand deaths than let you touch a hair on Trinlys's head—or Filibria's. I will never tell you."

"Then you do know?" The knife pushed harder, and a small trickle of warm blood ran down her neck, soaking into the collar of her dress.

"What would you gain by my death? My lips are sealed both in life and in the grave. You took my daughter and my son. You drove away my daughter-in-law. I owe you nothing. Yes," she said with satisfaction when his face paled, "I know you killed my daughter."

King Dalen's hand trembled. The knife tip dug deeper.

"I thought to save you from this," King Dalen said coldly. "If only you had stayed in your room."

"I am not a bird to be caged, Dalen, only brought out before the guests when it is time to sing. I have a life."

"You are my wife! You listen only to me!"

The Queen ripped her wrist free, eyes ablaze. "You lost my trust and loyalty. You drove away and killed my children. You plotted wars behind my back. Why should I listen to you!" She was too angry to fear him anymore.

King Dalen watched his wife's face. His hand quivered slightly in response to the rise and fall of her slender throat.

"Too long I have cowered before you. Do your worst." Her eyes gleamed like flint, striking fire in her husband's eyes.

He watched her, his fingers tightening on the back of her neck. Waiting for her to fold, to burst into tears, to cower, but she stood strong.

Then King Dalen exploded. It was over quickly. He straightened and stared coldly at the corpse of his wife, wiping the blood from his hands.

"She remained true to her word. A mother's lips are sealed unto death." He looked to Wrestan who stood shocked in the corner. "Send for the steward again. The death of her two children has been too much for the Queen. She could not bear life anymore. I tried to stop her, but when she heard of the loss of her daughter-in-law, she grabbed the knife and she..." King Dalen swallowed hard and his voice dropped—"she...I could not stop her."

Wrestan bowed. "It shall be done, Father."

King Dalen slipped the knife into his wife's stiffening hand and walked from the room. A single tear glimmered at the corner of the King's eye

CHAPTER

Twenty-One

FILIBRIA LEANED OVER THE stallion's neck. Night gathered early as angry clouds converged. Lightning lit up the dark forest and thunder rumbled in the distance. The first drops fell. Filibria's heart beat in rhythm to the powerful, fast hoofbeats.

She strained to remember the way. The coming storm added to her urgency, but clogged her memory with fear. With the rain, she would not be able to see anything. Just when she reached the valley where the royal barrows lay, the skies opened. Worse, the dip in the land was filled with mist. Filibria rode between the mounds and up into the forest. Branches lashed out at her. Rain fell steadily, even though the trees covered her. Her dress clung to her, soaked to the skin as water rolled down her face, making it hard to see through the darkness ahead. What if she got lost? What if Trinlys was not there? Filibria forced herself not to think of the possibilities.

Finally, she found what she was looking for: the narrow lane between the trees. She spurred Swift Foot into a faster gait. The towering trees flashed past and lightning crackled in the distance, lighting up the way. The horse flinched with each clap of thunder, but continued on. Once, far away, a dog barked. Was it

Keayn? Or maybe it was a persistent hunter, still out to find her, tracking her with his hound. Could it be Wrestan? The bark did not come again.

The stallion broke into the clearing. *There! The mound.* There was the spring she had drunk from, too, but where was Trinlys? The small glade was empty, save for the remains of an old fire. White light filled the clearing, illuminating everything, and thunder exploded. Filibria's horse reared. Her cold, stiff fingers failed to grip the reins and her weak legs lost their grip. She slipped from the horse's back and landed on the thick wet turf. Stars and darkness filled her vision, but before she lost consciousness, she was aware of a rough, warm tongue licking the rain off her face.

"K-Keayn?" Then everything faded.

When Wrestan entered the room, he found the King standing before the fireplace. Dalen's hollow eyes reflected the firelight. He still wore black. Wrestan waited respectfully, but it was a long time before King Dalen spoke. When he did, he did not break off his gaze off the flames.

"We are in danger," he said slowly, "If the Queen knew so much, others in the castle may also know too much."

"It would be unlikely, my King," Wrestan replied.

"Oh? What about, say, the head cook and maid-in-waiting?"

"Mother Brylla?" Wrestan fidgeted with the hilt of his dagger. "She was Filibria's only source of contact for a long time, and we know that she orchestrated communication between Filibria and Trinlys, but it would be madness to get rid of her."

King Dalen only raised an eyebrow.

"If you did, the servants would revolt! The Queen was easy, because she is your wife, because she never goes out, because you blamed it on grief. But if you kill any of the staff..."

King Dalen leaned forward. "I will do whatever needs to be done. I fear no one. Word of the princess's disappearance must not slip out beyond the castle though. We will control the story of how she disappeared. It will be spun as an abduction—by her brother. If I hear any other version, heads will roll. Do you understand?"

"Yes, my King."

"And what of the page boy?"

Wrestan swallowed. "He...He has not been found." Wrestan barely ducked a goblet; it smashed against the wall, spreading wine over the stones.

"Fool! First you let Trinlys disappear, and then you let the girl slip completely out of your hands and now the boy is missing too!"

"I...I..." Wrestan drew himself up, clutching his trembling hands behind his back. "We... are searching for him, even now. And even now, we still search for the princess." It was the wrong thing to say. He ducked just in time to avoid the pitcher.

"Enough!" Wrestan shouted. "You are going mad, Father! Stop this show of hysteria. It will solve nothing. Perhaps the death of your queen was too much for you. Perhaps it would be better if your heir steps into your place until you recover."

King Dalen leaned over his desk, breathing hard. "Are you threatening me?" His eyes were bloodshot.

"Anger is getting you nowhere. Princess Filibria has made her move and succeeded. You must decide on your counterattack."

King Dalen sank into his chair.

"Blame King Kial for abducting his sister. Anger him. Declare war."

"It is hardly a matter of war. She has no ties here, after all. Since her husband is dead, King Kial has the right to revoke the peace tie." King Dalen slapped the table. "I was a fool to listen to my wife! I should have married you to Filibria immediately."

"That is in the past. Right now, we need a reason to go to war against Delvaria."

King Dalen hung his head, thinking. When he looked up again, a cold smile sliced his lips. He had returned to normal. "Make it known Princess Filibria carries the heir to the Eirarin throne. By taking her, King Kial hopes to secure Eirarin. The two have been conspiring since the beginning. It was his plot to kill Princess Tiaeve, my only daughter. With Filibria's help, he also got rid of Trinlys."

Now, Wrestan smiled too and he nodded. "It shall be done."

"See to it—and keep searching the country. She is a lone woman. She could not have gotten far. Every minute she is not locked away is a danger to us. If she gets the truth to her brother…"

"What if," Wrestan began cautiously, "she has met up with Trinlys as I suspect?"

"We have searched every nook and cranny in the country for him. How could he still be here? How long could he last on his own even if he were? He kept his nose in books. He knows nothing of the wild."

"I was only wondering at the possibility."

"It could be likely. They might have had a plan all along. But all the better; if we find her, perhaps we will find them both. Two are easier to find than one."

Wrestan bowed. "I myself will lead the searches. I will not return until I have found her or news of her. She is, after all, my betrothed."

"And should you also find Trinlys…" The King stared into the fire. "You know what to do."

"Yes, my King. No one shall ever hear of him again."

Jarin struggled to open his eyes. He lay on something soft in a dark room, but it was not his own. What had happened? Why was his head pounding? He reached up and touched a thick knot over his temple. A cool hand caught his and pulled it away.

"Shh. Don't disturb it." The voice was Mother Brylla's.

As his senses returned, the door opened and closed, giving Jarin a glimpse of the busy kitchen. He knew the room. Kitchen helps often used it to watch over anything cooking throughout the night. Just then, the door opened once more as Mother Brylla bustled in with a tray.

"It looks like you got on the wrong side of Captain Wrestan," she said as she helped him sit up.

"Filibria!" Jarin cried out. "Did she escape?"

"Yes. Thank heavens, they have found no sign of her yet." Mother Brylla began to spoon feed Jarin.

"We need to help her!" Jarin said between eager mouthfuls.

"You did your best already, lad. That was a brave—albeit a stupid—thing you did to help her."

"But her brother needs to know what happened! Someone needs to let him know in case she doesn't make it to safety. Someone needs to let him know the truth."

"Shh. It's out of our hands now. Now stop worrying or you will start your head a'bleeding. Lie down again and rest a little more. You will feel much better tomorrow." Mother Brylla took up the tray. "And whatever you do, do not leave the room. The King and Wrestan are looking for you." She squeezed his hand. "You are in danger. As soon as you get better, we will form a plan for your safety. For now, rest." She softly closed the door behind her, leaving Jarin in darkness.

Jarin could not rest. What if Filibria did not make it to Delvaria? He should find her. Or he should go to her brother and tell him all he knew. Which was not a lot, but at least he could tell King Kial his sister was still alive and out of Eirarin's controlling grasp.

When Mother Brylla brought Jarin his breakfast, the room was empty.

"Filibria! Filibria! Fili! Wake up."

Filibria's blinked several times as her senses began to focus again. She came to, lying on wet and mushy turf. Her wet clothes clung to her, soiled with rain and mud, and her wet hair was plastered to her face. But she only felt strong arms wrapped around her, and her head pressed into something solid and warm. Her cold body drew from that warmth, stirring her awake. She heard her name repeated and the frantic thumping of two hearts, her own as well as another just above her ear. She opened her eyes and slowly focused on the figure cradling her.

"Trinlys?" Her voice sounded weak, weaker than she felt.

"Fili?" His warm tears streamed down his cheeks, dripping onto her face and mingling with her own.

CHAPTER

Twenty-Two

KING KIAL PACED IN front of his throne. "Lies. All lies. King Dalen would go to war over a lie! First, he accuses me of his daughter's death and now *this*!" He crumpled the letter and hurled it against the wall, narrowly missing Carna.

"What is your response, my King?" Carna asked.

"I am tired of dealing with him. Tell him he lies. He can send a man to rip my castle from its foundations, and he will not find Princess Filibria. And if war is what he wants, I will give it to him, if only to silence his running tongue."

"But remember, you must not rush into a war, Your Majesty. Keep a level head. He means to infuriate the senses out of you."

"I know what I am doing, Carna."

The steward bowed. As he headed for the door, King Kial called him back. "Carna, call my knights in."

"Yes, my King."

Ten men entered the room soon after and King Kial halted his pacing to face them.

The captain of the ten bowed. "My men and I are at your service, Your Majesty. How may we help you?"

211

"As you have heard, my sister is missing. King Dalen accuses me of spiriting her away. He lies. Either he has locked her away, or she really has truly escaped. I want you to find out. Go to Eirarin. Do not reveal yourselves to anyone. Find my sister and bring her back to me."

"But what about the war?"

"It will be fought either way. I will take care of it. Now go. Do not return without her or at least news of her. You are dismissed."

The captain paused in the doorway and turned back. "I have ridden into many perils with you, my King. Now you are elevated to a place where I cannot help you anymore, but I still can counsel you. Do what is wise. War must always be a last resort."

King Kial, who had his head bowed and his back to the door, remained silent. The captain lingered a little longer then walked away to fulfill the King's order.

"What are you doing here? How did you get Father's horse?" Trinlys asked. "You know the penalty for riding it is death."

"If the King finds me here, the penalty will be the same either way. I came to find you, Trin. I escaped."

Trinlys's eyes narrowed. "What were you thinking? It's too dangerous. You should not have come here. But...But I'm glad you are with me now. I have missed you. Let's get you dry and warm and then you can tell me all that has happened."

He helped her out of her wet dress and wrapped her in his cloak. When he was satisfied she had been sufficiently cared for, he lifted her head and slipped beneath it so she could rest in his lap.

"Things have changed since you left, Trin. Your father declared you dead and appointed Wrestan as his heir."

Trinlys expressed no surprise at her news.

"And he demanded I marry Wrestan." Beneath her, Trinlys's body tensed.

"Marry him? I would sooner you marry a corpse. You did not, did you?"

"No. I asked for a month to mourn you. Then your mother reminded the King about waiting three months to see if I carried an heir. He said I had already been locked away for a month, so I had only two months."

"Then why did you flee? You had more time."

"I fled for another reason." She went quiet, enjoying the searching look in Trinlys's eyes along with the growing impatience. When she smiled at him, his face grew puzzled. "I am carrying our child," she whispered.

"A child!" Trinlys clutched her, his eyes shining. Then, suddenly, he burst into tears, burying his head into her neck. When he at last pulled away, he was laughing. "A child. Ours. We are going to have a child."

All the fear and tension inside Filibria melted away in that moment. "Yes. Our child."

He moved his hand to her stomach. "A child," he whispered. "We are saved."

"No." Filibria grabbed his hand. "No. Your father did not hesitate to kill your sister and give you up for dead. And he is using me, no doubt to get rid of my family so I am queen and he can rule both kingdoms. Do you understand? Even now he hunts us. He would kill the child as soon as it was born. You know it's true. That is why I had to leave."

"You could have lost it coming here," Trinlys protested, though he crushed her in a hug. "I am so happy," he murmured into her ear. "Come what may, you are the best thing that has ever happened to me, Filibria. But now we must decide what to do next. We cannot stay here forever, especially with you carrying a child. And winter is coming now. Any day we will see the first snow."

"Your mother told us to go south to Delvaria. My brother would give us shelter and we could tell him the truth. Perhaps we could also keep him from war."

Trinlys frowned. "By going to your brother, you might start a war, Fili. My father would be furious. Does he know of the child?"

Filibria shook her head.

"Then if he caught word, he would burn Delvaria to the ground."

"My brother would protect us."

Trinlys hesitated. "Would he, Fili?"

Her brother had always valued war over peace. He had wanted her to return, but had it been for her own safety? She was done being part of another's devious designs.

With a heavy heart, Filibria shook her head. "I don't know anymore. But where can we go? We have nothing with which to start a new life." She thought wistfully of the green stone Steward Carna had given her—left behind in Eirarin. *Steward Carna.* Even if her brother refused to help them, Carna would. "We will find help in Delvaria. I know we will."

Trinlys took her hand. "Then we will go to Delvaria. But from now on, I put you and our child above everything, even if it means the downfall of our kingdom. Here." He pulled something out of the front of his shirt. She recognized the letter she had written to her brother. "I took this when I left. I meant to go to your brother when the hunts died down, to reason with him. But now that you're with me...I don't want to endanger you by taking you to your brother."

"It will work out, I promise. We'll tell him the truth together and stop this war."

Trinlys hugged her tight again.

They stayed a few more days in the glade to recover and lay low while King Dalen scoured the countryside for them. Filibria wanted to send Swift Foot away, but Trinlys refused, saying she could not walk on foot to Delvaria. But the very next day, beyond the thick hedge of trees, they heard horns blaring and dogs barking, closer than ever. Trinlys took Swift Foot under the cover of darkness and led the beast as far as he possibly could, hoping they'd hunt down the horse instead. He slunk back to the mound just before dawn, and as the sun rose, the hounds and hunters returned, passing further west. After a few days, the hunts lightened and Trinlys decided it was time to move out. The skies were dark, threatening snow—and snow meant trackable footprints.

Trinlys led the way that day, following the maps in his head. They kept off the roads and as far away from houses as they could manage. This resulted in fighting their way through bare brush. Snow began to fall and the wind howled. Trinlys made Filibria stop many times throughout the long day.

"I'm not an invalid," Filibria argued when Trinlys made her stop yet again.

"If anything...*anything,* happened to you or our child because I pushed you too hard, I would never forgive myself."

Filibria obediently sank under the bush Trinlys had found. Trinlys, ready to follow after her, suddenly stiffened. The wind blowing from behind them filled with the sounds of baying. Trinlys froze, torn between hiding and fleeing. The tone of the hounds changed as they picked up a scent, making the decision for Trinlys. He pulled Filibria out of the bush and they ran.

"We need to find a stream. We need to lose our scent," Trinlys cried. He grasped Filibria's hand as they crashed through bushes, dodging trees and rocks.

They broke out of the forest into a clearing where a new house and barn had been resurrected close to burned remains.

"To the barn," Trinlys gasped. "It will be warm in there and hopefully mask some of our scent."

They ran over to the building, but Filibria hung back at the door. She looked back at the house, searching for any signs of life, but it looked empty. The door was closed and no smoke rose from the chimney.

"What if we are found?"

"We can't go on. We can't risk it."

The door creaked as Trinlys pushed it open. The animals inside stirred and woke as they crept the length of the barn to the furthest corner. The last stall was empty, filled with shavings and a bit of moldy hay. Trinlys leaned back against the wall and took a deep breath of air. He let it out in a long sigh of relief. Tucked away with the animals, it would keep the cold night at bay and mask their scent.

Night closed in around them. Safe in Trinlys's arms, Filibria began to tremble uncontrollably. The adrenaline of the past few days crashed, leaving her empty and scared.

"Filibria?"

At the sound of his voice, one that she had believed she might never hear again, she burst into tears. Trinlys tightened his embrace, rocking her gently.

"Shh, you're safe, Fili. I've got you. You're safe."

Filibria wanted to believe him…but even in his arms, she could still feel the world crumbling around her.

Twenty-Three

"FILI. FILI, WAKE UP." Filibria stirred and rolled over to see Trinlys sitting next to her. Filibria reached out for him and he caught her hand, holding a finger to his lips. "Hush now. You need to get up." The tense tone of his voice cleared all the sleep away.

She sat up. "What is it?"

Two armed men stood at the head of the stall, but Filibria only saw the colors they wore. Delvarian colors. Her heart leapt joyfully, that is, until their grim faces and the manner in which they greeted them put her on edge.

"Bring the princess out."

Trinlys helped Filibria to her feet. He gathered up their belongings and they stepped out into the open, together. Ten men with horses waited outside. Filibria searched their faces, desperate to see someone familiar.

"Captain Galder!" she cried.

He nodded tersely.

"Did my brother send you to find us?"

"Yes," the captain said with a small bow. "We have orders to take you back to Falendle."

Filibria frowned. "Are we in Delvaria?"

"You are just over the border."

Filibria grabbed Trinlys's hand and squeezed it; they were safe. Trinlys smiled at her.

"The King of Eirarin has called for war again. He accuses your brother of stealing you away."

"If we go to Falendle, we will make the accusations true," Trinlys said quietly.

"Your father wants war either way. Let us get there quickly so we can set it all right."

"I suppose you are her husband, the dead prince?" Captain Galder asked.

Trinlys nodded.

"I do not know what lies you have been weaving in your kingdom, and it is not my place to know, but you will come with us as well. No doubt the King will find use for you." He turned to his men. "Give this man a horse. I will take the princess with me."

Filibria was reluctant to part with Trinlys, but the sturdiness of Galder behind her put her fears at ease. She was finally going home. She would be safe. Filibria slipped her hand over her stomach; her child would be safe. The future was filled with turmoil, but at least she had control over her life now.

Filibria tried talking to him, but he soon quelled the conversation with an unexpected brusqueness. For hours, they hardly stopped. When Trinlys tried to reason with the captain for a break, Filibria shot him a glare, warning him to stay silent. She did not want them to know about her child yet.

They approached the city by night. The looming castle of Delvaria, glowing out of each window, was a welcome sight. Almost a year had passed since Filibria had ridden through the gates, alone and afraid, married to a stranger and headed to a strange land. Now she returned, afraid and uncertain, beside the man she now loved as her husband. She looked back to smile at Trinlys. He stared at the approaching city, his face grim and tight. All she wanted to do was take his hand, to reassure him it was going to get better.

Instead of taking them through the main gate, the captain led them towards the rear portion of the wall, where the door to the kitchen was. It opened at his request.

"What sort of welcome is this?" Filibria demanded, but Captain Galder hushed her.

"Come with us." The captain lowered Filibria from the saddle. The guards flanked Trinlys and Filibria as they led them through the dimly lit kitchen, to a servant who was waiting in the dark hall outside.

"Send for King Kial," the captain ordered. "Tell him we have arrived." He hustled Trinlys and Filibria into a small dark room nearby. Trinlys groped through the dark for Filibria's hand. His warm hand curled around her cold fingers, spreading warmth through her body.

King Kial hurried into the room, still securing his cloak over his shoulders. He stopped in the doorway and searched the gloom.

"You brought them back?"

"We did." A torch flared to life, illuminating the small space, and the captain stepped aside, revealing Filibria and Trinlys. Filibria ran forward to hug her brother, but an arm shot out and pinned her in place. "None of that," Captain Galder hissed. King Kial looked from his sister to Trinlys.

"What is the meaning of this? Why is her husband here?"

"He is not as dead as we were made to believe, it seems. No doubt another trick of King Dalen. We found them on the border of Delvaria, hiding and we took them both."

"Very well. Take them upstairs and lock them in separate rooms. Do not let anyone see them."

"Wait, brother!" Filibria struggled against the captain's grip. "What are you doing? We are not prisoners. We were coming to you, to set things straight. There is still time to stop the war."

"Do you know what your father-in-law would do if he found me harboring you? I have only just managed to defuse war between the kingdoms and now he demands war again, accusing me of stealing you away. And then you show up here, making me look like a liar."

"But I am a peace weaver! I must help. I will set things straight."

"Is it true you carry Eirarin's heir?" Kial asked abruptly.

Filibria hesitated and shared a look with Trinlys, who nodded.

"Yes."

King Kial smiled. "Things are at last turning in my favor. Take them away." He gestured to the guards.

Filibria grabbed at her brother as they passed, but he twisted out of her grasp. "What are you doing? Why are you treating us like this? You cannot. Trinlys is not a prisoner. We..." The guards grabbed her shoulders, pulling her back.

King Kial leaned in closer, looming over her. "You had your chance to return safely to Delvaria after the death of our father and you refused me. I am in charge now."

"You cannot treat the peace weaver like that!" Trinlys growled. "You cannot treat my wife like that. Let her go. If my father finds out..."

"That what? That you're alive? That I am sheltering you? I am done with Eirarin's games. The time for peace is over. I will take the consequences. But you both are now nothing but a hindrance to me." King Kial waved at the guards; two secured Trinlys's arms behind his back.

The hot rage inside Filibria simmered down to tears as exhaustion and helplessness overtook her. What good would fighting do her?

"What are you doing?" she whimpered as the guards moved towards the door.

"What is best for my kingdom," King Kial responded, and the door closed behind him.

Filibria reached for Trinlys, but it was too late. Guards ripped her from her husband and locked her away in her old room. She fell into her bed and cried herself to sleep, too shocked and exhausted to make sense of anything. She was alone, trapped without Trinlys; nothing had changed.

In the morning, she had her first chance look about her room. It was exactly as she had left it. Dust lay thick over everything, including her harp. Somehow, that made her hurt more. She had changed so much, yet her old life here had stopped the moment she stepped out of the door. Filibria walked to the window, framed by cobwebs. In the early dawn light, the dry fields were yellow. Over the hills, the shepherd was holed up for the winter in his hut. A longing to see her siblings and mother gripped Filibria at that moment. Was her mother even still alive? Did she know Filibria was here?

The door opened and a serving woman entered the room with a tray. She stood in the doorway, waiting for Filibria to turn her way.

"Set it down," Filibria said without looking, "I will dress myself." She did not want the pity of the castle servants.

"Yes, my lady." Filibria turned at the voice.

Malda opened her arms wide, catching Filibria as she ran to her; they both began to weep.

"You have no idea what it has been like here," Malda sniffed. "So quiet and the King is always angry. He hates Eirarin. He hates that you stayed. Some whisper he wants war. Since the death of your father, your mother has not left her room. She just lies listlessly in her bed. We fear she might die."

"Does she know I am here? Can I go to her?"

Malda hesitated. "She does not know you are here. Your brother is keeping you a secret. I do not know why."

Filibria groaned. "Yes. I am no better off here than I was in Eirarin. A prisoner of power. I need to talk to him, Malda. I need him to listen to me. I can help."

"I will let him know you wish to have an audience, but I do not know if it will change anything. Eat now, and sleep if you can. You look terrible." She paused, blinking away tears. "Is it true? Are you with child?"

Filibria nodded wearily.

Malda smiled and clapped her hands. "I am so glad, Filibria. You have secured your line, bound the kingdoms."

"It seems to be the only thing I have accomplished. Please, see if my brother will talk to me."

"I will. Rest now."

Filibria watched Malda leave the room. On the landing just outside her door stood a guard. Her brother had taken more precautions than King Dalen, seemingly more comfortable in keeping her secret. She placed her hand over her stomach.

"I just want all of this to end," she whispered. To the room or to the child, she did not know. "I want to be safe, to be with Trinlys."

Malda woke her up the next day; it was already afternoon. "Hurry and dress," Malda urged.

Filibria shot out of bed. "Will my brother talk to me?"

Some of Malda's enthusiasm died as she shook her head. "He would not answer me, but he has given you permission to see your mother. He does have a heart after all."

A small victory. But if anyone could help her, it would be her strong, peace-weaving mother.

Outside Filibria's room, two guards waited to escort the women to the Queen's chamber. Filibria stepped hesitantly through the door into her mother's room. It was so familiar, yet so strange. The interior was dark without the huge bright windows her mother-in-law's room had—but now, every bit of light was blocked out. The Queen lay in her great bed. Her white face and tumbled black hair were almost lost in the pillows, which glowed white in the gloom. Filibria stepped up to her side.

"Mother?"

Her mother's eyes flickered open. "Filibria? Is that you?" Her hand groped over the cover. Filibria caught it and held it tight. "I knew you would come back," her mother whispered. Tears rolled down both their faces; for a long time, they said nothing.

"What are you doing here, Fili?"

"Kial brought me here. I had to flee with Trinlys from Eirarin." She sank to her knees and laid her head on the edge of the bed. "I failed you, Mother. I failed to keep peace." Her mother's hand found her hair and began to stroke it lovingly.

"You did not fail me, Filibria. Some situations are beyond our control. We can only do what we know is right. By fleeing, you did just that. Sit beside me and tell me about life in Eirarin." Filibria poured out her story, mixed with her tears, while her mother comforted her.

"You found something better than peace, Fili. You found love."

Filibria sniffled. "But my task was to keep peace."

"And you did your best." Queen Bryn squeezed her hand. "More importantly, you found love and happiness. You did what was right by going to Trinlys instead of staying behind and trying to keep the slender thread of peace together. Ultimately, you would have failed, but now you have a second chance. Your bond between the kingdoms is stronger, more genuine, because of your love for your husband. It will help you weather whatever comes."

"But I don't know what Kial intends to do with us. He treats Trinlys as a prisoner, and me too. I am scared."

Her mother smiled and struggled to sit up. She had grown stronger by the minute just having Filibria with her. "Have faith, daughter. I will talk to him. He may be King, but I am still his mother." At that moment, a guard entered the room.

"I am supposed to escort you back now," he said nervously. Filibria looked to her mother, who nodded.

"But you will be back again, love. You will sing and play the harp for me. You will bring my light back."

The next day, Filibria was allowed to see her mother again. The room was much brighter, and a brazier burned by the bed. Her mother had not had a chance to talk to Kial yet, but she promised to intervene soon. Filibria sang and played, and for a while, they were able to forget the darkness surrounding them. Back in her room though, Filibria wept alone for everything she had lost. The endless game of waiting was gnawing at her soul.

Filibria's mother was back in her bed the next time Filibria visited her. She was pale and listless again, drained of her liveliness.

"He would not listen to me. He is set in his ways. He does not take Eirarin's offenses lightly. I think you should talk to him, Fili. Tell him what you witnessed in Eirarin. Tell him King Dalen's plans. Perhaps your brother will see the light and change his mind."

"I will." Maybe she could use her information to bargain for Trinlys's life.

When Malda came in with dinner, Filibria asked her again to tell Kial she wanted to see him. Malda promised to do her best, but nothing happened that day, nor the next. Filibria was about to ask again when two guards unlocked her door; she'd been graciously allotted an hour to talk to her brother.

Kial was sitting in their father's private solar, slumped over the desk in their father's great chair. Steward Carna waited to his left and a few guards stood around the room, like statues—like she was a threat. When Filibria walked in, memories flooded her. Her father had never been close to her, never having the time, but often she had snuck in here as a child to watch him work. Being his only daughter for a while, she had once been the light of his eyes.

Kial eyed her coldly. Steward Carna nodded slightly to Filibria. She looked to the steward, pleading with him, but the stone face she received only hurt her.

"You've made quite a mess of things, sister. I wonder what our father would have to say about it all. As we speak, King Dalen marches to war against Delvaria."

King Kial did not invite her to sit down, but Filibria chose a chair all the same. She did not have the strength to fight her brother standing up.

"You have to stop the war."

"How? By giving you and your husband back to Eirarin? I'm sure King Dalen would be elated to have his son back from the dead. No. I am not a fool. He will get his son back. I will trade the prince for peace. But you, you are too valuable to return."

"King Dalen killed his own daughter to blame it on you and start this war," Filibria protested. "And he does not want his son back. He does not want peace. He wants war. He wants both kingdoms."

"So do I."

Filibria stared at her brother. He was no longer the boy she knew; in the boy's place was a stony, cruel man, carved from the same stuff as her father-in-law.

"Don't look so surprised, sister. It is what any aspiring ruler would want, and I will have it. Through war and through the child you carry. You brought the last piece of the puzzle straight to me."

"You mercenary!" Filibria lunged at her brother, but like before, a soldier caught her and held her back.

"Calm down, Filibria. We do not want anything to happen to your child."

"I would sooner disappear as a peasant in the Eirarin countryside than let you touch a hair on my child's head," Filibria hissed. "Let me keep peace. Before a war starts."

"You have already started a war. You were supposed to relinquish anything to keep peace. That includes your husband. If you had done your duty, you would have kept peace and not have been tangled up in love. This is the consequence."

"The consequence of having a heart? Our father would have found a way to keep peace. Our father would not have sold lives, nor would he stoop to murder."

King Kial stood up and held up a hand, gesturing for the guards to release her. She stood heaving, too angry to move.

"I am not our father." He stepped around the desk and leaned in close, nostrils flaring. "Never forget that. All he ever wanted was peace. All he ever cared about was you and marrying you off to another kingdom. I would never have married you off to our enemy. I would have subdued them. I am a warrior, not a coward."

A smack rang through the room and a small red imprint of a hand rose on Kial's cheek. His angry flush soon drowned it out.

"Take her away before I forget she is my own blood. Your duties as a peace weaver are over, sister. If you forget that, I might even remove Trinlys and sever the tie."

"Murderer!" The guards pulled Filibria back, but before they could haul her away, the door opened, and a nervous servant entered.

"My lord?"

"Yes?"

"There is someone at the gate requesting to see you. He is only a boy. He claims to be from Eirarin."

Filibria's heart leapt. Could it be?

"Send him in." King Kial turned back to Filibria. "You are dismissed."

"No, wait! I might know this boy."

King Kial hesitated, then shrugged. "Let him in."

The door opened again, and Jarin stepped through. His face was pale, his clothes ragged, and his hair unkempt. At first, all he noticed was King Kial and he bowed low. But when he straightened, he caught sight of Filibria, still held fast by the guards.

His weary face brightened. "You are safe!"

Filibria only nodded.

"What about Trinlys? Did you find him?"

Again, Filibria nodded. "He is here too." She glared at her brother.

Suddenly, remembering something, Jarin's smile fell. "The Queen is dead."

Filibria's head whipped towards the page boy. "What? Dead?"

"After you left, she died. The King claimed it was grief."

Filibria swayed, but the guards held her up. King Dalen had killed his own Queen, Filibria was sure of it—and it was her fault. She had told her mother-in-law too much. A sob ripped through Filibria.

"Enough of that," King Kial snapped. He turned back to Jarin. "Why have you come?"

Jarin paused, a stunned look on his face. "Well...I guess I thought I would come get help..." He looked towards Filibria, who gave him an encouraging smile. "Things have gotten out of control in Eirarin. We need help."

King Kial stood staring at the boy, as if not sure what to do next. Then his face hardened. "Likely story. More like all of you have come to infiltrate my castle on King Dalen's request."

He waved at the guards. "Take Filibria away. And you," he said to a servant, "take this boy to the kitchen and feed him. Let the kitchen staff take care of him. Do not let him leave the castle. We would not want him running back to Eirarin with reports."

"I'm not a spy," Jarin assured them, but no one listened.

As soon as they had left, King Kial sank back into his chair.

All through the meeting, Steward Carna had kept an impassive face and a quiet tongue. Now he spoke as King Kial cooled down.

"My lord, are you being too harsh with her? She is your sister." Carna had been at Kial's birth and had known all the royal children from infanthood. Though he had never played favorites, he had always kept a secret special place in his heart for Filibria. Unfortunately, duty came before emotions.

"She is a threat."

"But you cannot treat her as a piece on a board game. She is family. More importantly, she is a peace weaver—of Eirarin and *Delvaria*. You should be honoring her efforts to unite the kingdoms."

"Be assured what I do is best for Delvaria. If I want your counsel, I will ask for it," King Kial growled.

Carna bowed. "Just do as your father did, my King. Though he often put his country before his family, he knew where to draw limits. Look how far Delvaria came under him. He let nothing stand in his way, yet he never made a rash choice." The steward's words were calm and measured, hopefully making the impression he'd meant them to.

But King Kial only turned his back on the steward. "You are dismissed. Send in Trinlys."

Carna bowed, doing his best to conceal the disappointment he felt.

Trinlys, shackled and escorted by two guards, was allowed to take a seat. King Kial drew up a chair opposite him and sat uncomfortably close. Trinlys trained his eyes on the stone floor.

"The Prince of Eirarin," King Kial mused aloud, "you live in the shadows. No other title, no renown, not even a threat—just a prince. No one even knew you existed before you married my sister. Tell me, why were you declared dead?"

"Because I fled from my father."

"Why did you do that?"

"He wanted to kill me."

"It was a rash thing—fleeing. I imagine you put my sister's position in danger. How could she weave peace if her own husband had fled for his safety?"

Trinlys did not respond, but his hands clenched white.

Kial stroked his beard, pleased by Trinlys's reaction. "Put yourself in your father's place, Prince. Peace, war, kingdoms aside, he declared his son dead, even holding a funeral. Then suddenly his son appears, alive and well, and in the rival kingdom. It would be an embarrassment, I would imagine. A great enough embarrassment he might do anything to cover it up. Not to mention I now hold you as a prisoner."

"My father does not want me."

"So, you have said. So Filibria has said. It does not matter whether your father wants you dead or alive. What matters is how much your father values his pride. Will he pay to have you silenced once and for all?"

"This is how you stop a war?" Trinlys asked. "By selling people to be murdered?"

"What is one life against the safety of two countries? Surely, you should understand. You are married to a peace weaver."

"If you take me to my father, I will tell him the truth. I will tell him you have Filibria."

"What will you gain? You would not want any harm to come to your wife or child, would you?"

Trinlys clamped his lips shut.

King Kial smiled. "I knew you could be manipulated easily; love makes people weak. Remember I am only doing this for the sake of our two kingdoms."

"If you were doing this for the kingdoms, you wouldn't hold Filibria and her child prisoner, and you wouldn't threaten to hurt her. She is still bound to her duties. By keeping her, you are asking for war. Instead, you want the power for yourself. You are no better than my father."

"Men with common goals are often alike."

"You want both kingdoms."

"Is it such a secret? I am a king. Kings want power. King Dalen is trying to take Delvaria. He is stretching his hand out to grasp it. Now that I see his plan, I can grab his arm and twist it behind his back. I may even be able to avoid war. I cannot imagine the people of Eirarin are overly fond of their King. If I avoid war and unite both kingdoms, I will be a hero to the people of Delvaria and Eirarin. Eirarin will welcome my rule with open arms. A golden opportunity has fallen in my lap. Only a fool would not take it." King Kial gestured that their little chat was at an end.

"Then what will happen to Filibria?" Trinlys asked as the guards hauled him to his feet.

"That all depends on how you behave."

Twenty-Four

"Now what?" Wrestan demanded. "You promised me two thrones, but all you hold is a handful of dead promises. We searched everywhere for the princess. She has vanished. She could be in western Mygin Formhain by now. What plan do you have to fix all this?"

King Dalen held up a hand to subdue the man, but Wrestan was not going to be silenced. his eyes burned fire.

"We will still have war with Delvaria. If we win, we will slaughter the royal family and you will be king of two countries as I promised. You are still my heir." Wrestan stood up and paced the floor.

"If, if, if. I am tired of ifs and wills and whens!" He brought his fist down hard on the table and glared at his father. King Dalen's face hardened...like father, like son. They both had tempers and could hold out against each other.

"And you could do any better?" King Dalen hissed.

Their only difference was age; Wrestan was younger, stronger, and had much more to lose.

"I would not hole up in my castle hurling insults across the moat. I would march my army out immediately. I would take Delvaria by surprise, not sit around and threaten it with war. You let Filibria slip from your fingers, now you let this chance go.”

“If I recall correctly, you were the one who literally let her slip through your fingers, right past you, only to vanish into the countryside while you were only a few steps behind. Filibria was going to bind the loyalty of Delvaria to me. Now, without her, I will have to keep Delvaria on the end of a chain.”

“She would have stayed if you had not foolishly locked her away and then driven Trinlys off. If you had killed him quietly when I wanted to...”

“I have had enough of your tantrum,” King Dalen said steely, “Leave.” Wrestan’s look was pure hatred as he stormed out of the room. Another obstacle had risen in his path to power—the King of Eirarin. He would be easy to deal with, but not yet. Wrestan still had uses for the King.

“My King.”

Kial turned to face the messenger; the man’s haggard face held a frightened look. “Let me guess, war?”

The messenger nodded. “I have come from the border. King Dalen has mobilized his troops and is amassing them there. It is still unclear whether he plans to cross into Delvaria or not.”

“Good,” King Kial said, “I will have less distance to travel. Call in my knights, my steward, my marshal, and my advisors. I will meet them in the war chamber.”

King Kial arrayed himself carefully in his father’s robe, sword, and crown, studying himself in the mirror. He looked the part of a warrior king, but could he play the part? His blood raced with the thought of war; Delvaria would prove itself on the battlefield. King Kial strode to the war chamber where his men waited.

"You plan to go to war against Eirarin?" the marshal demanded. "It would take us too long to assemble an army. Too long. It would be foolish. We do not have enough men."

"We do not have a choice," King Kial said. "Gather all the warriors you can. Immediately. Call them to honor their oath. There is a chance I can avoid war, at least for a while. For now, we will take what men we have and march to the border. I have one last dice to toss—King Dalen's son."

The gaoler stopped in front of Trinlys's cell. The prince was slumped against the wall and did not even look up.

"You are to be moved out," the goaler said. Trinlys stirred, blinking in the harsh light of the torch. "I know who you are," the gaoler said, "and I don't know why you are here, but is there anything I can do for you?"

"Can I see Princess Filibria?"

The gaoler hesitated, hoping he would have been asked for something simpler. "I will ask the King," he said at last.

"Thank you."

The gaoler presented the request before his King, and to his surprise, King Kial considered it.

"What harm can it bring?" the gaoler pleaded. "He has done nothing wrong. Let him see his wife."

King Kial nodded. "You may bring her to see him—but only for a short time."

The gaoler bowed and sent servants hurrying away for the princess.

"My princess."

"What is it?" Filibria asked, wary of a gaoler she did not know.

"I have gained permission for you to see your husband. He is being moved out."

She paled. "Soon?"

"Tomorrow. Come. He asked to see you and the King was generous to grant his request." The gaoler gently took Filibria's arm and led her down the dark steps of the dungeon, followed by two guards. "It's not the nicest of places," he warned.

His warning went unheeded as Filibria broke from his support and ran across the room; nearly stumbling to the bars.

"Trinlys!"

The prince reached through the bars to touch her face. His hand brushed her stomach where the slightest bump pressed against her dress.

"Trinlys." She started weeping. "Trinlys. Your mother is dead. King Dalen killed her. It is all my fault..."

Trinlys slumped against the bars. "No," he whispered.

"It is my fault," Filibria cried again, "and now she is gone."

"No, Filibria, no. You had no idea Father would go that far. You only did what you believed was best. Listen, Filibria." Trinlys reached out and lifted her head, waiting for her to meet his eyes. "Never stop looking for a way out, Filibria. You need to escape if you can. Go anywhere, but stay away from your brother *and* my father. I'm sorry you had to marry me and get tangled into this."

"I'm not—"

"Be strong, Fili. Do not ever grovel for your life or mine. Bear yourself like a queen and peace weaver. It will speak better of you than groveling. Make me proud. Speak out for the truth."

"I will." Tears slid down her face. He brushed them away. "What will happen to you, Trinlys? You cannot return to Eirarin. He will kill you."

"Shh. Filibria, if it brings peace, I am willing to make the sacrifice. You aren't the only one who has to be a peace weaver." His attempt at a smile only made Filibria sob and he wiped her tears away as more gushed down her face.

"But there cannot be peace. Your father wants Delvaria and my brother wants Eirarin."

"Filibria, as long as you are safe, I am happy. I do not care what happens to me. You and our child are the only thing worth fighting for anymore. Besides, Mother Brylla will fight for me, you know that. My father will not get away with it easily if he desires to kill me."

The gaoler laid a hand on Filibria's shoulder. "The time is up, my princess."

"Just a little more time?" she pleaded.

The guards stepped forward.

"Maybe just a little longer?" the gaoler appealed to the guard, but the guard shook his head.

"The King gave his orders."

Filibria grew frantic. She reached through the bars to embrace Trinlys, holding onto him as the guard tried to rip her away. She screamed, clawing at the guard as he hooked his arm around her waist and pulled her away. Trinlys could only weep as Filibria was carried from the dungeon, hoarse from her protest.

CHAPTER

Twenty-Five

KING DALEN WAITED WITH his men on a small strip of open grass opposite King Kial's war camp. He stood proud and defiant, dressed in bold colors. The sun reflected off his splendid crown and his armor, emblazoned with the talon of a hawk. His long red cloak riffled softly in the breeze. Above him, the bold pennon of Eirarin scratched at the sky. He looked every inch a king.

Beside King Dalen stood Wrestan, arrayed like a warrior prince. Wrestan did nothing to hide the scorn and triumph in his features. He stood openly as the heir of Eirarin and he was finally going to war against Delvaria. His patience was paying off at last. His destiny unfolded before him. Shame was behind, power ahead; nothing could stop him.

King Kial rode out to meet them. He stepped down from his horse's saddle and approached on foot. He took his first look at his enemies. Side by side, it was not hard to see the resemblance between father and son. "I told you; you have no grounds for war," King Kial spoke. "Why do you come before me with a war host?"

"Because you lie," King Dalen spat.

King Kial raised an eyebrow. "I lie? The only liar here is you." King Kial held up a hand as Wrestan began drawing his sword with a scoff. "No, Wrestan, let your king hear me out."It is true you lie when you accuse me of sheltering my sister. Yet even if she *were* here, it would be her right. You claimed her husband was dead and you were going to marry her to your captain of the guards, whom you have suddenly named your heir. All this would have been against her will, and, if you had, you would have made a grave mistake, for your son is still living. Today, I came with a prisoner. The ransom? A lasting promise of peace." He motioned to his guard. From the nearest tent, the guard returned, prodding Trinlys out in front of him.

King Dalen gasped at the sight of his son. The color fled Wrestan's face, but only for a second. His hand clenched his sword.

"Your son, back from the dead."

King Dalen glared at King Kial. "So, you stole him, just as you murdered my daughter. You thought you could take the throne by taking him."

"No. I did not take him. My men found him in Delvaria. I was surprised because I believed, like everyone else, that he was dead. It must be an embarrassment to have him suddenly come to life after your claims and your funeral. Who was in the coffin? Some unfortunate peasant?

"Now you can right the wrong and cover up your disgrace. I will trade your son for peace between the kingdoms. My sister failed at her job so now it falls upon me to keep peace. What say you?"

King Dalen's face contorted as he spat at King Kial's feet. "You offer me a pawn! I do not want my son. He is useless. Give me your sister. I know you are hiding her. I will not end this war until she is returned to me. I have a daughter still unavenged."

"You killed her yourself."

King Dalen's face turned purple, then white. "You lie."

"Do I? Then why does my accusation upset you so much? You must also remember I have a father unavenged. If you still accuse me of your daughter's death, I would say we are equal, a life for a life. And now I offer you one more—the life of your son."

"It is worth nothing."

"Fine. I will return with him to Delvaria. I am sure he could tell me more about your kingdom."

King Dalen struggled with himself. Finally, he burst out, "No. I will take him."

"And call off the war?"

"Yes, I will call off the war."

The two men each took a stiff step forward. They gripped each other's forearms and shook; a cheer went up from both sides.

Wrestan sheathed his sword, but he was not done with it.

Trinlys was exchanged and the next day, King Dalen and his camp pulled out and returned to Eirarin. King Kial rode back to Delvaria, pleased with himself. Like King Dalen, he too had plans for the united kingdoms of Eirarin and Delvaria. But unlike King Dalen, he was content to wait. Time would be his war. He would wait for the birth of the heir, the tie between the kingdoms.

Wrestan was livid; his whole body quivering with self-control.

"What use do you have for your son?" he spat. "You were best to leave him in King Kial's hands."

"Silence!" King Dalen barked.

"No! You have always promised that I was your son, that I was the only one you cared about. Now you have traded war for your son. You named me heir and then you bought back your son, making me look like a fool."

"Listen," King Dalen hissed, "my son has shown me up, turning me into a liar. Who knows how much he has revealed about our kingdom? I must cover up this shame first, then we have war. You must learn patience. You will be the heir again, you only need to wait."

Wrestan threw his goblet onto the ground, splashing wine into the fire. "I am tired of patience! I have waited my whole life! I am tired of your reassuring words! They are nothing but wind, changing each day and carrying nothing but whispers and caresses. I want war! You made me your heir, you paraded me before the kingdoms, only to buy back your son! You are back to where you started, with a useless son—and I am worse off than I started. Let me finish him off."

"Not yet."

Wrestan's eyes narrowed. "Have you grown soft?"

"I have grown tired of your insolence, Wrestan. Am I not King? I will not kill my son until it plays a part in my plot. I do not believe in needless waste."

"You cannot bring yourself to kill him."

"Leave!"

Wrestan marched out of the chamber. He would hunt down Filibria himself; he would kill King Kial himself. It was time he stopped leaning on fickle, old men...to take his future into his own hands.

CHAPTER

Twenty-Six

"My lady?"

Filibria had spent the last two days moving only between her bed and window; the days had grown shorter and the people, rested from their recent harvest, took time to gather and dance. Bonfires burned in the night as the people reveled—free. The air grew colder too, and birds headed for warmer climates. The world was on the move, but Filibria was trapped.

Malda appeared in the doorway and walked into the room, leaving the door open. "My lady, the King has ordered us to pack."

"Us? Why?"

"He did not say, only you must pack everything and for me to pack as well." Malda opened the chest and began filling it. They heard footsteps in the passage and looked up to see Carna in the open doorway, watching in silence.

"Do you know the meaning of this?" Filibria asked the steward.

"It is no longer safe to keep you in the castle. Too many mouths to spread the word."

"Where am I going?"

"Somewhere you cannot be found. I tried to argue against it, but the King would not hear. You will be well protected wherever you go." He bowed and left them to their packing.

Filibria drifted back to the window. She looked down at the ribbon tied around her wrist, running her thumb along the twist of silken green. It was dirtied by her journey through the wild with Trinlys, but she did not care. It had been such a small gift that perfect day Trinlys had given it to her, but now it meant the world to her.

"Wait!" She dashed towards the door and flung it open. Carna was out of sight around the corner. "Carna!"

The steward appeared in the doorway again.

"Give this to Trinlys, should you ever see him again." Filibria held out the ribbon. Carna looked at it and his face softened as he took it. "And...and help him... find me...if...if he is still..."

"I will." Carna bowed.

Filibria returned to her room and collapsed on the bed, an emptiness settling in the pit of her stomach. Malda rubbed her back as she cried into the pillows.

"My lady, what your brother is doing is best for you. Away from the castle, you will be free, you will have peace, and you can raise your child."

"But what about Mother? What about Trinlys?"

Malda stopped packing. "Filibria, there is nothing more you can do for Trinlys. It is best to give him up. At least, where you are going, you will be safe from Wrestan and Eirarin. Find comfort in that at least. Come now, help me pack."

Servants removed the trunk from her room and placed into a closed wagon. As Filibria was escorted out of the castle to the courtyard, all the memories from her wedding day crashed around her. She tried to stay strong, but tears rolled down her face. Once again, she was uncertain and alone, leaving for an unknown future. Carna helped her into the wagon and led the way. Though this was not in his line of work, he had volunteered, and King Kial had eagerly agreed; Carna already knew about the princess and the less people that did, the better.

They traveled far southeast, following the main road for a way before turning off down an abandoned mining road. Ahead of them, the mountains rose, mangled by the hands of men, their roots stripped bare. The road was choked with rock dust.

Malda shivered. "Why did they send us to such a forsaken place? We are not war criminals."

Filibria did not reply. She simply watched the landscape go by, committing it to memory for a day when she might need it.

The wagon pulled to a stop at the base of one of the mountain's many slopes. Filibria and Malda sat quietly for a long time. Outside, they could hear the murmur of an argument between Carna and the guards. Filibria listened to her heart beat, fast and uneven and she slid a hand over her belly, willing her heart rate to settle.

Malda touched Filibria's hand. "The baby will be fine. No doubt he's as strong as his mother."

Filibria smiled bravely.

Carna's head appeared at the back of the wagon. His eyes were dark, his lips pursed in a tightline. Filibria had known him long enough to read it meant no good.

"We must walk from here," he said, helping them out of the wagon.

"Where to?"

"Up there."

The women followed his finger up through the mist of the mountains to a foreboding old watch tower. A perilous set of stairs carved into the mountainside wound down to where they stood.

Malda gasped. "You must be crazy! The princess cannot walk up there. She is with child!"

"I'm sorry. It is the King's orders. I tried to argue otherwise, but could only get so far. The soldiers will carry all of your things and you will take it slowly. I will go with you as well."

As if dashed against the mountain, Filibria's will began to crumple inside her. She reached out and grabbed Carna's hand, gripping it so tight he winced.

"Please." Her words burst out in gasps. "Please, Carna. *Please.* Trinlys won't be able to find me up here. Take me somewhere else, anywhere else. My brother doesn't have to know." Tears streamed unchecked down her face.

Carna's expression melted and he pulled her close to him.

"I wish I could, my dear, but I cannot go against orders. It breaks my heart, truly it does. I promise I will do whatever it takes to keep you safe and comfortable. At least, up there, you will be safe from Eirarin. We must start now."

The climb took half of the day. Filibria almost gave up many times, but Malda and Carna kept her on her feet, one step at a time. She struggled to continue, but she also had no choice.

At last, they reached the top. Soldiers unlocked the gate in the wall around the tower, swinging it open on well-oiled hinges. Snow lay in unsightly patches on the bare ground. Nothing grew in the small yard, though there were the sad remains of a garden. Filibria looked around, her mind spinning. Clearly this place had not been occupied since it had been abandoned who knows how long ago. By whom? And how many times? How many prisoners had her father snuck away to this forsaken place?

Inside the tower, it was bare but well-kept. The bunk rooms had been refurnished into tidy little bedrooms. Filibria chose hers and when Malda went to find her own, Filibria stopped her.

"Share my room, please?"

Malda smiled solemnly and nodded.

As the soldiers set the provisions down, Carna stood in the middle of the main room, rocking back and forth uncomfortably...then it was time to say goodbye.

Carna took Filibria's hand and brought it to his lips.

"I am sorry, my lady. I did all I could to sway your brother's mind, but he was set. I promise to do all I can to right the wrong and set you free."

"There is nothing to forgive you for, Carna. You did your duty. You must serve my brother faithfully as you served my father." She squeezed his hand. "My brother needs you, Carna. Perhaps he will see the light one day and then you will be there to guide him. But be careful and watch yourself. Do not trust him."

Carna bowed. "I will do my best, Princess."

He and the soldiers left soon after and Malda and Filibria were left alone in the desolate wasteland, far from help and from those who loved them.

Filibria would have sunk into depression, but Malda kept her up, putting the tower into good order.

If Trinlys did manage to escape, he would never find her.

"Bring Wrestan to me," King Dalen told his chamberlain, but the man only scratched his head nervously.

"About that...You see, Your Majesty...Captain Wrestan is not here." He took a step backwards to be a safe distance from King Dalen when he exploded.

"Not here?" The King's voice was dangerously level.

"Yes, Your Majesty. He came back with us to Eirarin, but left the day after."

"Where did he go?"

"None of us know, Your Majesty. We believed he went with your knowledge and blessing, so we did not ask. He took his horse and a pannier of belongings. He was dressed for a long journey."

"Has he taken things into his own hands now?" King Dalen muttered, grinding his teeth.

"What was that, Your Majesty?"

"Nothing. You may leave. When you hear word of Wrestan, tell me immediately. No wait!" he called after the servant. "Send men after Wrestan. He is going to Delvaria." Wrestan meant to get his hands on Filibria before King Dalen could.

"It will be done." The chamberlain hurried out of the room.

To punish Wrestan, King Dalen would keep Trinlys alive. As long as the true prince of Eirarin lived, the bastard had no claims and his kingdom would still have an heir.

Trinlys sank into the chair in front of his father. His face was pale and unkempt, his clothes ragged and unwashed. He was tired; tired of living, tired of being locked away, tired of being manipulated. He no longer had the strength to withstand his father or figure out him and his web of plans.

"Why am I still alive?" he asked. "You killed my sister and my mother." King Dalen, in the middle of pouring wine, jerked up, spilling wine over the table. Trinlys gathered satisfaction from his father's scared look. It gave him strength. "I know you killed my mother. She knew too much, didn't she? I know more. So why am I still alive?"

King Dalen offered a goblet of wine to Trinlys.

Trinlys refused.

"It's not poisoned, boy. Drink."

Trinlys reluctantly accepted it and took a sip.

King Dalen watched his son for a long time.

"Why am I still alive?" Trinlys repeated, breaking the eerie silence.

"Wrestan seems to have deserted me."

"You were a fool to trust him in the first place."

King Dalen twitched but kept his temper in check. "I fear he might have plans of his own. Plans that seek to undermine mine. While you remain alive, he cannot marry Filibria. If he cannot marry Filibria, he cannot be King of either Delvaria or Eirarin. In the end, I hold the reins."

"So, I am still a pawn? I am alive only because you still have a use for me?"

"You should be grateful," his father snarled. "If Wrestan cannot be trusted, I will take matters into my own hands. I will marry Filibria myself. We will have an heir worthy of the combined thrones."

"Filibria already carries an heir." Trinlys's eyes widened at what had just escaped his lips.

King Dalen pounced on him. "So, she did find you! And she does carry an heir. Where is she?"

Trinlys clamped his lips shut.

King Dalen shook him hard by the shoulders until his teeth rattled. "Tell me!" Hearing the commotion, an armed guard ran into the room, but King Dalen dismissed him. "Did she travel with you to Delvaria? Is she with her brother? Speak."

Trinlys shook his head. "You said you cannot kill me," he croaked.

"No—but I can make you wish for death." King Dalen called the guard back in and told him to throw Trinlys back in prison, then he summoned the chief gaoler.

"The boy has information I need. He knows where the princess is. Extract it from him. Break him, but do not kill him."

The gaoler bowed and shuffled off.

Trinlys sat on the hard bench, contemplating the chains connecting his hands. In the dim light, the metal glinted invitingly. How long would it take? Would he have the strength to do it? The thought of his father hunting down Filibria filled him, emboldening his helplessness. Trinlys twisted his arms around his head until the cool metal of the chain encircled his neck.

He started to pull, but then hesitated. Wrestan was somewhere out there, no doubt looking for Filibria. And he could be trusted with her less than his father. But sitting here, Trinlys could do nothing. The thought engulfed him and he started to pull harder.

"Don't."

The voice came from beyond his cell. Trinlys drowned it out. His ears began to sing as air left him. "Stop." When Trinlys did not obey, a key rattled in the lock and the door flew open.

The chief gaoler stepped inside. He grabbed Trinlys's hands and pushed them back towards his head, loosening the chains.

"I know why you're here," Trinlys gasped, his vision swimming. "You won't get information out of me."

"Stop this." The gaoler fought Trinlys until he could unwrap the chains from his neck.

Trinlys slumped against the wall in defeat. "Just let me die," he croaked.

"No." The gaoler withdrew another key and unlocked the shackles binding Trinlys's wrists. The chain fell to the floor.

"Get up and follow me."

Trinlys rose wearily and stumbled out of the cell. The goaler clamped a hand over his shoulder and led him through the maze of dungeon cells.

He pushed Trinlys into a dark room, an apprentice following behind with a torch. He touched it to the braziers and the space sprang to light. Trinlys swallowed as he viewed the tools and chains scattered over the walls. A table lay in the center of the floor.

"I will tell you nothing. Just kill me and be done with it," Trinlys pleaded.

The goaler did not reply. Instead, he motioned for the apprentice to leave, then he turned to Trinlys and bowed.

"I am your loyal servant. I will not lay a hand on you. To disobey the King's order is death, but I will do anything for you. And there are others too. You are the rightful heir of Eirarin. If you die, so too does the hope of Eirarin. You must live. For your kingdom. For your people."

Trinlys took a step back.

"What do you mean?"

"We will help you. We will get you to safety. You must find your bride and go to Delvaria."

Trinlys shook his head to clear it of the whirling confusion. "I cannot. Delvaria is compromised. King Kial himself gave me over to my father."

The gaoler's face fell, but only for a moment. The determination returned to his eyes. "That matters not then. We will find a way. We will free you and then you must return to free us and Eirarin."

"Who is *we*?"

"Many of us here in the castle. We have sat in the shadows for years, disapproving, but never fighting back. Now we fight back."

"And Mother Brylla?"

The gaoler chuckled. "She is our leader, our brain. And she is getting you out of here tonight. I only brought you to this room because I knew we would not be overheard in here. Come. I will take you back to your cell now."

The gaoler did not shackle Trinlys again. Instead, he removed the chains from the cell and locked the door behind him.

Trinlys sat on the bench, his mind spinning, his heart beating. A feeling he had given up on surged through him with every breath. *Hope.*

CHAPTER

Twenty-Seven

"The Prince Trinlys says the princess never made it to Delvaria," the chief gaoler said. "He was captured by King Kial's men, but Filibria managed to escape. She was headed west, last time the prince saw her."

King Dalen's eyes narrowed, measuring, and judging the open, honest face of the goaler. "This is the truth?"

The gaoler shook his head vigorously. "Few can lie under pain I am capable of inflicting. He is already a broken man. It did not take much."

"You have done well. Take care of him until I need him again."

"Yes, my King. It will be many moons before he is fit to see anyone. That is if his senses ever do return to him."

"But he will live?"

"Of course. I will keep him locked away in the dark and nurse him back to health until you have need for him. Only I must see him though."

"Good." The King flicked his hand towards the door, dismissing the man.

The chief gaoler nodded to the steward as they passed each other in the doorway. As the door closed behind the gaoler, he wiped his sweating hands on his cowl and hurried back to the safety of the castle dungeon.

"Trinlys. My prince."

Trinlys shifted and groaned, opening his eyes. A torch was burning in his cell and the chief gaoler stood in the room, holding the torch high. Behind him, the cell door was open.

"Get up."

Trinlys pulled himself up against the wall. "Did my father believe you?"

"He did." The gaoler tossed him a bundle of rough clothes and stood guard while Trinlys changed. When Trinlys finished, the goaler took him by the arm and led him out of the cell. He locked the door behind them. "Now listen, a horse is waiting for you…"

Trinlys pulled up short in the passageway.

"No. I cannot flee again. I am tired of running and hiding. I am better in there." He gestured back to the cell. "At least, while I am here, I can be sure Filibria cannot marry anyone else. If I disappear, my father will claim I am dead again. Besides," he said, "Eirarin needs me."

"Yes, Eirarin does need you, my prince. They need you alive. You have nothing here left to protect, except your life. I have told the King you need many weeks to recover. That will give you time before he discovers you are missing. Go to your wife before anyone else does…" The gaoler paused, knowing the weight of his next words. "Wrestan is missing."

Trinlys's head whipped up. "Since when?"

"A day or two. Without him, King Dalen is nothing, so we are safe. But I have no doubt Wrestan is going after Princess Filibria."

A fire lit in Trinlys's eyes. "Thank you for the news."

"This castle loves you, Trinlys." The gaoler clapped him on the shoulder. "We have been rooting for you since the day you were born. We cannot let Wrestan or your father triumph."

"How can I thank you?"

"Return and take your kingdom when you are ready. We will be waiting here for you."

"Tell Mother Brylla goodbye for me, please."

"Of course."

Outside, Trinlys looked up into the dark sky. The castle, his home, was a grey blob against the black. He was free. He should have felt relief, but he only felt terror squeezing at his heart. Wrestan was hunting down Filibria.

The ostler was waiting with the horse. He smiled and bowed when Trinlys entered the stables.

"Good luck, my prince."

Trinlys thanked him and swung into the saddle. The porter stood by the wide-open gate and he saluted Trinlys as he passed, securing the gate behind him.

When Trinlys had ridden a good distance away from the city, he turned back. The houses were dark shapes against the sky. Though some windows blazed with light and life, the castle itself was dark. In that moment, Trinlys knew he could not flee forever from Eirarin. He would not escape his life. He was bound to this kingdom by birth. When it was safe, he would return to Eirarin, with Filibria, and do what was right. There were lives in Eirarin that needed protecting; he was the only one who could do it right.

Trinlys rode all night towards Delvaria. He had no plan other than showing up at the castle and demanding Filibria be returned to him. They were bound by marriage. Her brother had no right to her. Yet at the same time, it meant his death if King Kial captured him and returned him to King Dalen again. More lives than Trinlys's would be in danger. but no other plan would come to him. He would simply have to be careful. He had to find Filibria and if only her brother knew, then he had to confront King Kial once again, no matter the cost.

Trinlys reached the royal city at dawn. He stopped at a rundown inn on the edge of the town where he was sure he would not be recognized and asked for breakfast and a room. After he ate, he fell fast asleep.

"Master?"

Trinlys rolled over to see a young boy standing at the side of his bed. He frowned through the fog of sleep, trying to understand the situation.

"My mother wants to know if you intend to pay for another night?"

"Another night?" Trinlys pushed himself up, legs dangling over the side of the bed. Deep golden rays of sunlight crept across the floor. He still had no plan. The boy waited respectfully for Trinlys to fight off the fog of sleep.

"Yes, I will."

The boy nodded and scampered off.

Trinlys walked to the window. From here, over the roofs of the houses, he could catch the slightest glimpse of the castle. Filibria was somewhere in there, likely in her room. His eyes went to the tower Filibria had described in detail. He had to find a way in without arousing suspicion. Her maid, *Malda.* The name hit him. Filibria had often talked fondly of her.

At the castle gates, Trinlys pulled his hood low over his face. It was evening and the flow of traffic through the gates was thick with people completing business and heading home. Trinlys slipped through and followed the smells to the kitchen, where beggars waited for handouts.

He hung around in the shadows until they left and then knocked on the door. It opened a minute or two after, and a red-faced woman glared at him. He ducked his head, cheeks burning with nervousness.

"Food line's closed," she barked.

"I'm...I'm looking for a woman named Malda," he said. "She's a maid here."

"Are you now? Well, skedaddle off right this minute. I can tell you Malda is not that kind of woman."

Trinlys's face burned even hotter. "No," he said, catching the door as it started to close. "You don't understand. I am a relative. A cousin. I have news about her family." The force on the door yielded and the woman propped her hand up on her hips, cocking an eyebrow.

"Not unwelcome news, I hope?"

"No, just sickness. Can I see her?"

"I'm afraid that is impossible at the moment. She left a week ago."

"Where?"

"No one knows. She just up and left."

"Did she go with anyone?"

The woman's eyes narrowed. "I'm not supposed to say. Now get out of here before they close the gates. Wait." She ducked back into the kitchen and returned shortly carrying a crust of bread and an end of a sausage. Trinlys accepted them humbly. He turned to leave the courtyard.

Behind him, a boy darted out of the kitchen door.

"Wait!" the boy called, but Trinlys did not turn back. "Wait!"

Trinlys slipped out of the gates and they closed with certainty behind him.

Back in his room at the inn, Trinlys paced the floor. Malda was gone, probably with Filibria. But where would King Kial have sent them? Surely the King would not be so foolish as to let Filibria out of his sight? King Kial did not know that there was a man out who would risk nothing to hunt her down. Trinlys's footsteps faltered; Filibria was in danger. He had to find her before Wrestan did. But how? He was helpless, and hopeless.

Just then, someone knocked on his door. Trinlys paused. He knew no one in Delvaria. He needed a weapon—anything. He glanced around the room, coming up empty. Finally, as the knocks came again, more desperate than the last, he snatched up a candlestick and eased open the door. He did not recognize the man standing on the dark landing and he quickly tried to close the door, but the man slipped a boot in the door, leaving a crack.

"Please, Prince Trinlys, hear me out."

At his name, Trinlys paused. "Who are you?"

"Carna, Steward of Delvaria. We met when you came before."

"How did you find me? What do you want?"

Carna slipped a hand through the crack in the door. His fingers uncurled, revealing a green ribbon.

Trinlys gasped.

CHAPTER

Twenty-Eight

"Filibria's ribbon! Did she give it to you? Where is she? Is she safe?"

"She is safe. She told me to give it to you should I ever see you again. I knew the chances were slim, but I did it for her." Carna relaxed in the chair. "I understand you came to the kitchen door this evening asking for Malda, posing as her family member. The servant who greeted you passed this on to the chief cook, who happens to be my wife.

"Malda has lived at the castle ever since her parents died. She has no relatives. My wife concluded either you were a ne'er-do-well—her words—or you were seeking someone other than Malda. My wife was one of the few who knew Princess Filibria was held in the castle. She told me of your strange appearance because she was worried. And then, a new boy, who came recently from Eirarin, claimed to recognize you—a page boy named Jarin. He said you were Prince Trinlys."

Trinlys's head shot up. "Jarin? But what is he doing here?"

"He brought a letter to King Kial and has been lodging with us ever since. My wife has grown fond of him. I reviewed your actions at the door and decided you were looking for the princess. It was quite possible you were a spy of Eirarin, but it was also possible, by some strange fate as the boy claimed, that you were actually the prince."

Trinlys could not wait for the explanation to end. He jumped up from his chair. "And you came here to tell me something. Where is Filibria?"

Carna laughed and held up a hand to ward off the eager young man.

"All in good time. You can do nothing tonight. But I do know where the princess is. First, I had to make sure you were really the prince. Afterwards, I intended to tell you. I am one of the few who know where she is being kept, because I am in charge of providing for her."

"Where?"

"Far from here. I will take you there."

"When?"

"We must give it time. I leave soon to bring her provisions, but I do not trust the guards I ride with. Give me a week and I will put together a retinue of guards I trust."

Trinlys sank back into his chair, his face desolate. "A week?!"

Carna laid a hand on his arm. "I know how you feel, but going too soon would arouse suspicion. The princess is closely guarded. I can only go when I have the King's pass. Do not worry about her. She is well looked after and well-guarded."

"Well-guarded? I have been told a man is out searching for her. He is the captain of Eirarin's guard and in close league with my father."

"He will not find her," Carna assured him. "And now I should leave. I will come for you in a week's time. Wait for me here."

"I will." Trinlys stood up again and escorted his guest to the door. "How...is Filibria...and the child she carries?"

"Well, though for how long, who knows? She does not like her captivity and she misses you. She will not stop talking or asking about you and I never have any news to give her. Now...now things shall be different." He smiled and bid goodnight. "I shall bring you instead of merely news."

"Could you bring me a weapon?" Trinlys asked. "A sword, perhaps? I did not bring my own."

Carna bowed. "I shall send one along tomorrow. Goodnight."

"Wait!"

Carna turned back.

"Could you send her a book? She will be bored. Something to help her escape for an hour or two. Say it is from me."

Carna smiled and nodded. "It will be done."

Trinlys went to the window to watch the steward ride away. For the first time in his life, fate just might be on his side. But a week?! Anything could happen—and Wrestan was still out there.

Early the next morning, Trinlys woke to a rapping on his door. Disregarding his safety, he jumped up, threw a cloak around himself, and opened it.

"Jarin!"

The boy grinned. He was dressed in Delvarian colors, looking grimmer and older.

"I brought this by order of Steward Carna." He held out a sword and all of its trappings.

"Thank you."

"I have seen her, Trinlys. I saw the Lady Filibria."

"When?"

Jarin frowned, mentally counting the days. "A week or two ago."

Trinlys deflated. He had seen her around the same time.

"I brought King Kial the letter Filibria had written him. It was too late, but I saw her. She was arguing with her brother. She was angry and soldiers had to hold her back. What happened? I thought you had been taken back to Eirarin."

"I had, but I escaped again. King Kial is just as greedy as my father. He tried to use me for leverage and now, he is keeping Filibria for the same purpose."

"What can I do to help?"

Trinlys looked the scrawny, quiet boy over. "Stay in the castle and gather what news you can."

"Delvaria is unhappy with their king just as Eirarin is with your father. And Delvaria does not even know about Filibria. When you overthrow both kingdoms..."

"Hold on." Trinlys held up his hands. "I do not plan to overthrow any kingdom. I am only going to rescue Filibria and get her to safety."

Jarin's face fell. "I at least want to help you rescue Lady Filibria."

"You cannot, you are too young. Now go back before they miss you, and thank Carna for sending the sword."

When the boy left, dejected, Trinlys dressed and buckled on the sword; it felt strange and heavy. He drew it and assessed its weight in his hand. He had learned to swordfight—his princely duties had demanded it—but his father had never insisted on his learning the art of war. Now, Trinlys knew why. His father had never intended him to live long, nor did he ever think Trinlys could fight back. Well, fight back he would.

Though it would be dangerous to stay at the inn for too long, Trinlys had no other place to go. He kept to his room each day, only visiting the common room late at night when most everyone had left. He made no trouble and attracted none, except for one particular evening.

The common room was empty besides Trinlys and a fellow sitting in the far corner. The fire was low enough to hide both men's faces in shadows while they ate. The innkeeper appeared in the door, clearing his throat to announce his presence, then he joined Trinlys at his table.

"Now look here, man, you have stayed a couple of days already and I have not seen a single coin for it. Now I don't mean to be pushy, but you have to understand this is my living. I've had too many up and leave without paying to be trusting any longer. You seem like a good man, but all the same, I'd appreciate a little payment."

"Of course." Trinlys pulled out his pouch and counted out the right number of coins, coins he had used all of his life. It was not until they were in the innkeeper's hands that Trinlys realized his mistake. The innkeeper peered at the coins.

"I haven't seen these in a long while. You'll have to excuse me, but Eirarin coins have gone down in value, what with rumors of war and all." Trinlys quickly made up the difference; he would have to get his other coins changed soon. It would also be safest to change inns.

Mortified at his mistake, Trinlys slunk back to his room and securely locked the door. The next morning, he paid for the rest of his keep and hunted around for another inn to hide out in. Each day crawled past, giving Trinlys plenty of time to doubt. Was he right to endanger the steward? He had already risked Brylla's life, the gaoler's life, and who knew how many countless others. When the week neared its end and he headed back to the first inn, he was almost ready to turn down Carna's offer. Almost, but not quite.

The great gate to the old watchtower swung open.

"My lady, Steward Carna is here."

Filibria roused from the settee and Malda wrapped a cloak around her before the two women walked out the door. Filibria ran out to embrace Carna.

"Any news?"

Carna held out a book. "A gift from a prince."

Filibria's face paled as she reached for the book. "From Trin—?"

Carna put a hand against Filibria's mouth, glancing back to see if the guards had heard anything. "Shhh. Do not speak his name," Carna hissed. "But have hope. I am going to find a way to reunite you both. Until then, he wanted something to help you escape mentally."

Filibria clutched her arms around the book and smiled. "Thank you."

Carna only grunted. He stood in the courtyard, overseeing the unloading of supplies carried up the mountain by guards. Then, after promising to return the next week, he and his men left, locking the gate firmly behind them.

"He's alive, Malda," Filibria sang when Carna had left, "and Carna has seen him."

"Now don't get your hopes up. What if he gave it to someone right before he was taken away and they gave it to Carna?"

"No. He wouldn't have. He's alive." Filibria sank back onto the settee, cradling the book like a child. There was no letter inside it, nothing from Trinlys...but he had sent her a book.

He was alive; she could feel it.

Twenty-Nine

"You could lose your position." Carna smiled despite Trinlys's serious face. "You could even lose your life."

"You had a week to think about it," Carna said at last, "and of course, you doubted. I am touched by your concern, but you seem to forget I also had a week to think through the consequences. Your wife was bound to her duties as a peace weaver. Instead, she had the courage to fight for love over peace. She abandoned her duties to do what was right. If a princess can do it, why can't I? She has been dear to me since she was a child. I will follow my heart, not my orders."

Trinlys conceded. "Thank you. Both of us are indebted to you."

"Now listen, tomorrow night, the wagon will come by. Filibria's guards have been relieved, and we are bringing new ones, along with supplies. The wagon—"

"Wait!" Trinlys interrupted. "She is unguarded for now?"

Carna fiddled with his sword hilt. "There was a misunderstanding. Her guards came back too early, but it will only be for a day. She will be safe. Now listen, the wagon will slow before this inn. That is when you must jump into the wagon and conceal yourself. Do you understand?"

Trinlys nodded.

"There is one other thing"—Carna's eyes dimmed—"your father has sent out word of your escape. He says since you are gone, the peace agreement is annulled. Even now, he is again amassing his army on the border. King Kial responded with anger. There will be war."

Trinlys buried his face in his hands and groaned.

"Come inside, my lady. You'll catch a cold. It's bad for you and the baby."

Filibria did not move from the doorway. She stared at the gate as if her willpower would fling it open and Trinlys would be standing on the other side.

Malda sighed. "At least wear a cloak." She draped one over Filibria, covering the hands clutching the book over her stomach.

"He's coming, Malda. I am going to be here when he comes."

Malda only shook her head and headed back to her chores.

"I know he'll come," Filibria whispered.

"I'm going to murder Carna," Malda muttered into the bread dough. She gave it an extra hard pound for good measure.

Like Trinlys, Wrestan had escaped from Eirarin without a plan. He was a man of arms, not a man of brains, yet he knew how to plan battles and make men do what he wanted. There were two ways to make a castle fall: Lay siege and then storm it or slowly infiltrate it from within until it crumbled. For lack of men and strength, Wrestan chose the latter. Dressing as a wandering hunter, he begged for shelter in the castle and was rewarded with a spare bed in the barracks. He could not have asked for more; soldiers were the most likely to talk. Wrestan spun tales to charm the guards and soldiers. He played dice with them, coming across as a rookie and gaining their pity. He bought them drinks to make their tongues run. He played every trick he knew and slowly, he picked up the talk he wanted.

He learned Princess Filibria had been in Delvaria. After a few days more, it became clear to Wrestan, she was no longer in the capital. He kept his ears open for any hints of the princess's location, but King Kial had hidden her well and covered his tracks.

At last, one guard gave Wrestan the exact information he was looking for. Unfortunately, to discover the information, Wrestan had to get him drunk to the point of incomprehension and then he had to prod him further with uncomfortably direct questions.

"You are a new face. I'm sure I would not have overlooked yours before now."

The guard's twisted, mangled visage opened in raucous laughter. The bright flush of alcohol did not improve his complexion. "Naw. I'm an old hand. Been here years. That's why I'm trusted." He winked at Wrestan.

Wrestan called for another drink. "Trusted for what?"

"Now, now, no tellin' that; that's a secret."

Wrestan set the fresh tankard in front of the man. He downed it in one gulp and came up frothing like a rabid dog. He grinned, displaying all ten of his teeth. Inwardly, Wrestan writhed with revulsion, but he kept his face passive, as if he was using this conversation merely to whittle away time.

"Well, from your tanned look, it looks as though you drew a bad lot. Lots of standing around in the sun."

The man shook his head vigorously. "Not bad. Not bad. Good pay. Very good pay."

"But you must miss your family being so far away."

The man frowned, then he laughed. "Don't have no family—and it's not far. A day?" He held up a finger and then added another one in dazed confusion. "Two days?"

"Near Eirarin? That border's dangerous. I could understand why the pay would be high."

"No. Not Eirarin. Southeast. Far southeast. Far from Eirarin. Nice place."

"I would understand your tan being up on those exposed hills."

"No. Not hills. Valleys...and secret places. Forgotten places." He chuckled and began a song about valleys and flowers.

Wrestan handed him another tankard, and once again, the man drank up. Then his bloated face hit the table and he gave a single loud snore.

Wrestan laid down his coins for the drinks. Before the tavernkeeper took them up, Wrestan's companion on his right snatched one of the coins.

With one hand, Wrestan reached for the coin; with his other, his dagger. The man placidly placed it back on the table and chuckled.

"I won't mess with you. I was just looking at the coin. Eirarin. You don't see a lot of those on this side of the border. 'Specially in these times."

"I was stationed there for a while," Wrestan said, "I have not had time to change them."

"No, not you. I saw another man who used them."

"In this town?"

"Yes, at the inn on the edge of town. A quiet, secretive fellow. He changed inns soon after."

Wrestan twisted a spare coin in his fingers. "I'll give you one of these if you can describe the man."

The man's eyes glinted, then he shut them, trying to recall details into his mind. "I don't remember much. It was dark in the room, see? Dark and smoky. Anyway, he was tall. His hair was light, I think, and cropped close. He had a thin, pale look—like a thief."

"What was he wearing?"

"I don't remember. A cloak hid most of it anyway."

Wrestan threw the man the coin and rose. Who would be from Eirarin? Was it chance? Or was someone tracking him? Maybe he had underestimated his father.

Outside, a boy stood by Wrestan's horse, holding the reins, and seemingly inspecting the bridle. Wrestan swatted at him. "Be gone, boy." The boy looked up and their eyes met; recognition flashed like lightning between them.

Before Wrestan could act, the boy scampered away out of sight. The Eirarin pageboy! Why was he here? Was he working for Filibria? Or for Trinlys? Or was he a spy for his father? Wrestan growled in frustration and yanked at the straps on his saddle bags, securing them tight.

"You are leaving?"

Wrestan looked over the back of his horse. A young soldier was watching him. For a moment, Wrestan panicked, but then he forced himself to stay calm. Why should the man suspect him?

"Yes. I suppose I have overstayed my welcome here."

"Not necessarily. If you asked in the right places, you could get yourself a job. You look like a fighting man."

"What sort of job?"

"Mercenary."

"Mercenaries are only hired in times of war."

The man nodded solemnly. "These are times of war. Have you not heard? The King of Eirarin's son is again missing. The King of Eirarin is calling for war yet again. We move out tomorrow. You will be well rewarded if you fight with us."

Wrestan shook his head. When the man had left, he laughed aloud. Join Delvaria to fight against his own kingdom? So, King Dalen had gone to war. Perhaps he was not as soft as Wrestan had judged him. Most of all, Trinlys was missing. How? And for how long? The man at the inn. The Eirarin coins. Could Trinlys be free and looking for Filibria too? Maybe he could find them both and kill Trinlys once and for all. Wrestan swung into his saddle. He would find Filibria first and deal with Trinlys later. He rode out of Delvaria, heading southeast.

The small guarded wagon rattled down the sleeping streets, slowing a little outside a brightly lit inn. In the shadows of the doorway waited a hooded man, a sword strapped to his side. When the wagon rattled past, the Prince of Eirarin caught ahold of it and pulled himself in, stretching out in the half-empty back. Soon after, the wagon rolled to a stop in front of the gates. Trinlys's heart tightened. He strained to hear the exchange between Carna and the guard. Finally, the gates creaked open and the wagon rumbled out into the country. It would be a long ride, so Carna had told him. Trinlys settled down among the supplies, but he knew he would not be able to sleep.

Wrestan rested behind an outcropping of rocks. By the light of his small fire, he ate and drank a little, then he settled back. Tomorrow, he would search for the right valley. For now, he had to be on his guard.

The rattle of a wagon and the steady beat of hooves jerked him out of the sleep he had not meant to take. Wrestan slithered up the rock and peered over the top. The dim light of the moon shone on the riders. They were concealed with cloaks, but their horses' trappings were rich, bearing the device of Delvaria. Wrestan clambered back off the rock to consider his good fortune. He would not need to waste time searching for the valley. He stomped out his fire, saddled his horse, and slipped onto the road, keeping back just enough so as not to be seen.

Once they were in the countryside, Trinlys came out of hiding. He moved to the back of the wagon and sat, dangling his legs over the edge. The guards acted as though he was not even there.

The barrels and sacks behind Trinlys shifted and he turned back, just in time to catch Jarin crawling out.

"Jarin! What are you doing here?"

Jarin clambered up beside Trinlys. "I tried to find you earlier, but I could not. You had left the inn. Wrestan is in Delvaria! I saw him up in the royal barracks. I saw his horse first and then he came out. He recognized me."

"Royal barracks?! How?"

Jarin shrugged. "He was drinking in the tavern. He came out and saw me, so I ran."

"You could have sent a message with Steward Carna instead of hiding in the wagon," Trinlys replied dryly, but his chest tightened. Wrestan was in Delvaria. How much did he know?

"No, that is not why I came. I came to help you rescue the princess." He gave Trinlys a winning smile.

"Keep out of sight and stay in the wagon."

Jarin obediently ducked back behind the barrels.

Trinlys returned his gaze to the road unraveling out behind them. At least if Wrestan was still in the capital, he did not know Filibria had been moved out.

On a long stretch of straight road, Trinlys thought he saw another rider behind them. He brushed it off, thinking it was only his sleep deprived eyes. A few minutes later though, he caught a glint of metal in the moonlight. Now he was sure they were being followed. Who else would be traveling on this forsaken road at night? Trinlys crept to the front of the wagon and called for Carna, who rode a little ahead. Carna dropped back.

"We are being followed."

"Are you sure?"

"Someone is riding a horse behind us. They are neither dropping behind nor gaining on us."

There was silence for a while as Carna processed his options.

"Keep a watch. Tell me if anything changes." Carna spoke softly to the driver. The wagon's pace increased and Trinlys resumed his place. The rider did not fall behind. Wrestan. It had to be Wrestan. What would he do when they stopped? Could all the guards fight him off?

"Trinlys?" Carna rode level with the wagon. "There has been a change of plans. When the wagon slows a little, jump off. Head for the mountains. You will find stairs leading up to an abandoned watchtower. That is where she is being kept."

"What about you?"

"We will keep going to draw this rider off."

"I think I know who he is. It's Wrestan, captain of the guards of Eirarin."

"I know of him. We will deal with him."

"Be careful. He is not a man to be reckoned with. He knows how to fight."

"When you reach Filibria, leave with her. Take her west, across Relcrios Lake. I will not come back but will return to the King and tell him we were pursued and so we did not go near Filibria. Farewell." Carna spurred his horse and rode to the head of the column again.

Trinlys readied himself, listening to the wagon, judging when it was slowing. He timed it to the beat of his heart, but as the wagon slowed, his heart only beat faster.

The time had come. Trinlys jumped from the back and rolled into the bushes by the side of the road. He would have gotten up then, but an impulse overcame him, and he stayed hidden.

The horse and rider drew closer. The man was dressed in leather armor without markings, and his hood was thrown back. Black hair gleamed in the moon's light. His cruel face was set in grim determination. *Wrestan.* A feeling of helplessness washed over Trinlys and he stayed on the ground long after Wrestan had passed. He did not have the skill or strength to fight the man for Filibria.

After a while, Trinlys forced himself to his feet. The only way he could save Filibria was if he got to her first and took her away. He followed Carna's directions and soon came upon a slightly worn track leading towards the mountains.

As the land rose into craggy arms, a set of stairs, carved into the mountainside appeared out of the gloom. Heart racing, Trinlys sprinted up them. His sword banged on his hip and he considered abandoning it, but thought better of it. The stairs ascended sharply into mist, forcing Trinlys's shaking legs to slow. Cold wind rattled through his gasping lungs. He doubled over once or twice to catch his breath. Filibria waited for him at the top of the stairs. His love; his wife—the woman who carried his children. The thought coursed warmth through his veins, enough to keep going a little longer.

As he rounded a bend, he stopped to draw yet another breath. The air so high up felt thinner. Clouds had gathered, concealing the moon and making footing treacherous. To his left, the stairs perilously clung to the side of the mountain. To his right, the world dropped away in a dizzying abyss. Dank cold air rose from the bottomless depths. Trinlys kicked a loose stone off the edge but never heard it hit the bottom. As his ears strained for the sound, he heard another, more distant noise from the stairs below him: The sound of boots on the stone. He paused, waiting to make sure the air was not playing tricks on him. His heart sank as the unmistakable sound of footsteps pierced the night air. He was being followed. Wrestan had caught up to him.

# CHAPTER

Thirty

FEAR SQUEEZED TRINLYS'S HEART as he gripped his sword, knuckles white. He pushed himself flat against the outcropping to keep hidden from below as the footsteps continued closer, steady and sure.

Deciding his only hope was the element of surprise, Trinlys waited until he could hear Wrestan's breath. Though heavy, it was smooth and even, untroubled by the height and pace.

Trinlys drew his sword and stepped out to face his foe. To his dismay, the rock beneath his foot shifted slightly, reminding him of his perilous balance.

Surprise flashed across Wrestan's face, only to be quickly replaced with a sneer.

"So you found her too? Did my father set you free?"

"Turn around Wrestan, and ride far from here. I will forgive you and forget all that is ill between us."

Wrestan's laugh fell into the abyss, echoing eerily against the rocks. "You always think there is a peaceful way out of everything, don't you? I shall strike you down where you stand and throw your body to the chasms where it will never be found. Then I will take your wife and bed her as my Queen to rule both kingdoms—and you will be forgotten."

Trinlys took a step back to strengthen his footing and gripped his sword tighter, hoping Wrestan could not see the slight tremble in the blade. Without a proper reply for Wrestan's taunt, he kept his mouth closed.

Wrestan laughed again. He spread out his hands, palms up. "What now, brother? You think you can strike me down? You know nothing of sword work or you would know your fighter's arm is pinned against the wall giving *me* the advantage."

"And you know nothing of me." Shifting the sword to his left hand, Trinlys swung inwards and downwards at Wrestan. Caught off guard, Wrestan jumped back. He teetered, but years of training steadied his feet again. Gone now were the taunts as Wrestan drew his sword.

Trinlys took another step back and Wrestan moved up, right where Trinlys wanted him; the rock shifted slightly beneath Wrestan's foot.

Taking advantage of Wrestan's uneven position, Trinlys threw himself at the man. He raised his sword, blocking Wrestan's. His weight caused both to lose hold of their swords; metal rang as the weapons skittered over the cliff.

Wrestan threw his weight towards the wall, pinning Trinlys to the rocks. Trinlys's face grated against the rough stone as strong hands wrapped around his throat, squeezing it shut.

As stars gathered in Trinlys's vision, he beat feebly on Wrestan's arm and chest, but Wrestan only laughed. The pressure around his neck increased, and the world began to go grey. This was it; Wrestan would win. Trinlys's broken body would be carrion food. And Filibria…

The thought of her sent a rush of energy through Trinlys's body. In a last effort, Trinlys twisted against the rocks. He kicked at Wrestan's leg, causing him to lose balance. While Wrestan fought to steady himself, Trinlys yanked himself free. Wrestan may have been strong, but Trinlys was fighting for more than his life now. Adrenaline raced through him. Every little scrap of training his father had forced him to take came back to him as he tackled Wrestan.

"She is my wife"—Trinlys panted—"and Eirarin is my kingdom."

A sharp pain pierced Trinlys's back. He screamed as Wrestan yanked the dagger out. Warm blood dripped onto the path. The pain coursed through Trinlys, clearing his mind and driving him mad. He charged at Wrestan and pushed him backwards, but Wrestan caught him by the arms and they both tumbled towards the edge. Wrestan's foot landed in the puddle of blood, found no footing, and he slipped over the edge, bringing Trinlys. Trinlys saw Wrestan's eyes widen with terror, and then they were falling. Trinlys's flailing arms caught the edge of the cliff. He felt Wrestan falling past him.

A curdling scream cut through the night air, growing fainter as it fell...then there was silence.

Grunting with pain, Trinlys slowly pulled himself back from the edge. His watery limbs betrayed him, forcing him to stretch out on the solid stairs. Deep breaths racked his body, already trembling uncontrollably.

Wrestan was gone; he had killed him...he had pushed him to his death. Wrestan, who had been a dark shadow looming over him his entire life. *Gone.*

Blood gushed from Trinlys's wound. He did his best to bandage it with his shirt, but the cloth quickly became soaked. Trinlys leaned his shoulder against the rocks, exhausted. Each step would leech a little more of his life. Would he survive all the way to the top? He had to try. Filibria was waiting for him up there. Slowly, on hands and knees, Trinlys began to crawl upwards.

A rosy light bloomed on the horizon as he mounted the last step. The tower loomed in shadows above him, but before him stood an impenetrable wall. He had no key for the gate. He had come this far. A wall could not stop him.

Filibria, well-wrapped at Malda's nagging insistence, stepped out the door to pace the small courtyard for fresh air—another one of Malda's insistences. As always, she stared up at the wall, hiding everything beyond from her. What was going on beyond? Had King Dalen found another excuse for war? And Trinlys, was he...? *No.* Filibria blocked the thought from her mind. She could only think of him when she was strong...and she wasn't often anymore, not in the long cold days.

As she turned to go back through the door, something heavy fell from the wall. She jumped, then she screamed when she realized it was a body, covered in dirt and blood.

"Fili," he croaked and rolled to look at her.

The man's face was pale, dirty, and haggard with several weeks' worth of unkempt beard growth. His clothes were dirty and tattered. But the fire burning in his eyes was the same. It was love.

"Trinlys?" Tears welled up, blurring her vision. "This is not some cruel trick?"

"No, my love. It's me."

She ran to him and knelt, hesitant to touch him. Laughing, he seized her outstretched hand and pulled her close. She embraced him—dirt, blood, and all.

"I knew you would come," she sobbed repeatedly, "I knew you would come. Carna gave me your book. I knew you were alive. I was so scared. What happened to you? How did you get over the wall?" Filibria ran her hands over his face, one she had almost given up hope of ever seeing again.

He was alive; he had found her. They were together again.

"A lot has happened to me. And after all I've done to get here, do you really think a wall would be able to separate me from you?" He kissed the top of her hair; it smelled fresh and warm, like sunshine. "We are safe now, my love. I have come to rescue you and set you free."

Suddenly, Trinlys crumpled in Filibria's arms.

"Trinlys!" A patch of red covered his back, and Filibria snapped her head towards the tower. "Malda! Malda, come quickly!" Filibria screamed.

The woman burst out of the tower, freezing at the sight of Trinlys.

"Help me!" Breathy sobs ripped from Filibria's body as Malda examined Trinlys.

"We need to get him inside," Malda said grimly.

Between the two women, they gingerly lifted Trinlys and carried him into the house. They lay him face down on the bed and Filibria sat stunned by his side while Malda raced around, boiling water and stripping cloth for bandages. With Filibria's help, she cut off Trinlys shirt and peeled it away from the wound.

"Is it dangerous?" Filibria asked, studying Malda's face for clues.

Malda pursed her lips. "It's high, but I don't think it is high enough or deep enough to have pierced a lung. It looks like a knife wound, but it was deflected by the rib bone. Help me wash the blood away."

Trinlys remained unconscious while they cleaned the wound and bound it. Malda snuck out of the room, but Filibria stayed, holding Trinlys's clammy hand and stroking his matted hair. She had once thought of him only as a pale scholar; how wrong she had been. He was a warrior... the best and bravest of warriors.

Trinlys groaned several times in his sleep, but by the end of the day, he was fully awake. His brow wrinkled in confusion, then he let out a deep sigh, relaxing when he recognized his wife. Filibria stroked the hair away from his face.

Trinlys took her hand. "Now we are both trapped here."

"Shh," Filibria laughed. "That does not matter right now. We are safe and together." She pressed her lips to his forehead.

A shadow darkened Trinlys's brow. "I don't know how long we can wait. Our kingdoms needs us."

"Can we not just stay here? Or go somewhere far from here?" Filibria pleaded. "I have what I want." She slid a hand over her stomach, touching Trinlys with the other. "I just want us all to be safe."

Trinlys took his hand in both of hers. "I know, but living a simple life was not what was dealt to us. We need to help our kingdoms. It is our sworn duty. My people risked their lives to free me. If I do not risk mine for them, that is a life debt unpaid."

"I know. I just want it to end now. There will be years of war and politics before it will all be sorted through and some sort of peace established."

"Yes...but they will be years with you—and our child." Trinlys moved his hand to rest on top of hers on her stomach. "We will do it together, I promise, then we will rest."

While he rested, Trinlys filled Filibria in on his journey back to Eirarin and then his escape back out of it. Filibria shook her head when he told her about Jarin sneaking along in the wagon.

"That boy deserves to be knighted...or thrown in prison," she said.

Trinlys laughed. It ended in a deep cough, which brought Malda running back in.

"He'll cough up his guts if you're not careful," she scolded Filibria. "Let him rest again."

"She's worse than Mother Brylla," Trinlys said with a smile when Malda left the room.

"They would make quite the pair. Both kingdoms would be whipped into shape in no time at all if they had any say in politics."

"Maybe they should."

Malda knocked, peeking around the door before they had time to answer. "I don't mean to disturb you, but there's someone at the door. He unlocked the gate, and he's demanding to see you."

Trinlys pushed himself up in bed. His first reaction was to search for a weapon...anything. His muscles relaxed when he remembered Wrestan was dead, but surely Carna would not have turned around so quickly.

Filibria was watching him, worry wrinkling her face. Who could it be?

"Let him in," Trinlys replied.

"He'll be no danger to you," Malda assured them. "He's just a lad."

Thirty-One

Jarin waltzed triumphantly into the room, holding a large key in his outstretched palm like a prize. "I had hoped to catch up with you before you reached the gate," he confessed, "because I knew you could not open it."

"How did you get the key?" Trinlys asked.

"I took it from Carna and followed you."

"Knighting," Filibria whispered under her breath, making Trinlys smile, "but only after a little imprisonment for his own safety."

"We can leave now!" Jarin said. "You can go stop the war."

"You'll do nothing of the sort," Malda interrupted from the doorway. "The prince is not fit to travel—and neither is the princess. She should not travel those perilous stairs in her condition."

Trinlys looked at Filibria, his face lighting up with a new thought.

"No," Filibria replied to his unspoken words, "I will not stay up here until the baby is born."

"But you will be far out of harm's way."

"While you are right in harm's way. My place is by your side, no matter what. We will leave when you are able, and we will fight for our kingdoms together."

"Together," Trinlys echoed. He smiled at Filibria. "A peace weaver and a scholar."

As Trinlys healed, he and Filibria spent their days enjoying each other's company; though their days were darkened by discussions of the future and unpleasant choices they would have to make. The more days that passed, the further they felt from the outside world.

Had war started? Or had peace been kept?

On the seventh day, another visitor found them.

Carna had returned to Delvaria. To keep suspicions low, he waited his normal week to return with provisions, but then he had ridden back out as quickly as he could.

"You are still here!" he exclaimed when they let him into the tower. "I had half-hoped you would have ridden off already, but no matter. I have a wagon for the women and a horse for you, Trinlys. Once you reach the bottom of the mountain, you can ride further south."

"We will not leave our kingdoms," Trinlys replied gravely.

Carna stopped and drew himself up in a long breath. When his breathing had settled his face grew grim. "Then I must be honest with you so you can weigh your options. There has been war, with many skirmishes along the border. King Kial fell in battle two days ago."

Filibria cried out.

Carna bowed his head. "Your mother is doing her best to lead your kingdom, but grief is heavy on her. That is why I came to find you, Filibria, if you were still here." He took both of her hands and his eyes shone. "You are free, but most importantly, you will be Queen of Delvaria on your return."

Filibria and Trinlys exchanged worried looks.

"Meaning Trinlys is king," Filibria murmured. "Now his father will want to kill him more than ever."

"Yes. You see now why you must flee, both of you. Do not worry about Delvaria. I will keep it until you return when it is safe."

"No," Trinlys said. He looked at Filibria. "Filibria will stay here, guarded for her safety, but I will ride to the border as King of Delvaria and face my father. With renewed hope, we will fight back."

"I will not stay here," Filibria replied, "you know that."

Trinlys looked again at Filibria, watching as she stood up; he did not like the determination on her face.

Carna looked from husband to wife, waiting for one of them to speak.

"My place is at Trinlys's side," Filibria spoke. "My place is with Delvaria."

"But you will not ride into battle," Trinlys said firmly.

"Of course not," Carna assured him. "There will be plenty for her to do at the castle. She will rally hope and men to your side."

Filibria agreed, much to Trinlys's relief.

"Let hope return to Delvaria!" Carna cried.

Jarin jumped up and down, cheering.

CHAPTER

Thirty-Two

Within half an hour, they had packed all they needed and were ready to descend. Like before, it took them almost half a day to reach the waiting wagon. Trinlys's wound forced him to take the steps slowly, and everyone else kept reminding Filibria to keep a gentle pace. She wanted nothing more than to throw off their guiding hands and hurry down the steps, but she let them help her. It allowed her to wrap herself up in her thoughts of the coming days.

They arrived in Delvaria in the middle of the night. The city was eerily quiet, and the castle even more so; the royal barracks were empty and cold, too. A pall of mourning lay over everything, but Filibria could not tell if it was for her brother, or for the fate of Delvaria.

A hollowness filled her heart as they moved through the city. Despite his flaws, Filibria had always looked up to her brother. Way back in their childhood, they had been close. Before politics, and war, and all the expectations placed upon them by their kingdom. When they had just been brother and sister. She cried for that memory now; the memory of everything that had been lost and could no longer be fixed.

Every person in the castle wore black. The staff padded silently past, hardly even looking up. When a few did, and they saw Filibria's face, it was as if a candle suddenly ignited in their eyes. Before long, the rumor had spread like fire through the castle.

The princess was alive, and she had returned to Delvaria. She would be their queen: she would right the wrongs.

Filibria would have liked to have time alone with Trinlys to plan, but as soon as they arrived, they joined the war council set up in the Great Hall. Carna and Malda had both advised Filibria to rest while they made plans, but she refused.

Her mother, swathed in fresh black, stood alone at the war table, staring deeply at a map. She barely looked up when they entered, but Filibria hurried to her, wrapping her arms tight around her mother.

Queen Bryn gasped and buried her lips into her daughter's hair. "Are you real? Or just another ghost come to torment me?"

"I'm real, Mother," Filibria whispered through her tears.

The Queen began to sob. "I failed you, Filibria. I failed my family. I focused so hard on weaving peace in this kingdom, that I neglected weaving it in our own family and look what became of it. Your brother would tell me nothing. I thought you were dead," she repeated in a whisper.

Filibria hugged her mother harder and wept.

"It is alright now, Mother. Please, go rest. We will see things from here."

Before she conceded, Queen Bryn looked her daughter over, her eyes bright with tears. "Look at you. I never thought I would see the day you would become Queen of this kingdom. I am so proud of you."

"Thank you, Mother," Filibria whispered.

"You should rest too, dear. It will be a long night and many long days to follow."

Filibria only nodded. She would not rest if Trinlys could not.

The room began to fill with knights and advisors and Queen Bryn bid her daughter goodbye, disappearing back to her chambers.

As the war council sat around the table covered in maps and candles, sleep did overtake Filibria. She ended up stretched out on a bench, covered with a cloak, her head in Trinlys's lap. As long as she pinned him down, he could not leave without her knowledge.

They must have come to some satisfying conclusion because before dawn, they roused Filibria.

"We still have not settled the question of crowning," Carna told her. "It would not be proper to crown you so soon after your brother's death, but in these days…it is your choice."

He looked around the council; everyone was waiting for Filibria's verdict.

"We will wait," she said, "but Trinlys shall go to battle dressed like a king."

Carna bowed. "That is good. He shall wear King Kial's armor."

If Trinlys had looked strange the day he had climbed over the wall, he looked even stranger when he returned from the armory. Despite her sorrow, Filibria smiled. Instead of making him look larger and stronger than he was, the armor—made for her taller, larger brother—dwarfed him. Trinlys looked like a snail with too big of a shell.

When Filibria laughed, Trinlys grimaced. "Not exactly the inspiration my troops are looking for."

Filibria reached up and kissed him. "I like the scholar Trinlys more, but I'm glad he has another side."

"When this is all over, your scholar will return to you."

Fear suddenly seized her, and she hugged him tightly. "Come back, Trinlys. Come back to us," she whispered.

"Shh. I will, my love." Trinlys wiped her tears away. His hands fell to her stomach to caress the gentle bump beneath her dress. Then he was walking down the hallway, away from her.

As the sun rose, the castle staff spilled out into the courtyard to watch their new King ride into battle. Though word had spread out into the city announcing Filibria's safety and return, no one was prepared for the arrival of the new King.

The streets were silent as Trinlys rode out on his charger. People pressed up against the edge of the street, straining to catch a glimpse of the elusive Prince of Eirarin.

Filibria stood by the gate to the palace, wrapped in a rich fur cloak to fend off the cold and smiled at her husband. She reached up her hand as he passed, and he leaned to take it, kissing it once, then twice, then once more for good measure. He and the few soldiers, who were left in the city, rode out down the streets. Filibria watched him until he was out of sight. Malda placed a gentle hand on her arm.

"We should go in, my lady."

"Not just yet."

On the wind, a murmur spread through the town. It increased in volume; a cheer, a cheer of hope. The people of Delvaria had accepted their King. Filibria stood taller, tears of happiness streaming down her face. Malda cried, too, and Carna's eyes were suspiciously moist as he led the women back into the castle.

The next few days that passed were the longest in Filibria's life. Not even when she thought Trinlys was dead did she worry like she did now. Every morning, right after eating breakfast, she would join the war council in the Great Hall, and when they broke up for the day, she remained in the room, unable to find rest.

Without a feast, a council, or her father who could fill up a room alone, the Great Hall loomed vast, empty, and silent, like a charnel house. Filibria leaned on the table, staring at the dais. On a stone slab, dressed in gold cloth lay the body of the King, her brother, awaiting his funeral.

Filibria's mind wandered back to the day she had stepped into this hall and had seen Trinlys. Her hands slipped over her stomach, and she smiled a little. How so much had changed in such a short time!

The one she loved was out waging war to bring peace. Filibria smiled at the absurdity of it, but soon, her smile burst into a flood of tears. A warm arm slipped around her shaking shoulders. Her mother ran her other hand up and down Filibria's back.

"I did not fail you, Mother," Filibria sobbed. "I found the balance between peace and love, but it was so hard. And now we fight a war for it."

"Balance," her mother murmured. "Everything in life is a dangerous balance. I am glad you have found yours, even with all that has happened. With firm footing, it is easy to keep balance—and I can see Trinlys is a firm place to put your trust."

Filibria stared at the body of her brother. "I wish he had not fallen into such evil."

"Me too"—Bryn rested her cheek against her daughter's forehead—"me too."

Every afternoon, a messenger rode into the castle with news from the battlefront; Filibria was always waiting along with Carna and Jarin, to hear the news.

"They have pushed the Eirarins back over the border."

"The battle line has changed little." And when he had nothing to report, he would encourage Filibria with news of her husband.

"The Delvarians have grown fond of their King," he would say one grey afternoon.

"The King has a wise and level head."

After major reports, the council would gather again and Filibria would join them. She lived and breathed nothing but the war. If they lost...she did not allow herself to think of the consequences.

Then one day, the messenger's horse came galloping up through the gates. The messenger did not even wait for the horse to stop before he jumped from the saddle. His face glowed.

"King Dalen has been captured! The Eirarin army has been routed well back into their own country. We will see victory." Bells began tolling throughout the city, and people swarmed into the streets to dance, laugh, and sing. *Victory!* Filibria waited for the messenger to calm down before she asked for news of Trinlys.

"The King has been wounded, but not badly, Your Majesty. The best physicians in Delvaria are attending to him. He claimed to be no warrior, but he led all the attacks and fought valiantly."

Pride, so large it felt like it would burst out of her, filled Filibria. "When will he be returning?"

"As soon as the dead are buried, the fields are cleaned, and the camp packed up. Soon," the messenger promised and then ran off to find a tavern to celebrate.

Though she inwardly rejoiced, Filibria would not join in the revelries, not until Trinlys was safe by her side.

Every day, she walked through the town, surrounded by guards, to watch on the northern wall. When she passed down the streets, people would turn out to hail and cheer her on. Young girls threw flowers at her feet and old women blessed her. The people she had grown up with treated her like a hero, but she did not deserve it. She had failed them. Their husbands, sons, and fathers were at war because she had not been able to keep peace. Yet when she saw the hope in their eyes, resolve grew; she would do her best to be worthy of their adoration. She would do her best to protect them, no matter the cost.

One day, Filibria's vigilance paid off. A smudge grew on the horizon until it was a dust cloud thundering down the road. Soon, Filibria could pick out the glint of armor, then the color of the horses and the clothes of their riders. The soldiers and their King were returning home. The bells in the city began tolling again.

Filibria stood on the wall as the first of the soldiers rode past her. She searched them for the royal crest on Trinlys's helmet, but did not see it. She paced the wall, watching each man. Slowly the stream of returning men dwindled and stopped. Filibria rushed down from the wall and confronted the first captain she met. She snagged the draped bit of his horse's reins, nearly upsetting the beast.

"Where is King Trinlys?"

The man was so startled that he stammered for several seconds searching for the words to an answer. "He stayed behind," he finally said. "He took his father to Eirarin, but he will be along soon, likely with the wounded and the caravans."

Filibria let go of his reins and the current of excitement pulled him past her, into the rejoicing city. She stared down the empty road before turning back to the wall.

The city soaked up the influx of men. Most crowded into taverns and inns to celebrate their victory and rest. Others returned to their houses, to their waiting wives and children. Though the city was full, the absence of those who had not returned was noticeable. On her walk to the northern wall, the black ribbons on the doors and the black curtains in the windows stared out at Filibria, accusing her. Like her, these women had waited for their husbands to return home, but unlike her, they now knew their husbands would never come back. The ribbons always filled her with regret. Filibria wanted nothing more than to stop at each house to offer her condolences, but Carna said there'd be time for such later; it was not safe now. Walking the streets was dangerous enough; to enter a house was downright risky. Filibria had to be content with letting Carna arrange for elaborate funerals and pensions for the widows. But still, she hid her face from the gaunt women who watched from the darkened windows.

Three days later, the first of the wounded arrived in the city, escorted by the well. No bells rang, no crowds gathered with chattering excitement. Only a few anxious women stood in the streets, straining, hoping against hope, to find a loved one. Faces peered from the windows, watching as each man was carried or helped up the street. Broken men came home, never to be the same.

At the gates, a single clear horn blew. A bell tolled, another answered. A cheer rose from the gates, spreading up the streets and the celebrations picked up again as the King of Delvaria was spotted. He held his head high as he rode through the gates.

Filibria ran down to the street, pushing her way like a commoner through the masses flooding the street. When people realized who she was, they quickly cleared a path, only to swell back behind her, blocking off her guards, Malda, Jarin, and Carna.

"Trinlys!" Filibria drew up on the edge of the road, searching the dirty, battered faces of men on horseback. Then she saw him. His armor was scuffed and dented, but it no longer swallowed him up. He looked like a noble warrior, like the king he was. Trinlys caught her eye and smiled, but the crowd of people still held them apart.

Carna mounted a hitching post and blew his horn. "All hail King Trinlys of Eirarin and Delvaria!"

Trinlys lifted his spear, shaking it in the air as the town swelled with cheers. Hats and ribbons filled the sky.

"All hail Queen and Peace Weaver Filibria of Delvaria and Eirarin!" Hats rose again as Filibria took the reins of Trinlys's horse. The procession fought its way through the ecstatic crowds into the courtyard of the castle. Women threw flowers in the path, and small children darted out in front of the horses to stare at the King and Queen. Finally, the procession passed through the gates, into the empty, quiet courtyard.

Trinlys at last dismounted and Filibria dropped the reins, running into his arms. The small party of people, mainly Malda, Jarin, Carna, Trinlys's men, and the several messengers, gave their own joyous cheer.

"Welcome home, King Trinlys," Filibria whispered.

CHAPTER

Thirty-Three

A ROYAL BANQUET WAS prepared; the castle and the whole city of Falendle glowed with the lights of celebration. But, the next morning, at the royal decree, the city was swathed in black. In the royal fields beside the castle, servants built a grand pyre for King Kial's body, and Filibria, again veiled in black, led the solemn funeral procession.

Once she reached the pyre and the body had been placed atop it, Carna handed her a torch. She touched it to the fuel-soaked wood before stepping back to allow others to contribute to the flames. As the fire caught, sending sparks into the sky, Filibria leaned against Trinlys.

"I once stood before your pyre," she whispered.

Trinlys slipped an arm around her and pulled her closer.

After war came the gritty details of kingdoms, alliances, diplomacy, kingship, and queenship. Councils gathered to argue and decide if Delvaria and Eirarin should be joined into one kingdom or kept separate. If not, what castle would the royal couple live in? Trinlys and Filibria decided the kingdoms would be kept separate for the time being. They had too many differences to be joined yet.

Sometime in the future, perhaps one kingdom would be possible, but until then, the royal couple would split their year equally between Eirarin and Delvaria.

There was also the matter of what to do with King Dalen.

"I will not execute him," Trinlys said firmly. "He is my father. Just because he tried to kill me does not mean he deserves death from my hand. He will be contained in the castle of Eirarin for now."

Everyone agreed this was the best course of action for the time being.

After many hours of politics and petitions, it was time for the celebration again. The whole city had worked night and day to prepare for the coronation. While cheering citizens looked on, Trinlys and Filibria were crowned King and Queen of Delvaria. A similar ceremony would be held again in Eirarin, and the two crowns from each kingdom would be forged anew into one crown—symbols of new beginnings, under a new peaceful rule.

There were tears when Trinlys and Filibria left for Eirarin. Carna stayed behind to man the castle in their absence, but Malda went with Filibria.

Filibria wanted to ride with Trinlys, but Malda put her foot down.

"Not in your condition."

So Filibria was consigned to a wagon, but Trinlys slowed his pace and they traveled together along the road they had rode on so many months before.

Soon, the border would be dissolved, though the kingdoms would retain their names. The lonely road would be bustling with travelers, merchants, and messengers. It would no longer be a single ribbon, but a strong tie between the kingdoms; a strong highway of trade and possibilities.

Filibria and Trinlys rode into the royal city of Eirarin to the cheers of their subjects. In the courtyard, Trinlys helped Filibria out of the carriage. Around them, the courtyard burst into celebration. They were all dear familiar faces. Even the gaoler turned out of his dank dungeon to see them.

"Welcome home, Queen Filibria." Trinlys pulled her tighter to him and whispered into her ear. "The love and light of my life."

At that moment, Mother Brylla broke through the crowd and pulled Filibria into a hug. "You never expected to keep peace this way, did you?" Brylla laughed. "You bound two kingdoms so tightly you've almost made them one."

When Mother Brylla let go, Filibria looked up at the castle—a strong, stone bulwark, full of memories that would haunt her. But she was home. They would rebuild; they would forge new memories together. She smiled at Trinlys and took his proffered hand.

He led her through the crowd into the castle and the doors closed behind them.

A new year began for the combined kingdoms; a year of sorrows and victories, hurts and healing lay behind them, but much still lay ahead. Though it would take many generations for the kingdoms to become seamless, both had flourished through Eirarin's trade and Delvaria's open trade route to the West.

Filibria stood in front of the large glass window, happy to see their world was at peace. In the fields beyond, a shepherd herded his ewes and frisky lambs out to the spring pasture. Even over the distance and through the thick glass, she could hear the tune he played on his whistle. It was bright and hopeful, a spring song...a song for a new year and new hopes.

Trinlys stepped beside Filibria and gently lifted the sleeping infant from her arms. Little Tiaeve, their precious little girl. He smiled down at the baby's face and then kissed Filibria's forehead. "You succeeded, peace weaver."

THE END

Acknowledgements

Just as it's so hard to write a blurb for a book—to condense so much into so few words—so too is it hard to acknowledge all the people who helped me along the way to publishing *Peace Weaver*.

For the longest time, I felt alone on this journey of writing. But when I sit and actually think about it, there are so many people who helped me—even just in little ways—that kept me going.

The first is my friend and coworker, Keli, who tricked me into a pinky promise to get this book published. She also reintroduced into reading in my adult years.

I also want to thank my brilliant cover artist, Lyndsey graphics, and my interior design artist, MGdesiigns (check them out on Instagram at those handles). Many thanks to my editor, WLHelgren, who took my hand and walked me through the long process of making this book the best it could be.

Out of all the beta readers who gave their time to read my rough drafts, I want to specifically thank Jennifer Lane, a writer herself and an unlikely beta swap, who was so encouraging and helpful.

I want to thank my mom for encouraging the love of writing and story telling in me (and for reading through all of the creative assignments that inevitably turned into novellas). And God, for instilling the love of writing in me in the first place.

My fantasy world of Eldrim would not have become the world it is today without the imagination and input of my brother. Any success I achieve will be because of what he and I started so long ago.

It may take one person to write a book, but it truly does take a village to get it independently published.

About the Author

MEGAN REES HAS BEEN weaving stories ever since she learned how to write. Her stories are fueled by wild imagination, history, and lots of tea. When she is not crafting tales, she can found with a book or visiting another country, searching for history and folklore to weave into her next writing project.